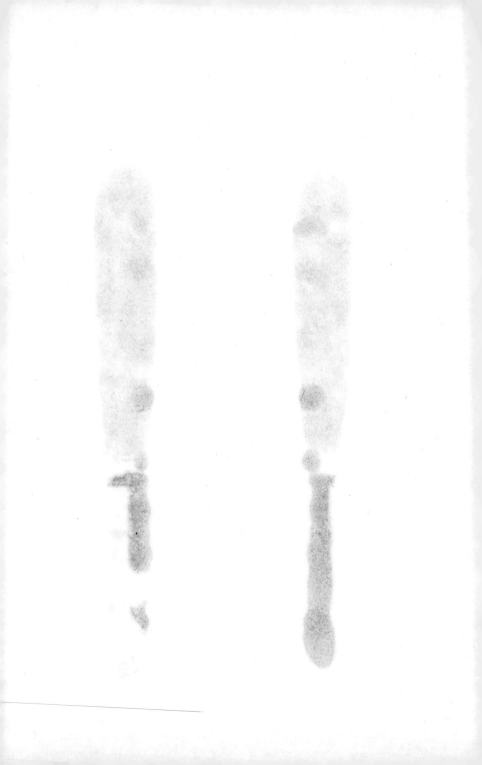

M A R I E   G R U B B E

MARIE GRUBBE

A Lady of the Seventeenth Century

J. P. JACOBSEN

SECOND EDITION

TRANSLATED FROM THE DANISH BY
HANNA ASTRUP LARSEN

REVISED AND WITH AN INTRODUCTION BY
ROBERT RAPHAEL

LIBRARY OF SCANDINAVIAN LITERATURE

TWAYNE PUBLISHERS
A DIVISION OF G. K. HALL & CO.
&
THE AMERICAN-SCANDINAVIAN FOUNDATION

The Library of Scandinavian Literature

Erik J. Friis, *General Editor*

Volume 30

Copyright © 1975, by The American-Scandinavian
Foundation

First Edition, 1917, by The American-Scandinavian
Foundation

Twayne Publishers ISBN 0-8057-8151-X

The American-Scandinavian Foundation
ISBN 0–89067–053–6

MANUFACTURED IN THE UNITED STATES OF AMERICA

INTRODUCTION

Along with the educator and theologian N. F. S. Grundt-
vig and the philosopher Søren Kierkegaard, Georg Mor-
ris Cohen Brandes (1842–1927) was the first of Danish
intellects to generate tangible eddies in the flow of literary ideas throughout Scandinavia generally, rather than
in Denmark alone. Norway's Ibsen, Bjørnson, Kielland,
and Lie, together with Sweden's Strindberg, were clearly
stimulated by Brandes' lectures and essays on literature
and literary men which came forth in the generation
between 1870 and 1890. In the twenty years when the
influence of Brandes was at its strongest, Scandinavian
letters and artistic thought became more unified than
they had ever before been, or have been since. Georg
Brandes and his group who, beside Ibsen, included the
Danes Holger Drachmann and Sophus Schandorph, for
a time considered themselves a roving element in the
North's "Modern Breakthrough," the trend which had
been announced and initiated in 1871 by Brandes himself with his introductory lecture in the series known as
Main Currents in Nineteenth-Century Literature. In it,
the young Brandes proclaimed what was to be the theory
behind much of Scandinavian, and European, writing
over the next twenty years: modern literature's over-
riding task was to put forward the social problems of
the day for argument and debate. Although no one
knew it then, Georg Brandes was propelling Scandinavia into the same current that was starting to sweep
out of France. For there, in 1871, Émile Zola brought
out the first two parts of his *Rougon-Macquart* series,

that microscopic "natural and social history of a Second Empire family." Both here and in Brandes, then, existed the ground for a novel literary orientation that in great part was to characterize the 1870s and 1880s. It was an orientation that eschewed metaphysical experience or reflection. Guided by the boundless scientific optimism of the age, this new literature made it a point to scrutinize the morass of society's problems with the rigor and objectivity of the laboratory. Progress, or perhaps a kind of redemption, might be achieved by having to face the revelations obtained through the author's dispassionate, microscopic observation. Social man, it was believed, found himself imprisoned by heredity, and milieu. The author's mission, and that of the reader, was to face the fact and try to improve man's lot by altering social conditions. If, however, society was beyond help, then one might, as Ibsen intimated in his social plays, simply blow it up. Thus derived the hope, and the optimism—such as it was—that moved the hand of the naturalist.

Jens Peter Jacobsen, however, was not, in any true sense of the term, a naturalist. If he shared his colleagues' enthusiasm for objective observation—he did, after all, begin as a botanist—it was with an entirely different purpose in mind. Man, subject to outside conditions beyond his control, was also the prisoner of his instincts, the unguarded victim of all its hellish urgings and half-hidden drives. The individual personality, not society, was a morass. Darwin, Swinburne, and Walter Pater became for Jacobsen what Darwin, Brandes, and Zola were for a time for Ibsen and Strindberg. He, like the naturalists, shunned any kind of metaphysics but for a different reason and with a different purpose. Because if, in Pater's words, "the whole scope of observation is dwarfed to the narrow chamber of the individual mind . . . each mind keeping as a solitary prisoner its own dream of a world," then, Pater concludes, living must remain "one desperate effort to see and touch; we shall hardly have time to make theories about the things we see and touch"; a deep-seated esthetically valid self-realization, therefore, must be the end in view, not the scrutiny of society or its betterment. With a keen, microscopic eye of his own, Jacobsen was bent on bringing to light not the problems of social man but the terrors and the glory of the individual psyche.

Furthermore, although he was a Darwinist *par excellence*, having literally transmitted Darwin's thinking into Scandinavia by his own translations in the early 1870s, Jacobsen did not keep in step with any of the other literary Darwinists of his time. While they were bringing up social problems for debate, Jacobsen remained intent on the perfection of a literary style he called his "pearl embroidery." Jacobsen's whole artistic orientation became, therefore, far more akin to the opulence of Pater or Swinburne than it was to any of his naturalist contemporaries and their objective dissections of society.

J. P. Jacobsen (1847–1885) was born in the small town of Thisted in the northwest corner of Denmark's Jutland peninsula, where he spent nearly twenty-two of his thirty-eight years, passing away there on April 30, 1885. In boyhood, his dominant interests were botany and literature. As early as his ninth year, inspired by reading Danish poets, Jacobsen began writing short verses. By the time he entered Copenhagen's university, in 1867, he could not decide, as he phrased it, "between the lyre or the microscope." Nor was it always a simple thing for him during his young adulthood to keep a proper balance between the compelling sadomasochism which fed his fantasies on the one hand, and the pristine gaze of the cool scientist on the other. In fact, his growing maturity both as a poet and as a naturalist led him in time to achieve a fruitful union of erotic insights, keenness of observation, and literary inventiveness. All of that came with age. By 1868, Jacobsen's literary activity had reached, in the dramatic poem *Gurresange,* those contrasts of shade and light and the exquisite texture that were to become the wings of his lasting fame. Arnold Schönberg set the German translation to music in 1910. In that same period, Jacobsen the scientist made his debut with the first translations into a Scandinavian language of Darwin's *On the Origin of the Species* (1871–1873) and *The Descent of Man* (1874). Although Darwin had already been a topic of debate in Denmark, it was Jacobsen's translations which made Darwin generally known throughout the Nordic countries, and which caused the English scientist's thinking to become a part of the new spirit of "breakthrough" in Scandinavia's literature. Fluent in English since boyhood, Jacobsen, the ruthless naturalist and the atheist who had been influenced by Strauss and Feuerbach, was very susceptible to Darwin's theories about man's evolution and biological fate.

In the novella *Mogens*, which was composed during the spring of 1872, Jacobsen not only made his debut in literary prose, but he also revealed that he was a contributor to the spirit of "breakthrough" which was thriving around him. For in *Mogens*, nature and human action are both viewed with a hard objectivity and magnified detail such as had not existed in the romantic prose of an earlier day. With his sharp scientific gaze intensified by Darwin, but softened by his sure poetic instincts, Jacobsen makes of *Mogens* a portrait of man and nature as a wholesome totality, wherein human feeling and action are sound—perhaps because they need not rely upon a heaven which is empty. In the end, *Mogens* seemed to blast like a hurricane against the reaction and conservatism that prevailed in Danish letters. The work's atheism and its naturalism, its very fresh and inventive style and its high level of esthetic communication, left no doubt that Jacobsen was fulfilling the challenge of Georg Brandes that the modern artist be a new kind of aristocrat. Jacobsen's cultural contemporaries were well aware of that fact. What they, however, could not surmise was that in depicting preconscious and even subconscious thought in what seemed apparently irrational deed, Jacobsen was placing himself as an artist under the kind of extreme pressure that can only produce novel, often unique, orientations. It was what Carlyle and Baudelaire had done before him, and what Proust, Thomas Mann, and Kafka were to do after him.

With the appearance of the novel *Marie Grubbe* late in 1876, readers no doubt surmised from its subtitle, "A Lady of the Seventeenth Century," as some believe still, that Jacobsen's major aim was to depict veraciously the times and the existence of history's Marie Grubbe, at least from her fourteenth year in 1657 until her death in 1718. The store of detail vividly culled from Danish history, together with the bounty of elegant vignettes and earthy color recalled from everyday life in Denmark's baroque age, gives ample cause for this belief to appear a fact. Despite the novel's historical authenticity and richness, Jacobsen's object is not an elaborate recreation of seventeenth-century Denmark.

This novel is essentially about the personality and development of Marie Grubbe alone, thus much of the author's detailed historical background ultimately bears little, if any, relevance to the profound changes within her, viewed—as they always are—from the author's unique and innovative perspective. Yet the antique settings and picturesque dialogue may be seen as germane, if only because these elements provided him with a unifying scrim, a strategic artistic leverage that allowed him to maintain firm stylistic control of all his esthetic data. During 1873, the writer scrupulously gathered as much historical detail as possible from documents and letters of the period in Copenhagen's Royal Library. In this endeavor Jacobsen's strategy was hardly different from that of European contemporaries who successfully exploited the materials of history with the same artistic intent. Gustave Flaubert, in his novel *Salammbô* of 1862, used ancient Carthage as a means of gaining stylistic control of, and unity in, his material precisely in the way Richard Wagner did when he used nearly every facet of sixteenth-century Nuremberg in order to manipulate and clarify the artistic environment of his *Die Meistersinger*, which premiered in 1868.

Using the external authority of history, Jacobsen had a solid platform of fact on which he could juxtapose and control all of the major data relating to the historical Marie Grubbe and her age with such success that he achieved exactly what he was after from the beginning: a unique and unifying vision of Marie's existence and psyche as it resided in his artist's eye. Moving within his historic frame, Jacobsen was free to bore into layers of personality that had scarcely been revealed with such unrelenting light before; he was, in fact, now able to turn himself into his main characters whenever and however he chose. This technique had, of course, been fruitfully employed a generation before by Flaubert, who, using his observations of the French provincial middle class, transformed himself into Emma Bovary. Jacobsen, indeed, could have said about his *Marie Grubbe* what the French writer, in that legendary statement, proposed about his own book: "Madame Bovary c'est moi." Emma and Marie are certainly akin in many essential ways. Both are youthful victims of powerful illusions regarding romantic love, illusions that were largely shaped by their adolescent reading. But, whereas Emma is ostensibly ruined by her books, Marie, in the end, proves to be not nearly so blind. Marie learns relatively soon about the sham of society's mores, its ideas of status, and its precarious system of social roles, and she grows to scorn them. At the same time, she also learns to spurn all notions about eroticism but her own, gradually becoming strengthened to confront—just as Jacobsen

did—the innermost abyss of her personality. Unlike
Emma Bovary, who perceives these things too late and
remains powerless to react or change, Marie Grubbe
is able to survive her final years of poverty and obscur-
ity by regarding the world and herself without flinching.
Her surroundings have ceased to be relevant in any way.
That is why she can accept death, as she informs Holberg in the novel's last pages, without fear or the
consolation of belief in a hereafter. Marie may be said
to face the same kind of "difficult death" that Niels
Lyhne was to do, and for nearly the same reason.

Jacobsen was perhaps the most creative Darwinist in
the Europe of his day. This clearly distinguishes him
from Flaubert, whose most renowned work appeared
two years before *On the Origin of the Species* was published in 1859. As a scientist, the Danish author was in a
position to understand Darwin's significance as few
other Europeans, among them Zola and Swinburne,
could. Like them, Jacobsen found himself quickly re-
sponding to the English scientist's shattering effect on
traditional ideas concerning God, the universe, and man's
fate. Finding his own insights confirmed in Darwin,
Jacobsen rejected once and for all the long sacrosanct
teleological view of the origins and destiny of man.
The Dane came to see that the final goal of human
evolution was *not* the perfect adaptation of the organism
to its environment, an adaptation that would reveal
the perfection of God's plan, to say nothing of the
perfectibility of man himself. Instead, Jacobsen understood what only a bare handful of intellectuals, by 1872,
were able to: the venerated teleological concept of

existence simply did not correspond to fact; evolution and the human predicament were not purposive at all. Far from being naturally perfectible, man was but the helpless victim of heredity and milieu, depending as every other creature on laws of natural selection. If man achieved any advance over his condition, it was strictly by random chance.

It is no surprise, therefore, that Marie Grubbe herself may be regarded as the genuine offspring of the author's Darwinism; the novel was begun the same year he was translating *On the Origin of the Species*. When one speaks of *Marie Grubbe* as Scandinavia's first naturalistic novel, therefore, it is because one notices the way in which the author shows the life of the protagonist evolving almost inevitably out of inborn propensities which are lucidly revealed in the novel's first episode. Developing through conflict with—and perceptions about —her milieu, Marie, in the last pages of the work, may even be looked on as a Darwinist in her own right. Certainly her atheism and Darwinism are implied when she proclaims to Ludvig Holberg (who was a major figure of the Enlightenment, supporting its confident, teleological views of God and His universe) lack of belief in an after life and asserts her strong belief in self.

All this evidence, however, does not make *Marie Grubbe* a naturalistic work. If it were that, Jacobsen could never have permitted himself the apparent luxury of what he termed the "pearl embroidery" of his distinctive style. This style had come into being in the exquisite images and phrases of the *Gurresange* before any real contact with Darwin. It was a style that no naturalist ever could devise. In the novella *Mogens* Jacobsen developed it further, to a point where the whole of nature, rather than being portrayed naturalistically, is perceived as a purely esthetic experience from first to last. No naturalist, Jacobsen should rather be regarded as a stylist, a term which applies to those European artists who now are seen to have created under the headings impressionism, estheticism, or decadence. In its salient aspects, Jacobsen's art may therefore be viewed as being far more in tune with that of such writers as Wilde, Hofmannsthal, or D'Annunzio, members of the generation that followed his, than he was with contemporaries such as Zola or Ibsen. But by the 1870s, the chief stylists of Jacobsen's time had already emerged clearly into sight. They were England's Walter Pater and, above all, Algernon Swinburne. Indeed, it scarcely astonishes us to learn that by 1870, Jacobsen, whose command of English was excellent, ordered his publisher to get copies of everything Swinburne had in print. Jacobsen devoured all of it with unceasing fascination. Swinburne can be seen as an interest that preceded, and survived, the author's active preoccupation with Darwin, and with good cause.

The content, but more particularly the style, of Swinburne's *Atalanta in Calydon* (1865) and the famous *Poems and Ballads* (1866) confirmed by resplendent example what Jacobsen had already begun to surmise: Art could be more than a tool with which one fashioned profound and disturbing vistas of the personality, it might also provide a usefully complete and wholly self-justifying end in itself. The terrors of personality and existence could be squarely confronted when perceived from the distance of a lovely esthetic surface; perceived, that is, *with style*.

Using unending beauty of esthetic surface, Jacobsen provided himself with an observation tower from which he was able to survey in the peculiarly impersonal manner of the stylist the often highly disturbing emotions of Marie Grubbe. Like Swinburne, who was an admitted sadomasochist, Jacobsen reveals, from the outset, the horrors of Marie's intensely eroticized personality, which parallels his own. In the sexual fantasies with which the novel opens, eroticism is seen as something that is scarcely separable from psychic and physical torment. Jacobsen's vision of eroticism as a series of sadistic violation and masochistic self-violation was shared by not just a few of his contemporaries besides Swinburne, among them Baudelaire, Huysmans, Wagner, and Strindberg. This vision was to culminate in the gorgeous textures and frightening content of Oscar Wilde's play *Salome* in 1893, a work whose lurid depictions had already been prefigured in 1876 in Gustave Moreau's painting based on the same theme, and by Wagner's *Parsifal* of 1882.

Through the acute lens of his sustained and exquisite style, Jacobsen probes the abyss of Marie's erotic life, delving first into her fantasy of self-violation in the role of Griselda, and, pursuing her sexual daydream further, the author details a second violation that would end in self-destruction were the dreamer not to awaken from her reverie, as she, of course, must. "Stripped by a black and shaggy hand..."—it is clear that the owner of the hand is Bertel of the turnpike house to whom Marie is strongly attracted—the fourteen-year-old girl imagines herself in the role of Brynhild, a character from the romantic legends of her reading. Tossed into the dust by sadistic "Bertel," who grasps her by strands of long black hair, Marie's ankles are tied to the long tail of a snorting black stallion. At this moment, Marie's free association breaks off, and none too soon.

These astonishing episodes are detailed by Jacobsen by means of an uncanny use of the interior monologue technique that appears as modern and effective as Molly Bloom's soliloquy at the close of Joyce's *Ulysses*. This technique had, of course, already been employed with some subtlety by Laurence Sterne in his novel of 1759, *Tristram Shandy*. The principles of eighteenth-century empirical psychology and mental association, however, were later exploited by romantic poets to produce a *de facto* kind of stream-of-consciousness, or interior monologue, in works by authors such as Novalis, Lamartine, de Vigny, Leopardi, and Wordsworth. Even the apprenticeship novels of Charles Dickens written in the first person may, from a certain point of view, be described as a stream-of-consciousness approach. Certainly Dujardin who, in his *Les lauriers sont coupés* of 1887, wrote a novel in the form of the interior monologue, cannot be said to have achieved, in the retrospect of today, Jacobsen's merit as the progenitor of this technique in its modern form, even if Joyce in his *A Portrait of the Artist* of 1916 deliberately borrowed the technique from the Frenchman.

After the author brilliantly lights up the erotic cran-

nies of Marie's psyche through her daydreaming in the
novel's initial episode, he does not spare us its conse-
quences. Jacobsen's microscopic eye pursues Marie's erotic
frustrations and masochistic gratifications into adult life
and old age, and reveals how his protagonist learns to
regard and accept unflinchingly the experiences and drives
of her personality that cannot simply be wished away.
In the end, unlike Emma Bovary, Marie Grubbe learns
to fashion a durable inner life that provides her with
solace even in her old age.

The position of Jacobsen's cultural niche in the nine-
teenth century is clear. Although he enlists both heredity
and milieu as major factors in the lives of Marie Grubbe,
and Niels Lyhne, his Darwinism does not make of him
a naturalist in the manner of Zola or Hauptmann or the
Strindberg of *Miss Julie* or anyone else. Moreover,
other important writers who were never in the cause of
naturalism, not least among them Thomas Mann, were
sometimes at pains to detail the effects of environment
and heredity. In Jacobsen's case, Darwinism and all
that it implied for his age was only a part of the means.
The artistic end was style, those esthetic arabesques and
excesses, that "pearl embroidery" whose excruciating
limits were finally achieved a decade or two after him,
first in Huysman's *A Rebours* and the poetry of Mal-
larmé, and ultimately in the stylistic floods we associate
with *art nouveau* and the *fin de siècle*. Jacobsen belongs
in the society of "the melancholy company," those deca-
dents and esthetes spoken of at length by Marie Grubbe's
onetime lover, the voluptuary Sti Høg, who is none
other than the author's own representative and spokes-

man. Sti Høg, just as the artist Jacobsen himself, burns
with that "hard, gemlike flame" described by Walter
Pater in his depiction of the beautiful experience. For
through the consistently sensuous, esthetic flow created
by a beautiful style, Jacobsen knew, the terrors of the
mind and experience could be faced and endured as
never before.

ROBERT RAPHAEL.

Queens College

MARIE GRUBBE

MARIE GRUBBE

CHAPTER I

THE air beneath the linden crowns had flown in across brown heath and parched meadow. It brought the heat of the sun and was laden with dust from the road, but in the cool, thick foliage it had been cleansed and freshened, while the yellow linden flowers had given it moisture and fragrance. In the blissful haven of the green vault it lay quivering in light waves, caressed by the softly stirring leaves and the flutter of white-gold butterfly wings.

The human lips that breathed this air were full and fresh; the bosom it swelled was young and slight. The bosom was slight, and the foot was slight, the waist small, the shape slim, and there was a certain lean strength about the whole figure. Nothing was luxuriant except the partly loosened hair of dull gold, from which the little dark blue cap had slipped until it hung on her back like a tiny cowl. Otherwise there was no suggestion of the convent in her dress. A wide, square-cut collar was turned down over a frock of lavender homespun, and from its short, slashed sleeves billowed ruffles of fine holland. A bow of red ribbon was on her breast, and her shoes had red rosettes.

Her hands behind her back, her head bent forward, she went slowly up the path, picking her steps daintily. She did not walk in a straight line but meandered, sometimes almost running into a tree at her left, then again seeming on the point of strolling out among the bushes to her right. Now and then she would stop, shake the hair from her cheeks, and look up to the light. The softened glow gave her child-white face a faint golden sheen and made the blue shadows under the eyes less marked. The scarlet of her lips deepened to red-brown, and the great blue eyes seemed almost black. She was lovely—lovely!—a straight forehead, faintly arched nose, short, clean-cut upper lip, a strong, round chin and finely curved cheeks, tiny ears, and delicately pencilled eyebrows. . . .

She smiled as she walked, lightly and carelessly, thought of nothing, and smiled in harmony with everything around her. At the end of the path, she stopped and began to rock on her heel, first to the right, then to the left, still with her hands behind her back, head held straight, and eyes turned upward, as she hummed fitfully in time with her swaying.

Two flagstones led down into the garden, which lay glaring under the cloudless, whitish blue sky. The only bit of shade hugged the feet of the clipped box hedge. The heat stung the eyes, and even the hedge seemed to flash light from the burnished leaves. The amber bush trailed its white garlands in and out among thirsty balsamines, nightshade, gillyflowers, and pinks, which stood huddling like sheep in the open. The peas and beans flanking the lavender border were ready to fall from their trellis with heat. The marigolds had given up the struggle and stared the sun straight in the face, but the poppies had shed their large red petals and stood with bared stalks.

The child in the linden lane jumped down the steps, ran through the sun-heated garden with head lowered as one crosses a court in the rain, made for a triangle of dark yew-trees, slipped behind them, and entered a large arbor, a relic from the days of the Belows. A wide circle of elms had been woven together at the top as far as the branches would reach, and a framework of withes closed the round opening in the centre. Climbing roses and Italian honeysuckle, growing wild in the foliage, made a dense wall, but on one side they had failed, and the hopvines planted instead had but strangled the elms without filling the gap.

Two white seahorses were mounted at the door. Within the arbor stood a long bench and table made of a stone slab which had once been large and oval but now lay in three fragments on the ground while only one small piece was unsteadily poised on a corner of the frame. The child sat down before it, pulled her feet up under her on the bench, leaned back, and crossed her arms. She closed her eyes and sat quite still. Two fine lines appeared on her forehead, and sometimes she would lift her eyebrows, smiling slightly.

"In the room with the purple carpets and the gilded alcove, Griselda lies at the feet of the margrave, but he spurns her. He has just torn her from her warm bed. Now he opens the narrow, round-arched door, and the cold air blows in on poor Griselda, who lies on the floor weeping, and there is nothing between the cold night air and her warm, white body except the thin, thin linen. But he turns her out and locks the door on her. And she presses her naked shoulder against the cold, smooth door and sobs, and she hears him walking inside on the soft carpet, and through the keyhole the light from the scented taper falls and makes a little sun on her bare breast. And she steals away, and goes down the dark staircase, and it is quite still, and she hears nothing but the soft patter of her own feet on the ice-cold steps. Then she goes out into the snow — no, it's rain, pouring rain, and the heavy cold water splashes on her shoulders. Her shift clings to her body, and the water runs down her bare legs, and her tender feet press the soft, chilly mud which oozes out beside them. And the wind—

the bushes scratch her and tear her frock—but no, she
hasn't any frock on—just as they tore my brown petticoat! The nuts must be ripe in Fastrup Grove—such heaps
of nuts there were at Viborg market! God knows if Anne's
teeth have stopped aching... No, No, Brynhild!—the
wild steed comes galloping ... Brynhild and Grimhild—
Queen Grimhild beckons to the men, then turns, and
walks away. They drag in Queen Brynhild, and a squat,
black yokel with long arms—something like Bertel in
the turnpike house—catches her belt and tears it in two,
and he pulls off her robe and her underkirtle, and his
huge black hands brush the rings from her soft white
arms, and another big, half-naked, brown and shaggy
churl puts his hairy arm around her waist, and he
kicks off her sandals with his clumsy feet, and Bertel winds
her long black locks around his hands and drags her along,
and she follows with body bent forward, and the big fellow
puts his sweaty palms on her naked back and shoves her
over to the black, fiery stallion, and they throw her down
in the gray dust in the road, and they tie the long tail of the
horse around her ankles—

The lines came into her forehead again and stayed there
a long time. She shook her head and looked more and more
vexed. At last she opened her eyes, half rose, and glanced
around her wearily and discontentedly.

Mosquitoes swarmed in the gap between the hopvines,
and from the garden came puffs of fragrance from mint and
common balm, mingling sometimes with a whiff of sow-
thistle or anise. A dizzy little yellow spider ran across her
hand, tickling her, and made her jump up. She went to
the door and tried to pick a rose growing high among the
leaves, but could not reach it. Then she began to gather

the blossoms of the climbing rose outside and, getting more and more eager, soon filled her skirt with flowers which she carried into the arbor. She sat down by the table, took them from her lap, and laid one upon the other until the stone was hidden under a fragrant cover of pale rose.

When the last flower had been put in its place, she smoothed the folds of her frock, brushed off the loose petals and green leaves that had caught in the nap, and sat with hands in her lap gazing at the blossoming mass.

This bloom of color, curling in sheen and shadow, white flushing to red and red paling to blue, moist pink that is almost heavy, and lavender light as wafted on air, each petal rounded like a tiny vault, soft in the shadow, but gleaming in the sun with thousands of fine light points, with all its fair blood-of-rose flowing in the veins, spreading through the skin—and the sweet, heavy fragrance rising like vapor from that red nectar that seethes in the flower-cup. . . .

Suddenly she turned back her sleeves and laid her bare arms in the soft, moist coolness of the flowers. She turned them round and round under the roses until the loosened petals fluttered to the ground, then jumped up and with one motion swept everything from the table and went out into the garden, pulling down her sleeves as she walked. With flushed cheeks and quickened step she followed the path to the end, then skirted the garden toward the turnpike. A load of hay had just been overturned and was blocking the way to the gate. Several other wagons halted behind it, and she could see the brown polished stick of the overseer gleaming in the sun as he beat the unlucky driver.

She put her fingers in her ears to shut out the sickening sound of the blows, ran toward the house, darted within the open cellar door and slammed it after her.

The child was Marie Grubbe, the fourteen-year-old
daughter of Squire Erik Grubbe of Tjele Manor.

The blue haze of twilight rested over Tjele. The falling
dew had put a stop to the haymaking. The maids were in
the stable milking while the men busied themselves about
the wagons and harness in the shed. The tenant farmers,
after doing their stint of work for the squire, were standing
in a group outside the gate, waiting for the call to supper.

Erik Grubbe stood at an open window, looking out into
the court. The horses, freed from harness and halter, came
slowly, one by one, from the stable and went up to the wa-
tering trough. A red-capped boy was hard at work putting
new tines in a rake, and two greyhounds played around the
wooden horse and the large grindstone in one corner of
the yard.

It was growing late. Every few minutes the men would
come out of the stable door and draw back, whistling or
humming a tune. A maid carrying a full bucket of milk
tripped with quick, firm steps across the yard, and the farmers were straggling in, as though to hasten the supper bell.
The rattling of plates and trenchers grew louder in the
kitchen, and presently someone pulled the bell violently,
letting out two groups of rusty notes which soon died away
in the clatter of wooden shoes and the creaking of doors.
In a moment the yard was empty, except for the two dogs
barking loudly out through the gate.

Erik Grubbe drew in the window and sat down thoughtfully. The room was known as the winter parlor, though
it was in fact used all the year round for dining room and
sitting room, and was practically the only inhabited part
of the house. It was a large room with two windows and

a high oak panelling. Glazed Dutch tiles covered the walls with a design of blue nosegays on a white ground. The fireplace was set with burned bricks, and a chest of drawers had been placed before it as a screen against the draught that came in whenever the door was opened. A polished oak table with two rounded leaves hanging almost to the floor, a few high-backed chairs with seats of leather worn shiny, and a small green cupboard set high on the wall— that was all there was in the parlor.

As Erik Grubbe sat there in the dusk, his housekeeper, Anne Jensdaughter, entered, carrying in one hand a lighted candle and in the other a mug of milk warm from the udder. Placing the mug before him, she seated herself at the table. One large red hand still held the candlestick, and as she turned it round and round, numerous rings and large brilliants glittered on her fingers.

"Alack-a-day!" she groaned.

"What now?" asked Erik Grubbe glancing up.

"Sure, I may well be tired after stewing 'roun' till I've neither stren'th nor wit left."

"Well, 'tis busy times. Folks have to work up heat in summer to sit in all winter."

"Busy—ay, but there's reason in everythin'. Wheels in ditch an' coach in splinters 's no king's drivin', say I. None but me to do a thing! The indoor wenches 're nothin' but draggle-tails—sweethearts an' town talk's all they think of. Ef they do a bit o' work, they boggle it, an' it's fer me to do over. Walbor's sick, an' Stina an' Bo'l—the sluts —they pother an' pother till the sweat comes, but naught else comes o't. I might ha' some help from M'ree ef you'd speak to her, but you won't let her put a finger to anything."

"Hold, hold! You run on so fast you lose your breath
and the King's Danish too. Don't blame me; blame yourself. If you'd been patient with Marie last winter, if you'd
taught her gently the right knack of things, you might have
had some help from her now, but you were rough and cross-
grained, she was sulky, and the two of you came nigh to
splitting each other alive. 'Tis to be more than thankful
for there's an end on 't."

"Ay, stand up fer M'ree! You're free to do it, but ef
you stand up fer yours, I stand up fer mine, and whether
you take it bad or not, I tell you M'ree 's more sperrit than
she can carry through the world. Let that be fer the fault
it is, but she's bad. You may say 'No,' but I say she is. She
can never let little Anne be—never. She's a-pinchin' and
a-naggin' her all day long and a-castin' foul words after
her till the poor child might wish she'd never been born
—and I wish she hadn't, though it breaks my heart. Alack-
a-day, may God have mercy upon us! Ye're not the same
father to the two children, but sure it's right that the sins
of the fathers should be visited upon the children unto the
third and fourth generation—and the sins of the mother
too, and little Anne 's nothin' but a whore's brat—ay, I tell
ye to yer face, she's nothin' but a whore's brat, a whore's
brat in the sight of God and man. But you, her father!—
shame on ye, shame!—yes, I tell ye, even 'f ye lay hands
on me, as ye did two years ago come Michaelmas, shame
on ye! Fie on ye that ye let yer own child feel she's conceived in sin! Ye do let her feel it, you and M'ree both of
ye let her feel it —even ef ye hit me, I say ye let her feel
it—"

Erik Grubbe sprang up and stamped the floor.

"Gallows and wheel! Are you spital-mad, woman?

You're drunk, that's what you are. Go and lie down on your bed and sleep off your booze and your spleen too! 'T would serve you right if I boxed your ears, you shrew! No—not another word! Marie shall be gone from here before tomorrow is over. I want peace—in times of peace."

Anne sobbed aloud.

"O Lord, O Lord, that such a thing should come to pass—an everlastin' shame! Tell *me* I'm tipsy! In all the time we've ben together or all the time before, have ye seen me in the scullery with a fuddled head? Have y' ever heard me talkin' drivel? Show me the spot where ye've seen me o'ercome with drink! That's the thanks I get. Sleep off my booze! Would to God I might sleep! Would to God I might sink down dead before you, since ye put shame upon me—"

The dogs began to bark outside, and the beat of horses' hoofs sounded beneath the windows.

Anne dried her eyes hastily, and Erik Grubbe opened the window to ask who had come.

"A messenger riding from Fovsing," answered one of the men about the house.

"Then take his horse and send him in," and with these words the window was closed.

Anne straightened herself in her chair and held up one hand to shade her eyes, red with weeping.

The messenger presented the compliments of Christian Skeel of Fovsing and Odden, Governor of the Diocese, who sent to apprise Erik Grubbe of the notice he had that day received by royal courier, saying that war had been declared on June first. Since it became necessary that he should travel to Aarhus and possibly even to Copenhagen, he made inquiry of Erik Grubbe whether he would accompany him on the road so far as served his convenience, for they might at least end the suit they were bringing against certain citizens of Aarhus. With regard to Copenhagen, the Governor well knew that Erik Grubbe had plenty of reasons for going thither. At all events, Christian Skeel would arrive at Tjele about four hours after high noon on the following day.

Erik Grubbe replied that he would be ready for the journey, and the messenger departed with this answer.

Anne and Erik Grubbe then discussed at length all that must be done while he was away and decided that Marie should go with him to Copenhagen and remain for a year or two with her Aunt Rigitze.

The impending farewells had calmed them both, though the quarrel was on the point of blazing out again when it came to the question of letting Marie take with her sundry dresses and jewels that had belonged to her dead mother. The matter was settled amicably at last and Anne went to bed early, for the next day would be a long one.

Again the dogs announced visitors, but this time it was only the pastor of Tjele and Vinge parish, Jens Jensen Paludan.

"Good even to the house!" he said as he stepped in.

He was a large-boned, long-limbed man with a stoop in his broad shoulders. His hair was rough as a crow's nest, grayish and tangled, but his face was of a deep yet clear pink, seemingly out of keeping with his coarse, rugged features and bushy eyebrows.

Erik Grubbe invited him to a seat and asked about his haymaking. The conversation dwelt on the chief labors of the farm at that season and died away in a sigh over the

poor harvest of last year. Meanwhile the pastor was casting sidelong glances at the mug and finally said: "Your
honor is always temperate—keeping to the natural drinks.
No doubt they are the healthiest. New milk is a blessed
gift of heaven, good both for a weak stomach and a sore
chest."

"Indeed the gifts of God are all good, whether they come
from the udder or the tap. But you must taste a keg of genuine mum that we brought home from Viborg the other
day. She's both good and German, though I can't see that
the customs have put their mark on her."

Goblets and a large ebony tankard ornamented with silver rings were brought in and set before them.

They drank to each other.

"Heydenkamper! Genuine, peerless Heydenkamper!"
exclaimed the pastor in a voice that trembled with emotion.
He leaned back blissfully in his chair and very nearly shed
tears of enthusiasm.

"You are a connoisseur," smirked Erik Grubbe.

"Ah, connoisseur! We are but of yesterday and know
nothing," murmured the pastor absent mindedly, "though
I'm wondering," he went on in a louder voice, "whether
it be true what I have been told about the brew house of
the Heydenkampers. 'T was a free-master who related it in
Hanover the time I travelled with young Master Jörgen.
He said they would always begin the brew on a Friday
night, but before anyone was allowed to put a finger to it,
he had to go to the oldest journeyman and lay his hand on
the great scales and swear by fire and blood and water
that he harbored no spiteful or evil thoughts, for such
might harm the beer. The men also told me that on Sundays, when the church bells sounded, they would open all

the doors and windows to let the ringing pass over the beer. But the most important of all was what took place when they set the brew aside to ferment, for then the master himself would bring a splendid chest from which he would take heavy gold rings and chains and precious stones inscribed with strange signs, and all these would be put into the beer. In truth, one may well believe that these noble treasures would impart to it something of their own secret potency given them by nature."

"That is not for us to say," declared Erik Grubbe. "I have more faith, I own, in the Brunswick hops and the other herbs they mix."

"Nay," said the pastor, "it were wrong to think so, for there is much that is hidden from us in the realm of nature—of that there can be no doubt. Everything, living or dead, has its *miraculum* within it, and we need but patience to seek and open eyes to find. Alas, in the old days when it was not so long since the Lord had taken his hands from the earth, then all things were still so engirded with his power that they exhaled healing and all that was good for time and eternity. But now the earth is no longer new nor fine: it is defiled with the sins of many generations. Now it is only at particular times that these powers manifest themselves, at certain places and certain seasons when strange signs may be seen in the heavens —as I was saying to the blacksmith when we spoke of the awful flaming light that has been visible in half the heavens for several nights recently. . . . That reminds me, a mounted courier passed us just then; he was bound this way, I think."

"So he was, Pastor Jens."

"I hope he rode with none but good tidings?"

"He rode with the tidings that war has been declared."

"Lord Jesu! Alas the day! Yet it had to come some time."

"Ay, but when they'd waited so long, they might as well have waited till folks had their harvest in."

"'T is the Skaanings who are back of it, I make no doubt. They still feel the smart of the last war and would seek balm in this."

"Oh, it's not only the Skaanings. The Sjælland people are ever spoiling for war. They know it will pass them by as usual. Well, it's a good time for neats and fools when the Councillors of the Realm have gone mad one and all!"

"'T is said the Lord High Constable did not desire war."

"May the devil believe that! Perhaps not—but there's little to be made of preaching quiet in an ant hill. Well, the war's here, and now it's every man for himself. We shall have our hands full."

The conversation turned to the journey of the morrow, passed on to the bad roads, lingered on fatted oxen and stall-feeding, and again reverted to the journey. Meanwhile they had not neglected the tankard. The beer had gone to their heads, and Erik Grubbe, who was just telling about his voyage to Ceylon and the East Indies in the "Pearl," had difficulty in making headway through his own laughter whenever a new joke came to his mind.

The pastor was getting serious. He had collapsed in his chair, but once in a while he would turn his head, look fiercely around and move his lips as though to speak. He was gesticulating with one hand, growing more and more excited, until at last he happened to strike the table with his fist, and sank down again with a frightened look at Erik Grubbe. Finally, when the squire had got himself quite tangled up in a story of an excessively stupid scullery lad, the pastor rose and began to speak in a hollow, solemn voice.

"Verily," he said, "verily, I will bear witness with my mouth — with my mouth — that you are an offence and one by whom offence cometh, that it were better for you that you were cast into the sea — verily, with a millstone and two barrels of malt, the two barrels of malt that you owe me, as I bear witness solemnly with my mouth — two heaping full barrels of malt in my own new sacks. For they were not my sacks, never kingdom without end, 'twas your own old sacks, and my new ones you kept — and it *was* rotten malt — verily! See the abomination of desolation, and the sacks are mine, and I will repay — vengeance is mine, I say. Do you tremble in your old bones, you old whoremonger? You should live like a Christian, but you live with Anne Jensdaughter and make her cheat a Christian pastor. You're a — you're a — Christian whoremonger — yes —"

During the first part of the pastor's speech, Erik Grubbe sat smiling fatuously and holding out his hand to him across the table. He thrust out his elbow as though to poke an invisible auditor in the ribs and call his attention to how delightfully drunk the parson was. But at last some sense of what was being said appeared to pierce his mind. His face suddenly became chalky white; he seized the tankard and threw it at the pastor, who fell backward from his chair and slipped to the floor. It was nothing but fright that caused it, for the tankard failed to reach its mark. It merely rolled to the edge of the table and lay there while the beer flowed in rivulets down on the floor and the pastor.

The candle had burned low and was flaring fitfully, sometimes lighting the room brightly for a moment, then leaving it almost in darkness, while the blue dawn peeped in through the windows.

The pastor was still talking, his voice first deep and threatening, then feeble, almost whining.

"There you sit in gold and purple, and I'm laid here, and the dogs lick my sores—and what did you drop in Abraham's bosom? What did you put on the contribution plate? You didn't give so much as a silver eightpenny bit in Christian Abraham's bosom. And now you are in torments—but no one shall dip the tip of his finger in water for you,"—and he struck out with his hand in the spilled beer, "but I wash my hands—both hands. I have warned you—hi! there you go—yes, there you go in sackcloth and ashes—my two new sacks—malt—"

He mumbled yet a while, then dropped asleep. Meanwhile Erik Grubbe tried to take revenge. He caught the arm of his chair firmly, stretched to his full length, and kicked the leg of the chair with all his might, in the hope that it was the pastor.

Presently all was still. There was no sound but the snoring of the two old gentlemen and the monotonous drip, drip of the beer running off the table.

CHAPTER II

MISTRESS RIGITZE GRUBBE, relict of the late lamented Hans Ulrik Gyldenlöve, owned a house on the corner of Östergade and Pilestræde. At that time Östergade was a fairly aristocratic residence section. Members of the Trolle, Sehested, Rosencrantz, and Krag families lived there; Joachim Gersdorf was Mistress Rigitze's neighbor, and one or two foreign ministers usually had lodgings in Carl van Mandern's new red mansion. Only one side of the street was the home of fashion, however; on the other side Nikolaj Church was flanked by low houses where dwelt artisans, shopkeepers, and shipmasters. There were also one or two taverns.

On a Sunday morning early in September, Marie Grubbe stood looking out of the dormer window in Mistress Rigitze's house. Not a vehicle in sight! Nothing but staid footsteps, and now and then the long-drawn cry of the oystermonger. The sunlight, quivering over roofs and pavements, threw sharp, black, almost rectangular shadows. The distance swam in a faint bluish heat mist.

" At-tention!" called a woman's voice behind her, cleverly mimicking the raucous tones of one accustomed to much shouting of military orders.

Marie turned. Her aunt's maid, Lucie, had for some time been sitting on the table appraising her own well-formed feet with critical eyes. Tired of this occupation, she had called out and now sat swinging her legs and laughing merrily.

Marie shrugged her shoulders with a rather bored smile and would have returned to her window gazing, but Lucie jumped down from the table, caught her by the waist, and forced her down on a small rush-bottomed chair.

"Look here, Miss," she said, "shall I tell you something?"

"Well?"

"You've forgot to write your letter, and the company will be here at half-past one o'clock, so you've scarce four hours. D'you know what they're going to have for dinner? Clear soup, flounder or some such broad fish, chicken pasty, Mansfeld tart, and sweet plum compote. Faith, it's fine, but not fat! Your sweetheart's coming, Miss?"

"Nonsense!" said Marie crossly.

"Lord help me! It's neither banns nor betrothal because I say so! But, Miss, I can't see why you don't set more store by your cousin. He is the prettiest, most bewitching man I ever saw. Such feet he has! And there's royal blood in him—you've only to look at his hands, so tiny and shaped like a mould, and his nails no larger than silver groats and so pink and round. Such a pair of legs he can muster! When he walks it's like steel springs, and his eyes blow sparks—"

She threw her arms around Marie and kissed her neck so passionately and covetously that the child blushed and drew herself out of the embrace.

Lucie flung herself down on the bed, laughing wildly.

"How silly you are today," cried Marie. "If you carry on like this, I'll go downstairs."

"Merciful! Let me be merry once in a while! Faith, there's trouble enough, and I've more than I can do with. With my sweetheart in the war, suffering ill and worse— it's enough to break one's heart. What if they've shot him dead or crippled! God pity me, poor maid, I'd never get over it." She hid her face in the bedclothes and sobbed, "Oh, no, no, no, my own dear Lorens — I'd be so true to you if the Lord would only bring you back to me safe and sound! Oh, Miss, I *can't* bear it!"

Marie tried to soothe her with words and caresses, and at last she succeeded in making Lucie sit up and wipe her eyes.

"Indeed, Miss," she said, "no one knows how miserable I am. You see, I can't possibly behave as I should all the time. 'T is no use I resolve to set no store by the young men. When they begin jesting and passing compliments, my tongue's got an itch to answer them back, and then 't is true more foolery comes of it than I could answer for to Lorens. But when I think of the danger he's in, oh, then I'm more sorry than any living soul can think. For I love him, Miss, and no one else, upon my soul I do. And when I'm in bed, with the moon shining straight in on the floor, I'm like another woman, and everything seems so sad, and I weep and weep, and something gets me by the throat till I'm like to choke — it's terrible! Then I keep tossing in my bed and praying to God, though I scarce know what I'm praying for. Sometimes I sit up in bed and catch hold of my head, and it seems as if I'd lose my wits with longing. Why, goodness me, Miss, you're crying! Sure you're not longing for anyone in secret — and you so young?"

Marie blushed and smiled faintly. There was something flattering in the idea that she might be pining for a lover.

"No, no," she said, "but what you say is so sad. You make it seem as if there's naught but misery and trouble."

"Bless me, no, there's a little of other things too," said Lucie, rising in answer to a summons from below and nodding archly to Marie as she went.

Marie sighed and returned to the window. She looked down into the cool, green graveyard of St. Nikolaj, at the red walls of the church, over the tarnished copper roof of the castle, past the royal dockyard and ropewalk around to the slender spire of East Gate, past the gardens and wooden cottages of Hallandsaas, to the bluish Sound melting into the blue sky where softly moulded cloud masses were drifting to the Skaane shore.

Three months had passed since she came to Copenhagen. When she left home, she had supposed that life in the residential city must be something vastly different from what she had found. It had never occurred to her that she might be more lonely there than at Tjele Manor, where in truth, she had been lonely enough. Her father had never been a companion to her, for he was too entirely himself to be anything to others. He never became young when he spoke to fourteen years nor feminine when he addressed a little maid. He was always on the shady side of fifty and always Erik Grubbe.

As for his concubine, who ruled as though she were indeed mistress of the house, the mere sight of her was enough to call out all there was of pride and bitterness in Marie. This coarse, domineering peasant woman had wounded and tortured her so often that the girl could hardly hear her step without instantly and half unconsciously hardening into obstinacy and hatred. Little Anne, her half sister, was sickly and spoiled, which did not make it easier to get along with her; and to crown all, the mother made the child her excuse for abusing Marie to Erik Grubbe.

Who, then, were her companions?

She knew every path and road in Bigum woods, every cow that pastured in the meadows, every fowl in the hencoop. The kindly greeting of the servants and peasants when she met them seemed to say: Our young lady suffers wrong, and we know it. We are sorry, and we hate the woman up there as much as you do.

But in Copenhagen?

There was Lucie, and she was very fond of her, but after all she was a servant. Marie was in Lucie's confidence and was pleased and grateful for it, but Lucie was not in her confidence. She could not tell her troubles to the maid. Nor could she bear to have the fact of her unfortunate position put into words or hear a servant discuss her unhappy family affairs. She would not even brook a word of criticism against her aunt, though she certainly did not love her father's kinswoman and had no reason to love her.

Rigitze Grubbe held the theories of her time on the salutary effects of harsh discipline, and she set herself to bring up Marie accordingly. She had never had any children of her own, and she was not only a very impatient foster-mother but also clumsy, for mother love had never taught her the useful little arts that smooth the way for teacher and pupil. Yet a severe training might have been very good for Marie. The lack of watchful care in her home had allowed one side of her nature to grow almost too luxuriantly, while the other had been maimed and stunted by capricious cruelty, and she might have felt it a relief to be guided in the way she should go by the hard and steady hand of one who in all common sense could wish her nothing but good.

Yet she was not so guided. Mistress Rigitze had so many irons in the fire of politics and court intrigue that she was often away for days, and when at home she would be so preoccupied that Marie did with herself and her time what she pleased. When Mistress Rigitze had a moment to

spare for the child, the very consciousness of her own neglect made her doubly irritable. The whole relation therefore wore to Marie an utterly unreasonable aspect and was
fitted to give her the notion that she was an outcast whom
all hated and none loved.

As she stood at the window looking out over the city,
this sense of forlornness came over her again. She leaned
her head against the casement and lost herself in contem-
plation of the slowly gliding clouds.

She understood what Lucie had said about the pain of
longing. It was like something burning inside of you, and
there was nothing to do but to let it burn and burn — how
well she knew it! What would come of it all? One day
just like another — nothing, nothing — nothing to look forward to. Could it last? Yes, for a long time yet! Even when
she had passed sixteen? But things did happen to other
people! At least she wouldn't go on wearing a child's cap
after she was sixteen; sister Anne Marie hadn't — *she* had
been married. Marie remembered the noisy carousing at
the wedding long after she had been sent to bed — and the
music. Well, at least she could be married. But to whom?
Perhaps to the brother of her sister's husband. To be sure,
he was frightfully ugly, but if there was nothing else for
it — No, that certainly was nothing to look forward to.
Was there anything? Not that she could see.

She left the window, sat down by the table thoughtfully,
and began to write:

My loving greeting always in the name of Our Lord, dear
Anne Marie, good sister and friend! God keep you always
and be praised for His mercies. I have taken upon myself to write *pour vous congratuler* inasmuch as you have

been fortunately delivered of child and are now restored to good health. Dear sister, I am well and hearty. Our Aunt, as you know, lives in much splendor, and we often have company, chiefly gentlemen of the court, and with the exception of a few old dames, none visit us but men folks. Many of them have known our blessed mother and praise her beauty and virtue. I always sit at table with the company, but no one speaks to me except Ulrik Frederik, whom I would prefer to do without, for he is ever given to bantering and *raillerie* rather than sensible conversation. He is yet young and is not in the best repute; 'tis said he frequents both taverns and alehouses and the like. Now I have nothing new to tell except that today we have an assembly, and he is coming. Whenever I speak French he laughs very much and tells me that it is a hundred years old, which may well be, for Pastor Jens was a mere youth at the time of his travels. Yet he gives me praise because I put it together well, so that no lady of the court can do it better, he says, but this I believe to be but compliments, about which I care nothing. I have had no word from Tjele. Our Aunt cannot speak without cursing and lamenting of the enormity that our dear father should live as he does with a female of such lowly extraction. I grieve sorely, but that gives no boot for bane. You must not let Stycho see this letter, but give him greeting from my heart. September 1657.

Your dear sister,

MARIE GRUBBE.

The honorable Mistress Anne Marie Grubbe, consort of Stycho Höegh of Gjordslev, my good friend and sister, written in all loving-kindness.

The guests had risen from the table and entered the drawing room, where Lucie was passing the golden Dantzig brandy. Marie had taken refuge in a bay window, half hidden by the full curtains. Ulrik Frederik went over to her, bowed with exaggerated deference, and with a very grave face expressed his disappointment at having been seated so far from mademoiselle at the table. As he spoke, he rested his small brown hand on the windowsill. Marie looked at it and blushed scarlet.

"*Pardon*, Mademoiselle, I see that you are flushing with anger. Permit me to present my most humble service! Might I make so bold as to ask how I have had the misfortune to offend you?"

"Indeed I am neither flushed nor angry."

"Ah, so 't is your pleasure to call that color white? *Bien!* But then I would fain know by what name you designate the rose commonly known as red!"

"Can you never say a sensible word?"

"Hm — let me see — ay, it has happened, I own, but rarely —

> Doch Chloë, Chloë zürne nicht!
> Toll brennet deiner Augen Licht
> Mich wie das Hundsgestirn die Hunde,
> Und Worte schäumen mir vom Munde
> Dem Geifer gleich der Wasserscheu —"

"Forsooth, you may well say that!"

"*Ach*, Mademoiselle, 't is but little you know of the power of Eros! Upon my word there are nights when I have been so lovesick I have stolen down through the Silk Yard and leaped the balustrade into Christen Skeel's garden, and there I've stood like a statue among fragrant roses **and**

violets till the languishing Aurora has run her fingers
through my locks."

"Ah, Monsieur, you were surely mistaken when you
spoke of Eros; it must have been Evan—and you may
well go astray when you're brawling around at night-time.
You've never stood in Skeel's garden; you've been at the
sign of Mogens in Cappadocia among bottles and Rhenish
wineglasses, and if you've been still as a statue, it's been
something besides dreams of love that robbed you of the
power to move your legs."

"You wrong me greatly! Though I may go to the
vintner's house sometimes, 'tis not for pleasure nor revelry but to forget the gnawing anguish that afflicts me."

"Ah!"

"You have no faith in me; you do not trust to the con-
stancy of my *amour!* Heavens! Do you see the eastern
louver-window in St. Nikolaj? For three long days have
I sat there gazing at your fair countenance, as you bent
over your broidery frame."

"How unlucky you are! You can scarce open your
mouth but I can catch you in loose talk. I never sit with
my broidery frame toward St. Nikolaj. Do you know this
rigmarole?

> 'T was black night;
> Troll was in a plight,
> For man held him tight.
> To the troll said he:
> 'If you would be free,
> Then teach me quick
> Without guile or trick,
> One word of perfect truth.'

Up spake the troll: 'In sooth!'
Man let him go.
None on earth, I trow,
Could call troll liar for saying so."

Ulrik Frederik bowed deferentially and left her without a word.

She looked after him as he crossed the room. He did walk gracefully. His silk hose fitted him without fold or wrinkle. How pretty they were at the ankle, where they met the long, narrow shoe! She liked to look at him. She had never before noticed that he had a tiny pink scar in his forehead.

Furtively she glanced at her own hands and made a slight grimace—the fingers seemed to her too short.

CHAPTER III

WINTER came with hard times for the beasts of the forest and the birds of the fields. It was a poor Christmas within mud-walled huts and timbered ships. The Western Sea was thickly studded with wrecks, icy hulks, splintered masts, broken boats, and dead ships. Argosies were hurled upon the coast, shattered to worthless fragments, sunk, swept away, or buried in the sand; for the gale blew toward land with a high sea and deadly cold, and human hands were powerless against it. Heaven and earth were one reek of stinging, whirling snow that drifted in through cracked shutters and ill-fitting hatches to poverty and rags and pierced under eaves and doors to wealth and fur-bordered mantles. Beggars and wayfaring folk froze to death in the shelter of ditches and dikes; poor people died of cold on their bed of straw, and the cattle of the rich fared not much better.

The storm abated, and after it came a clear, tingling frost which brought disaster on the land — winter pay for summer folly! The Swedish army *walked* over the Danish waters. Peace was declared, and spring followed with green budding leaves and fair weather; but the young men of Sjælland did not ride a-Maying that year, for the Swedish soldiers were everywhere. There was peace indeed, but it carried the burdens of war and seemed not likely to live long. Nor did it. When the May garlands had turned dark and stiff under the midsummer sun, the Swedes went against the ramparts of Copenhagen.

During vesper service on the second Sunday in August, the tidings suddenly came: "The Swedes have landed at Korsör." Instantly the streets were thronged. People walked about quietly and soberly, but they talked a great deal; they all talked at once, and the sound of their voices and footsteps swelled to a loud murmur that neither rose nor fell and never ceased but went on with a strange, heavy monotony.

The rumor crept into the churches during the sermon. From the seats nearest the door it leaped in a breathless whisper to someone sitting in the next pew, then on to three people in the third, then past a lonely old man in the fourth on to the fifth, and so on till the whole congregation knew it. Those in the centre turned and nodded meaningly to people behind them; one or two who were sitting nearest the pulpit rose and looked apprehensively toward the door. Soon there was not a face lifted to the pastor. All sat with heads bent as though to fix their thoughts on the sermon, but they whispered among themselves, stopped for a tense moment and listened in order to gauge how far it was from the end, then whispered again. The muffled noise from the crowds in the streets grew more distinct: it was not to be borne any longer! The church people busied themselves putting their hymnbooks in their pockets.

"Amen!"

Every face turned to the preacher. During the litany prayer all wondered whether the pastor had heard anything. He read the supplication for the Royal House, the Councillors of the Realm, and the common nobility, for all who were in authority or entrusted with high office —and at that tears sprang to many eyes. As the prayer went on, there was a sound of sobbing, but the words came from hundreds of lips: "May God in His mercy deliver these our lands and kingdoms from battle and murder, pesti-

lence and sudden death, famine and drouth, lightning
and tempest, floods and fire, and may we for such
fatherly mercy praise and glorify His holy name!"

Before the hymn had ended, the church was empty, and
only the voice of the organ sang within it.

On the following day the people were again thronging
the streets but by this time they seemed to have gained
some definite direction. The Swedish fleet had that night
anchored outside of Dragör. Yet the populace was calmer
than the day before, for it was generally known that two
of the Councillors of the Realm had gone to parley with
the enemy and were—so it was said—entrusted with
powers sufficient to ensure peace. But when the Councillors
returned on Tuesday with the news that they had been
unable to make peace, there was a sudden and violent
reaction.

This was no longer an assemblage of staid citizens
grown restless under the stress of great and ominous tidings. No, it was a maelstrom of uncouth creatures, the
like of which had never been seen within the ramparts of
Copenhagen. Could they have come out of these quiet, respectable houses bearing marks of sober everyday business? What raving in long-sleeved sack and great-skirted
coat! What bedlam noise from grave lips and frenzied gestures of tight-dressed arms! None would be alone; none
would stay indoors; all wanted to stand in the middle of
the street with their despair, their tears, and wailing. See
that stately old man with bared head and bloodshot eyes!
He is turning his ashen face to the wall and beating the
stones with clenched fists. Listen to that fat tanner cursing the Councillors of the Realm and the miserable war!
Feel the blood in those fresh cheeks burning with hatred

of the enemy who brings the horrors of war, horrors that youth has already lived through in imagination! How they roar with rage at their own fancied impotence, and God in heaven, what prayers! What senseless prayers!

Vehicles are stopping in the middle of the street. Servants are setting down their burdens in sheds and doorways. Here and there people come out of the houses dressed in their best attire flushed with exertion, look about in surprise, then glance down at their clothes, and dart into the crowd as though eager to divert attention from their own finery. What have they in mind? And where do all these rough, drunken men come from? They crowd; they reel and shriek; they quarrel and tumble; they sit on doorsteps and are sick; they laugh wildly, run after the women, and try to fight the men.

It was the first terror, the terror of instinct. By noon it was over. Men had been called to the ramparts, had labored with holiday strength, and had seen moats deepen and barricades rise under their spades. Soldiers were passing. Artisans, students, and noblemen's servants were standing at watch, armed with all kinds of curious weapons. Cannon had been mounted. The King had ridden past, and it was announced that he would stay. Life began to look reasonable, and people braced themselves for what was coming.

In the afternoon of the following day, the suburb outside of West Gate was set on fire, and the smoke, drifting over the city brought out the crowds again. At dusk, when the flames reddened the weatherbeaten walls of Vor Frue Church tower and played on the golden balls topping the spire of St. Peter's, the news that the enemy was coming down Valby Hill stole in like a timid sigh. Through avenues and alleys sounded a frightened "The Swedes! The

Swedes!" The call came in the piercing voices of boys running through the streets. People rushed to the doors, booths
were closed, and the iron-mongers hastily gathered in their
wares. The good folk seemed to expect a huge army of the
enemy to pour in upon them that very moment.

The slopes of the ramparts and the adjoining streets
were black with people looking at the fire. Other crowds
gathered farther away from the centre of interest at the
Secret Passage and the Fountain. Many matters were discussed, the burning question being, Would the Swedes
attack that night or wait till morning?

Gert Pyper, the dyer from the Fountain, thought the
Swedes would be upon them as soon as they had rallied
after the march. Why should they wait?

The Icelandic trader, Erik Lauritzen of Dyers' Row,
thought it might be a risky matter to enter a strange city
in the dead of night, when you couldn't know what was
land and what was water.

"Water!" said Gert Dyer. "Would to God we knew
as much about our own affairs as the Swede knows! Don't
trust to that! His spies are where you'd least think. 'T is
well enough known to Burgomaster and Council, for the
aldermen have been round since early morning hunting
spies in every nook and corner. Fool him who can! No,
the Swede's cunning—especially in such business. 'Tis
a natural gift. I found that out myself—'tis some half-
score years since, but I've never forgotten that mum-
mery. You see, indigo she makes black, and she makes light
blue, and she makes medium blue, all according to the
mordant. Scalding and making the dye vats ready — any
'prentice can do that if he's handy—but the mordant—
there's the rub! That's an art! Use too much, and you

burn your cloth or yarn so it rots. Use too little, and the color will ne-ever be fast—no, not if it 's dyed with the most pre-cious logwood. Therefore the mordant is a closed *geheimnis* which a man does not give away except it be to his son, but to the journeymen—never! No—"

"Ay, Master Gert," said the trader, "ay, ay!"

"As I was saying," Gert went on, "about half a score of years ago I had a 'prentice whose mother was a Swede. He 'd set his mind on finding out what mordant I used for cinnamon brown, but as I always mixed it behind closed doors, 'twas not so easy to smoke it. So what does he do, the rascal? There 's so much vermin here round the Fountain it eats our wool and our linen, and for that reason we always hang up the stuff people give us to dye in canvas sacks under the loft-beams. So what does he do, the devil's *gesindchen*, but gets him one of the 'prentices to hang him up in a sack. And I came in and weighed and mixed and made ready and was half done when it happened so curiously that the cramp got in one of his legs up there and he began to kick and scream for me to help him down. Did I help him? Death and fire! But 'twas a scurvy trick he did me, yes, yes, yes! And so they are, the Swedes; you can never trust 'em over a doorstep."

"Faith, they 're ugly folk, the Swedes," spoke Erik Lauritzen. "They 've nothing to set their teeth in at home, so when they come to foreign parts they can never get their bellyful. They 're like poor-house children; they eat for to-day's hunger and for tomorrow's and yesterday's all in one. Thieves and cut-purses they are too—worse than crows and corpse-plunderers—and so murderous. It 's not for nothing people say, Quick with the knife like Lasse Swede!"

"And so lewd," added the dyer. "It never fails, if you see the hangman's man whipping a woman from town, and you ask who's the hussy, but they tell you she's a Swedish trull."

"Ay, the blood of man is various, and the blood of beasts, too. The Swede is to other people what the baboon is among the dumb brutes. There's such an unseemly passion and raging heat in the humors of his body that the natural intelligence which God in His mercy hath given all human creatures cannot hinder his evil lusts and sinful desires."

The dyer nodded several times in affirmation of the theories advanced by the trader. "Right you are, Erik Lauritzen, right you are. The Swede is of a strange and peculiar nature different from other people. I can always smell when an outlandish man comes into my booth whether he's a Swede or from some other country. There's such a rank odor about the Swedes—like goats or fish lye. I've often turned it over in my mind, and I make no doubt 'tis as you say; 'tis the fumes of his lustful and bestial humors. Ay, so it is."

"Sure, it's no witchcraft if Swedes and Turks smell different from Christians!" spoke up an old woman who stood near them.

"You're drivelling, Mette Mustard," interrupted the dyer. "Don't you know that Swedes are Christian folks?"

"Call 'em Christian if you like, Gert Dyer, but Finns and heathens and troll men have never been Christians by my prayer book, and it's true as gold what happened in the time of King Christian—God rest his soul!—when the Swedes were in Jutland. There was a whole regiment of 'em marching one night at new moon, and at the

stroke o' midnight they ran one from the other and
howled like a pack of werewolves or some such devilry,
and they scoured like mad round in the woods and fens
and brought ill luck to men and beasts."

"But they go to church on Sunday and have both pastor
and clerk just like us."

"Ay, let a fool believe that! They go to church, the
filthy gang, like the witches fly to vespers when the Devil
has St. John's mass on Hekkenfell. No, they 're bewitched,
an' nothing bites on 'em, be it powder or bullets. Half of
'em can cast the evil eye too, else why d' ye think the small-
pox is always so bad wherever those hell hounds 've set
their cursed feet? Answer me that, Gert Dyer, answer me
that, if ye can."

The dyer was just about to reply when Erik Lauritzen, who for some time had been looking about uneasily,
spoke to him, "Hush, hush, Gert Pyper! Who's the man
talking like a sermon yonder with the people standing
thick around him?"

They hurried to join the crowd, while Gert Dyer explained that it must be a certain Jesper Kiim, who had
preached in the Church of the Holy Ghost but whose doc-
trine, so Gert had been told by learned men, was hardly
pure enough to promise much for his eternal welfare or
clerical preferment.

The speaker was a small man of about thirty with something of the mastiff about him. He had long, smooth black
hair, a thick little nose on a broad face, lively brown eyes,
and red lips. He was standing on a doorstep, gesticulating forcefully and speaking with quick energy, though in
a somewhat thick and lisping voice.

"The twenty-sixth chapter of the Gospel according to

St. Matthew," he said, "from the fifty-first to the fifty-
fourth verse reads as follows: 'And, behold, one of them
which were with Jesus stretched out his hand, and drew
his sword, and struck a servant of the high priest's, and
smote off his ear. Then said Jesus unto him, Put up again
thy sword into his place: for all they that take the sword
shall perish with the sword. Thinkest thou that I cannot
now pray to my Father, and he shall presently give me
more than twelve legions of angels? But how then shall
the scriptures be fulfilled, that thus it must be?'

"Ay, my beloved friends, thus it must be. The poor
walls and feeble garrison of this city are at this moment
encompassed by a strong host of armed warriors, and their
king and commander has ordered them by fire and sword,
by attack and siege to subdue this city and make us all his
servants.

"And those who are in the city and see their peace
threatened and their ruin contrary to all feelings of hu-
manity determined upon, they arm themselves, they bring
catapults and other harmful implements of war to the ramparts, and they say to one another, 'Should not we with
flaming fire and shining sword fall upon the destroyers of
peace who would lay us waste? Why has God in heaven
awakened valor and fearlessness in the heart of man if
not for the purpose of resisting such an enemy?' And, like
Peter the Apostle, they would draw their glaive and smite
off the ear of Malchus. But Jesus says, 'Put up again thy
sword into his place: for all they that take the sword shall
perish with the sword.' 'Tis true, this may seem like a
strange speech to the unreason of the wrathful and like
foolishness to the unseeing blindness of the spiteful. But
the Word is not like a tinkle of cymbals for the ear only.

No, like the hull of a ship which is loaded with many useful things, so the Word of God is loaded with reason and
understanding. Let us therefore examine the Word and
find, one by one, the points of true interpretation. Wherefore should the sword remain in his place and he who
takes the sword perish with the sword? This is for us to
consider under three heads:

"Firstly, man is a wisely and beyond all measure glori-
ously fashioned microcosm or, as it may be interpreted,
a small earth, a world of good and evil. For does not the
Apostle James say that the tongue alone is a world of
iniquity among our members? How much more then the
whole body — the lustful eyes, the hastening feet, the cov-
etous hands, the insatiable belly, but even so the prayerful
knees, and the ears quick to hear! And if the body is a
world, how much more, then, our precious and immortal
soul! Ay, it is a garden full of sweet and bitter herbs, full
of evil lusts like ravening beasts and virtues like white
lambs. And is he who lays waste such a world to be regarded as better than an incendiary, a brawler, or a field
robber? And ye know what punishment is meted out to
such as these."

Darkness had fallen, and the crowd around the preacher
appeared only as a large, dark, slowly shifting and growing
mass.

"Secondly, man is a microtheos, that is, a mirror and
image of the Almighty God. Is not he who lays hands on
the image of God to be regarded as worse than he who
merely steals the holy vessels or vestments of the church or
who profanes the sanctuary? And ye know what punishment is meted out to such a one.

"Thirdly and lastly, it is the first duty of man to do

battle for the Lord without ceasing, clothed in the shining mail of a pure life and girded about with the flaming sword of truth. Armed thus, it behooves him to fight as a warrior before the Lord, rending the throat of hell and trampling upon the belly of Satan. Therefore the sword of the body must remain in its place, for verily we have enough to strive with that of the spirit!"

Meanwhile stragglers came from both ends of the street, stopped, and took their place in the outskirts of the crowd. Many were carrying lanterns, and finally the dark mass was encircled with an undulating line of twinkling lights that flickered and shifted with the movements of the people. Now and then a lantern would be lifted, and its rays would move searchingly over whitewashed walls and black window-panes till they rested on the earnest face of the preacher.

"But how is this? you would say in your hearts. 'Should we deliver ourselves bound hand and foot into the power of the oppressor, into a bitter condition of thralldom and degradation?' Oh, my well-beloved, say not so! For then you will be counted among those who doubt that Jesus could pray to his Father and He should send twelve legions of angels. Oh, do not fall into despair! Do not murmur in your hearts against the counsel of the Lord, and make not your liver black against His will! For he whom the Lord would destroy is struck down, and he whom the Lord would raise abides in safety. He has many ways by which He can guide us out of the wilderness of our peril. Has He not power to turn the heart of our enemy, and did He not suffer the angel of death to go through the camp of Sennacherib? And have you forgotten the engulfing waters of the Red Sea and the sudden destruction of Pharaoh?"

At this point Jesper Kiim was interrupted.

The crowd had listened quietly except for a subdued angry murmur from the outskirts, but suddenly Mette's voice pierced through: "Faugh, you hell-hound! Hold your tongue, you black dog! Don't listen to him! It's Swede money speaks out of his mouth!"

An instant of silence, then bedlam broke loose! Oaths, curses, and foul names rained over him. He tried to speak, but the cries grew louder, and those nearest to the steps advanced threateningly. A white-haired little man right in front, who had wept during the speech, made an angry lunge at the preacher with his long, silver-knobbed cane.

"Down with him, down with him!" the cry sounded. "Let him eat his words! Let him tell us what money he got for betraying us! Down with him! Send him to us; we'll knock the maggots out of him!"

"Put him in the cellar!" cried others. "In the City Hall cellar! Hand him down! hand him down!"

Two powerful fellows seized him. The wretch was clutching the wooden porch railing with all his might, but they kicked both railing and preacher down into the street, where the mob fell upon him with kicks and blows from clenched fists. The women were tearing his hair and clothes, and little boys, clinging to their fathers' hands, jumped with delight.

"Bring Mette!" cried someone in the back of the crowd. "Make way! Let Mette try him."

Mette came forward. "Will you eat your devil's nonsense? Will you, Master Rogue?"

"Never, never! We ought to obey God rather than men, as it is written."

"Ought we?" said Mette, drawing off her wooden shoe

and brandishing it before his eyes. "But men have shoes, and you're in the pay of Satan and not of God. I'll give you a knock on the pate! I'll plaster your brain on the wall!" She struck him with the shoe.

"Commit no sin, Mette," groaned the scholar.

"Now may the Devil——" she shrieked.

"Hush, hush!" some one cried. "Have a care, don't crowd so! There's Gyldenlöve, the lieutenant-general."

A tall figure rode past.

"Long live Gyldenlöve! The brave Gyldenlöve!" bellowed the mob. Hats and caps were swung aloft, and cheer upon cheer sounded until the rider disappeared in the direction of the ramparts. It was the lieutenant-general of the militia, colonel of horse and foot, Ulrik Christian Gyldenlöve, the King's half-brother.

The mob dispersed little by little till only a few remained.

"Say what you will, 'tis a curious thing," said Gert the dyer. "Here we're ready to crack the head of a man who speaks of peace, and we cry ourselves hoarse for those who've brought this war upon us."

"I give you good night, Gert Pyper!" said the trader hastily. "Good night and God be with you!" He hurried away.

"He's afraid of Mette's shoe," murmured the dyer, and at last he too turned homeward.

Jesper Kiim sat on the steps alone holding his aching head. The watchman on the ramparts paced slowly back and forth, peering out over the dark land where all was wrapped in silence, though thousands of enemies were encamped round about.

CHAPTER IV

FLAKES of orange-colored light shot up from the sea-gray fog bank on the horizon, and lit the sky overhead with a mild, rose-golden flame that widened and widened, grew fainter and fainter, until it met a long, slender cloud, caught its waving edge, and fired it with a glowing, burning radiance. Violet and pale pink, the reflection from the sunrise clouds fell over the beaches of Kallebodstrand. The dew sparkled in the tall grass of the western rampart; the air was alive and quivering with the twitter of sparrows in the gardens and on the roofs. Thin strips of delicate mist floated over the orchards, and the heavy, fruit-laden branches of the trees bent slowly under the breezes from the Sound.

A long-drawn, thrice repeated blast of the horn was flung out from West Gate and echoed from the other corners of the city. The lonely watchmen on the ramparts began to pace more briskly on their beats, shook their mantles, and straightened their caps. The time of relief was near.

On the bastion north of West Gate, Ulrik Frederik Gyldenlöve stood looking at the gulls sailing with white wings up and down along the bright strip of water in the moat. Light and fleeting, sometimes faint and misty, sometimes colored in strong pigments or clear and vivid as fire, the memories of his twenty years chased one another through his soul. They brought the fragrance of heavy roses and the scent of fresh green woods, the huntsman's cry and the fiddler's play, and the rustling of stiff, billowy silks. Distant but sunlit, the life of his childhood in the red-roofed Holstein town passed before him. He saw the tall form of his mother, Mistress Margrethe Pappen, a black

hymnbook in her white hands. He saw the freckled chambermaid with her thin ankles and the fencing-master with
his pimpled, purplish face and his bow-legs. The park of
Gottorp castle passed in review, and the meadows with
fresh hay-stacks by the fjord, and there stood the gamekeeper's clumsy boy Heinrich, who knew how to crow like
a cock and was marvellously clever at playing ducks and
drakes. Last came the church with its strange twilight, its
groaning organ, its mysterious iron-railed chapel, and its
emaciated Christ holding a red banner in his hand.

Again came a blast of the horn from West Gate, and
in the same moment the sun broke out bright and warm,
routing all mists and shadowy tones.

He remembered the chase when he had shot his first
deer, and old von Dettmer had made a sign in his forehead
with the blood of the animal while the poor hunters' boys
blew their blaring fanfares. Then there was the nosegay
to the castellan's Malene and the serious interview with his
tutor, then his first trip abroad. He remembered his first
duel in the fresh, dewy morning and Annette's cascades
of ringing laughter, and the ball at the Elector's and his
lonely walk outside of the city gates with head aching the
first time he had been tipsy. The rest was a golden mist,
filled with the tinkling of goblets and the scent of wine,
and there were Lieschen and Lotte and Martha's white
neck, and Adelaide's round arms. Finally came the journey to Copenhagen and the gracious reception by his royal
father, the bustling futilities of court duties by day and
the streams of wine and frenzied kisses at night, broken by
the gorgeous revelry of the chase or by nightly trysts and
tender whisperings in the shelter of Ibstrup park or the
gilded halls of Hilleröd castle.

Yet clearer than all these he saw the black, burning eyes of Sofie Urne; more insistent than aught else her voice sounded in his spell-bound memory — beautiful and voluptuously soft, its low notes drawing like white arms, or rising like a flitting bird that soars and mocks with wanton trills while it flees. . . .

A rustling among the bushes of the rampart below waked him from his dreams.

"Who goes there!" he cried.

"None but Daniel, Lord Gyldenlöve, Daniel Knopf," was the answer as a little crippled man came out from the bushes, bowing.

"Ha! Hop-o'-my-Thumb? A thousand plagues, what are you doing here?"

The man stood looking down at himself sadly.

"Daniel, Daniel!" said Ulrik Frederik, smiling. "You didn't come unscathed from the 'fiery furnace' last night. The German brewer must have made too hot a fire for you."

The cripple began to scramble up the edge of the rampart. Daniel Knopf, because of his stature called Hop-o'-my-Thumb, was a wealthy merchant of some and twenty years, known for his fortune as well as for his sharp tongue and his skill in fencing. He was boon companion with the younger nobility, or at least with a certain group of gallants, *le cercle des mourants*, consisting chiefly of younger men about the court. Ulrik Frederik was the life and soul of this crowd, which, though convivial rather than intellectual and notorious rather than beloved, was in fact admired and envied for its very peccadillos.

Half tutor and half mountebank, Daniel moved among these men. He did not walk beside them on the public streets or in houses of quality, but in the fencing school, the wine cellar, and the tavern he was indispensable. No one else could discourse so scientifically on bowling and dog training or talk with such unction of feints and parrying. No one knew wine as he did. He had worked out profound theories about dicing and love making and could speak learnedly and at length on the folly of crossing the domestic stud with the Salzburger horses. To crown all, he knew anecdotes about everybody, and—most impressive of all to the young men—he had decided opinions about everything.

Moreover, he was always ready to humor and serve them, never forgot the line that divided him from the nobility, and was decidedly funny when, in a fit of drunken frolic they would dress him up in some whimsical guise. He let himself be kicked about and bullied without resenting it and would often good-naturedly throw himself into the breach to stop a conversation that threatened the peace of the company.

Thus he gained admittance to circles that were to him as the very breath of life. To him, the citizen and cripple, the nobles seemed like demigods. Their cant alone was human speech. Their existence swam in a shimmer of light and a sea of fragrance while common folk dragged out their lives in drab-colored twilight and stuffy air. He cursed his citizen birth as a far greater calamity than his lameness, and grieved over it in solitude with a bitterness and passion that bordered on insanity.

" How now, Daniel," said Ulrik Frederik when the little man reached him. " 'Twas surely no light mist that clouded your eyes last night, since you've run aground here on the rampart, or was the clary at flood tide, since I find you high and dry like Noah's Ark on Mount Ararat?"

"Prince of the Canaries, you rave if you suppose I was in your company last night!"

"A thousand devils, what's the matter then?" cried Ulrik Frederik impatiently.

"Lord Gyldenlöve," said Daniel, looking up at him with tears in his eyes, "I'm an unhappy wretch."

"You're a dog of a huckster! Is it a herring boat you're afraid the Swede will catch? Or are you groaning because trade has come to a standstill, or do you think the saffron will lose its strength and the mildew fall on your pepper and paradise grain? You've a ha'penny soul! As if good citizens had naught else to think about than their own trumpery going to the devil—now that we may look for the fall of both King and realm!"

"Lord Gyldenlöve—"

"Oh, go to the devil with your whining!"

"Not so, Lord Gyldenlöve," said Daniel solemnly, stepping back a pace. "For I don't fret about the stoppage of trade, nor the loss of money and what money can buy. I care not a doit nor a damn for herring and saffron, but to be turned away by officers and men like one sick with the leprosy or convicted of crime, that's a sinful wrong against me, Lord Gyldenlöve. That's why I've been lying in the grass all night like a scabby dog that's been turned out; that's why I've been writhing like a miserable crawling beast and have cried to God in heaven asking Him why I alone should be utterly cast away, why my arm alone should be too withered and weak to wield a sword, though they're arming lackeys and 'prentice boys—"

"But who the shining Satan has turned you away?"

"Faith, Lord Gyldenlöve, I ran to the ramparts like the others, but when I came to one party, they told me they

had room for no more, and they were only poor citizens
anyway and not fit to be with the gentry and persons of
quality. Some parties said they would have no crooked
billets, for cripples drew the bullets and brought ill luck,
and none would hazard life and limb unduly by having
amongst them one whom the Lord had marked. Then I
begged Major-General Ahlefeldt that he would order me to
a position, but he shook his head and laughed: things hadn't
come to such a pass yet that they had to stuff the ranks
with stunted stumps who'd give more trouble than aid."

"But why didn't you go to the officers whom you
know?"

"I did so, Lord Gyldenlöve. I thought at once of the
cercle and spoke to one or two of the *mourants*, King
Petticoat and the Gilded Knight."

"And did they give you no help?"

"Ay, Lord Gyldenlöve, they helped me—Lord Gyldenlöve, they helped me, may God find them for it!
'Daniel,' they said, 'Daniel, go home and pick the maggots out of your damson prunes!' They had believed I had
too much tact to come here with my buffoonery. 'Twas
all very well if they thought me fit to wear cap and bells at
a merry bout, but when they were on duty, I was to keep
out of their sight. Now, was that well spoken, Lord Gyldenlöve? No, 'twas a sin, a sin! Even if they'd made free
with me in the wine-cellars, they said, I needn't think
I was one of them, or that I could be with them when
they were at their post. I was too presumptuous for them,
Lord Gyldenlöve! I'd best not force myself into their
company, for they needed no merry-andrew here. That's
what they told me, Lord Gyldenlöve! And yet I asked but
to risk my life side by side with the other citizens."

"Oh, ay," said Ulrik Frederik, yawning, "I can well understand that it vexes you to have no part in it all. You might find it irksome to sweat over your desk while the fate of the realm is decided here on the ramparts. Look you, you *shall* be in it! For—" He broke off and looked at Daniel with suspicion. "There's no foul play, sirrah?"

The little man stamped the ground in his rage and gritted his teeth, his face pale as a whitewashed wall.

"Come, come," Ulrik Frederik went on, "I trust you, but you can scarce expect me to put faith in your word as if 'twere that of a gentleman. And remember, 'twas your own that scorned you first. Hush!"

From a bastion at East Gate boomed a shot, the first that had been fired in this war. Ulrik Frederik drew himself up, while the blood rushed to his face. He looked after the white smoke with eager, fascinated eyes, and when he spoke, there was a strange tremor in his voice.

"Daniel," he said, "toward noon you can report to me, and think no more of what I said."

Daniel looked admiringly after him, then sighed deeply, sat down in the grass, and wept as an unhappy child weeps.

In the afternoon of the same day, a fitful wind blew through the streets of the city whirling up clouds of dust, whittlings, and bits of straw and carrying them hither and thither. It tore the tiles from the roofs, drove the smoke down the chimneys, and wrought sad havoc with the tradesmen's signs. The long, dull blue pennants of the dyers were flung out on the breeze and fell down again in spirals that tightened around their quivering staffs. The turners' spinning wheels rocked and swayed; hairy tails flapped over the doors of the furriers, and the resplendent glass suns

of the glaziers swung in a restless glitter that vied with the
polished basins of the barber-surgeons. Doors and shutters
were slamming in the back-yards. The chickens hid their
heads under barrels and sheds, and even the pigs grew
uneasy in their pens when the wind howled through sunlit
cracks and gaping joints.

The storm brought an oppressive heat. Within the
houses the people were gasping for breath, and only the flies
were buzzing about cheerfully in the sultry atmosphere.
The streets were unendurable, the porches were draughty,
and hence people who possessed gardens preferred to seek
shelter there.

In the large enclosure behind Christoffer Urne's house
in Vingaardsstræde, a young girl sat with her sewing under
a Norway maple. Her tall, slender figure was almost frail,
yet her breast was deep and full. Luxuriant waves of black
hair and almost startlingly large dark eyes accented the
pallor of her skin. The nose was sharp, but finely cut,
the mouth wide, though not full, and with a morbid
sweetness in its smile. The lips were scarlet, the chin
somewhat pointed, but firm and well rounded. Her dress
was slovenly: an old black velvet robe embroidered in
gold that had become tarnished, a new green felt hat
from which fell a snowy plume, and leather shoes that
were worn to redness on the pointed toes. There was lint
in her hair, and neither her collar nor her long, white
hands were immaculately clean.

The girl was Christoffer Urne's niece, Sofie. Her father,
Jörgen Urne of Alslev, Councillor of the Realm, Lord
High Constable, and Knight of the Elephant, had died
when she was yet a child, and a few years ago her mother,
Mistress Margrethe Marsvin, had followed him. The el-

derly uncle with whom she lived was a widower, and she was therefore, at least nominally, the mistress of his household.

She hummed a song as she worked and kept time by swinging one foot on the point of her toe.

The leafy crowns over her head rustled and swayed in the boisterous wind with a noise like the murmur of many waters. The tall hollyhocks, swinging their flower-topped stems back and forth in unsteady circles, seemed seized with a sudden tempestuous madness, while the raspberry bushes, timidly ducking their heads, turned the pale inner side of their leaves to the light and changed color at every breath. Dry leaves sailed down through the air, the grass lay flat on the ground, and the white bloom of the spirea rose and fell froth-like upon the light green, shifting waves of the foliage.

There was a moment of stillness. Everything seemed to straighten and hang breathlessly poised, still quivering in suspense, but the next instant the wind came shrieking again and caught the garden in a wild wave of rustling and glittering and mad rocking and endless shifting as before.

> "In a boat sat Phyllis fair;
>   Corydon beheld her there,
>   Seized his flute, and loudly blew it.
>   Many a day did Phyllis rue it;
>   For the oars dropped from her hands,
>   And aground upon the sands,
>   And aground——"

Ulrik Frederik was approaching from the other end of the garden. Sofie looked up for a moment in surprise, then bent her head over her work and went on humming. He strolled slowly up the walk, sometimes stopping to look at a flower, as though he had not noticed that there was anyone else in the garden. Presently he turned down a side-path, paused a moment behind a large white syringa to smooth his uniform and pull down his belt, took off his hat and ran his fingers through his hair, then walked on. The path made a turn and led straight to Sofie's seat.

"Ah, Mistress Sofie! Good-day!" he exclaimed as though in surprise.

"Good-day!" she replied with calm friendliness. She carefully disposed of her needle, smoothed her embroidery with her hands, looked up with a smile, and nodded. "Welcome, Lord Gyldenlöve!"

"I call this blind luck," he said, bowing. "I expected to find none here but your uncle, madam."

Sofie threw him a quick glance and smiled. "He's not here," she said, shaking her head.

"I see," said Ulrik Frederik, looking down.

There was a moment's pause. Then Sofie spoke, "How sultry it is today!"

"Ay, we may get a thunderstorm, if the wind goes down."

"It may be," said Sofie, looking thoughtfully toward the house.

"Did you hear the shot this morning?" asked Ulrik Frederik, drawing himself up as though to imply that he was about to leave.

"Ay, and we may look for heart-rending times this summer. One may well-nigh turn light-headed with the thought of the danger to life and goods, and for me, with so many kinsmen and good friends in this miserable affair, who are like to lose both life and limb and all they possess, there's reason enough for falling into strange and gloomy thoughts."

"Nay, sweet Mistress Sofie! By the living God, you must not shed tears!? You paint all in too dark colors—

> Tousiours Mars ne met pas au jour
> Des objects de sang et de larmes,
> Mais"—

and he seized her hand and lifted it to his lips—

> "... tousiours l'Empire d'amour
> Est plein de troubles et d'alarmes."

Sofie looked at him innocently. How lovely she was! The intense, irresistible night of her eyes, where day welled out in myriad light points like a black diamond flashing in the sun, the poignantly beautiful arch of her lips, the proud lily paleness of her cheeks melting slowly into a rose-golden flush like a white cloud kindled by the morning glow, the delicate temples, blue veined like flower-petals, shaded by the mysterious darkness of her hair . . .

Her hand trembled in his, cold as marble. Gently she drew it away, and her eyelids dropped. The embroidery slipped from her lap. Ulrik Frederik stooped to pick it up, bent one knee to the ground, and remained kneeling before her.

"Mistress Sofie!" he said.

She laid her hand over his mouth and looked at him with gentle seriousness, almost with pain.

"Dear Ulrik Frederik," she begged, "do not take it ill that I beseech you not to be led by a momentary senti-ment to attempt a change in the pleasant relations that have hitherto existed between us. It serves no purpose but to bring trouble and vexation to us both. Rise from this foolish position and take a seat in mannerly fashion here on this bench so that we may converse in all calmness."

"No, I want the book of my fate to be sealed in this hour," said Ulrik Frederik without rising. "You little know the great and burning passion I feel for you, if you imagine I can be content to be naught but your good friend. For the bloody sweat of Christ, put not your faith in anything so utterly impossible! My love is no smouldering spark that will flame up or be extinguished according as you blow hot or cold on it. *Par dieu!* 'Tis a raging and devouring fire, but it's for you to say whether it is to run out and be lost in a thousand flickering flames and will-o'-the-wisps, or burn forever, warm and steady, high and shining toward heaven."

"But, dear Ulrik Frederik, have pity on me! Don't draw me into a temptation that I have no strength to withstand! You must believe that you are dear to my heart and most precious, but for that very reason I would to the uttermost guard myself against bringing you into a false and foolish position that you cannot maintain with honor. You are nearly six years younger than I, and that which is now pleasing to you in my person, age may easily mar or distort to ugliness. You smile, but suppose that when you are thirty, you find yourself saddled with an old wrinkled hag of a wife who has brought you but little fortune, and not otherwise aided in your preferment! Would you not then wish that at twenty you had married a young royal lady, your equal in age and birth, who could have advanced you better than a common gentlewoman? Dear Ulrik Frederik, go speak to your noble kinsmen; they will tell you the same. But what they cannot tell you is this: if you brought to your home such a gentlewoman, older than yourself, she would strangle you with her jealousy. She would suspect your every look, nay, the innermost thoughts of your heart. She would know how much you had given up for her sake, and therefore she would strive the more to have her love be all in all to you. Trust me, she would encompass you with her idolatrous love as with a cage of iron, and if she perceived that you longed to quit it for a single instant, she would grieve day and night and embitter your life with her despondent sorrow."

She rose and held out her hand. " Farewell, Ulrik Frederik! Our parting is bitter as death, but after many years, when I am a faded old maid or the middle-aged wife of an aged man, you will know that Sofie Urne was right. May God the Father keep thee! Do you remember the Spanish romance book where it tells of a certain vine of India which winds itself about a tree for support, and goes on encircling it, long after the tree is dead and withered, until at last it holds the tree that else would fall? Trust me, Ulrik Frederik; in the same manner my soul will be sustained and held up by your love long after your sentiment shall be withered and vanished."

She looked straight into his eyes and turned to go, but he held her hand fast.

" Would you make me raving mad? Then hear me! Now I know that thou lovest me, no power on earth can part us! Does nothing tell thee that 'tis folly to speak of what thou wouldst or what I would when my blood is drunk with thee and I am bereft of all power over myself! I am possessed with thee, and if thou turnest away thy heart from me in this very hour, thou shouldst yet be mine in spite of thee, in spite of me! I love thee with a love like hatred —I think nothing of thy happiness. Thy weal or woe is

nothing to me — only that I be in thy joy, I be in thy sorrow, that I — "

He caught her to him violently and pressed her against
his breast.

Slowly she lifted her face and looked long at him with
eyes full of tears. Then she smiled. " Have it as thou wilt,
Ulrik Frederik," and she kissed him passionately.

Three weeks later their betrothal was celebrated with
much pomp. The King had readily given his consent, feeling that it was time to make an end of Ulrik Frederik's
rather too convivial bachelorhood.

CHAPTER V

AFTER the main sallies against the enemy on the second of September and the twentieth of October, the town rang with the fame of Ulrik Christian Gyldenlöve. Colonel Satan, the people called him. His name was on every lip. Every child in Copenhagen knew his sorrel, Bellarina, with the white socks, and when he rode past—a slim, tall figure in the wide-skirted blue uniform of the guard with its enormous white collar and cuffs, red scarf, and broad sword-belt—the maidens of the city peeped admiringly after him, proud when their pretty faces won them a bow or a bold glance from the audacious soldier. Even the sober fathers of families and their matrons in beruffled caps, who well knew how naughty he was and had heard the tales of all his peccadillos, would nod to each other with pleasure in meeting him, and would fall to discussing the difficult question of what would have happened to the city if it had not been for Gyldenlöve.

The soldiers and men on the ramparts idolized him, and no wonder, for he had the same power of winning the common people that distinguished his father, King Christian the Fourth. Nor was this the only point of resemblance. He had inherited his father's hot-headedness and intemperance, but also much of his ability, his gift of thinking quickly and taking in a situation at a glance. He was extremely blunt. Several years at European courts had not made him a courtier, nor even passably well mannered. In daily intercourse he was taciturn to the point of rudeness, and in the service he never opened his mouth without cursing and swearing like a common sailor.

With all this, he was a genuine soldier. In spite of his

youth—for he was but eight-and-twenty—he conducted the defence of the city, and led the dangerous but important sallies, with such masterful insight and such mature perfection of plan that the cause could hardly have been in better hands with anyone else among the men who surrounded Frederik the Third.

No wonder, therefore, that his name outshone all others, and that the poetasters, in their versified accounts of the fighting, addressed him as "thou vict'ry-crowned Gyldenlöv', thou Denmark's saviour brave!" or greeted him, "Hail, hail, thou Northern Mars, thou Danish David bold!" and wished that his life might be as a cornucopia, yea, even as a horn of plenty, full and running over with praise and glory, with health, fortune, and happiness. No wonder that many a quiet family vespers ended with the prayer that God would preserve Mr. Ulrik Christian, and some pious souls added a petition that his foot might be led from the slippery highways of sin, and his heart be turned from all that was evil, to seek the shining diadem of virtue and truth, and that he, who had in such full measure won the honor of this world, might also participate in the only true and everlasting glory.

Marie Grubbe's thoughts were much engrossed by this kinsman of her aunt. As it happened, she had never met him either at Mistress Rigitze's or in society, and all she had seen of him was a glimpse in the dusk when Lucie had pointed him out in the street.

All were speaking of him. Nearly every day some fresh story of his valor was noised abroad. She had heard and read that he was a hero, and the murmur of enthusiasm that went through the crowds in the streets as he rode past, had given her an unforgettable thrill.

The hero-name lifted him high above the ranks of ordinary human beings. She had never supposed that a hero could be like other people. King Alexander of Macedonia, Holger the Dane, and Chevalier Bayard were tall, distant, radiant figures—ideals rather than men. Just as she had never believed, in her childhood, that anyone could form letters with the elegance of the copy-book, so it had never occurred to her that one could become a hero. Heroes belonged to the past. To think that one might meet a flesh-and-blood hero riding in Store Færgestræde was beyond anything she had dreamed of. Life suddenly took on a different aspect. So it was not all dull routine! The great and beautiful and richly colored world she had read of in her romances and ballads was something she might actually see with her own eyes. There was really something that one could long for with all one's heart and soul; all these words that people and books were full of had a meaning. They stood for something. Her confused dreams and longings took form, since she knew that they were not hers alone, but that grown people believed in such things. Life was rich, wonderfully rich and radiant.

It was nothing but an intuition, which she knew to be true, but could not yet see or feel. He was her only pledge that it was so, the only thing tangible. Hence her thoughts and dreams circled about him unceasingly. She would often fly to the window at the sound of horses' hoofs, and, when out walking, she would persuade the willing Lucie to go round by the castle, but they never saw him.

Then came a day toward the end of October, when she was plying her bobbins by the afternoon light, at a window in the long drawing room where the fireplace was. Mistress Rigitze sat before the fire, now and then

taking a pinch of dried flowers or a bit of cinnamon bark
from a box on her lap and throwing it on a brazier full
of live coals that stood near her. The air in the low-ceil-
inged room was hot and close and sweet. But little light
penetrated between the full curtains of motley, dark-
flowered stuff. From the adjoining room came the whirr
of a spinning wheel, and Miss Rigitze was nodding
drowsily in her cushioned chair.

Marie Grubbe felt faint with the heat. She tried to cool
her burning cheeks against the small, dewey windowpane
and peeped out into the street, where a thin layer of new-
fallen snow made the air dazzlingly bright. As she turned
to the room again, it seemed doubly dark and oppressive.
Suddenly Ulrik Christian came in through the door, so
quickly that Mistress Rigitze started. He did not notice
Marie, but took a seat before the fire. After a few words of
apology for his long absence, he remarked that he was tired,
leaned forward in his chair, his face resting on his hand, and
sat silent, scarcely hearing Mistress Rigitze's lively chatter.

Marie Grubbe had turned pale with excitement, when
she saw him enter. She closed her eyes for an instant with
a sense of giddiness, then blushed furiously and could
hardly breathe. The floor seemed to be sinking under her,
and the chairs, tables, and people in the room falling through
space. All objects appeared strangely definite and yet flickering, for she could hold nothing fast with her eyes, and
moreover, everything seemed new and strange.

So this was he. She wished herself far away or at least in
her own room, her peaceful little chamber. She was frightened and could feel her hands tremble. If he would only
not see her! She shrank deeper into the window recess
and tried to fix her eyes on her aunt's guest.

Was this the way he looked?—not very, very much taller? And his eyes were not fiery black; they were blue —such dear blue eyes, but sad—that was something she could not have imagined. He was pale and looked as if he were sorry about something. Ah, he smiled, but not in a really happy way. How white his teeth were, and what a nice mouth he had, so small and finely formed!

As she looked, he grew more and more handsome in her eyes, and she wondered how she could ever have fancied him larger or in any way different from what he was. She forgot her shyness and thought only of the eulogies of him she had heard. She saw him storming at the head of his troops amid the exultant cries of the people. All fell back before him, as the waves are thrown off when they rise frothing around the broad breast of a galleon. Cannon thundered, swords flashed, bullets whistled through dark clouds of smoke, but he pressed onward, brave and erect, and on his stirrup Victory hung—in the words of a chronicle she had read.

Her eyes shone upon him full of admiration and enthusiasm.

He made a sudden movement and met her gaze, but turned his head away, with difficulty repressing a triumphant smile. The next moment he rose as though he had just caught sight of Marie Grubbe.

Mistress Rigitze said this was her little niece, and Marie made her courtesy.

Ulrik Christian was astonished and perhaps a trifle disappointed to find that the eyes that had given him such a look were those of a child.

"*Ma chère,*" he said with a touch of mockery, as he looked down at her lace, "you 're a past mistress in the art of working quietly and secretly; not a sound have I heard from your bobbins in all the time I've been here."

"No," replied Marie, who understood him perfectly; "when I saw you, Lord Gyldenlöve,"—she shoved the heavy lacemaker's cushion along the windowsill—"it came to my mind that in times like these 'twere more fitting to think of lint and bandages than of laced caps."

"Faith, I know that caps are as becoming in wartimes as any other day," he said, looking at her.

"But who would give them a thought in seasons like the present!"

"Many," answered Ulrik Christian, who began to be amused at her seriousness, "and I for one."

"I understand," said Marie, looking up at him gravely; "'tis but a child you are addressing." She courtesied ceremoniously and reached for her work.

"Stay, my little maid!"

"I pray you, let me no longer incommode you!"

"Hark'ee!" He seized her wrists in a hard grip and drew her to him across the little table. "By God, you're a thorny person, but," he whispered, "if one has greeted me with a look such as yours a moment ago, I will not have her bid me so poor a farewell—I will not have it! There—now kiss me!"

Her eyes full of tears, Marie pressed her trembling lips against his. He dropped her hands, and she sank down over the table, her head in her arms. She felt quite dazed. All that day and the next she had a dull sense of bondage, of being no longer free. A foot seemed to press on her neck and grind her helplessly in the dust. Yet there was no bitterness in her heart, no defiance in her thoughts, no desire for revenge. A strange peace had come over her soul and had chased away the flitting throng of dreams and longings. She could not define her feeling for Ulrik Christian; she only knew that if he said Come, she must go to him, and if he said Go, she must quit him. She did not understand it, but it was so and had always been so, thus and not otherwise.

With unwonted patience she worked all day long at her sewing and her lacemaking, meanwhile humming all the mournful ballads she had ever known, about the roses of love which paled and never bloomed again, about the swain who must leave his truelove and go to foreign lands, and who never, never came back anymore, and about the prisoner who sat in the dark tower such a long dreary time, and first his noble falcon died, and then his faithful dog died, and last his good steed died, but his faithless wife Malvina lived merrily and well and grieved not for him. These songs and many others she would sing, and sometimes she would sigh and seem on the point of bursting into tears, until Lucie thought her ill and urged her to put way-bread leaves in her stockings.

When Ulrik Christian came in, a few days later, and spoke gently and kindly to her, she too behaved as though nothing had been between them, but she looked with childlike curiosity at the large white hands that had held her in such a hard grip, and she wondered what there could be in his eyes or his voice that had so cowed her. She glanced at the mouth too under its narrow, drooping moustache, but furtively and with a secret thrill of fear.

In the weeks that followed, he came almost every day, and Marie's thoughts became more and more absorbed in him. When he was not there, the old house seemed dull and desolate, and she longed for him as the sleepless long for daylight, but when he came, her joy was never full and free, always timid and doubting.

One night she dreamed that she saw him riding through the crowded streets as on that first evening, but there were no cheers, and all the faces seemed cold and indifferent. The silence frightened her. She dared not smile at him, but hid behind the others. Then he glanced around with a strange, questioning, wistful look, and this look fastened on her. She forced her way through the mass of people and threw herself down before him, and his horse set its cold, iron-shod hoof on her neck.

She awoke and looked about her, bewildered, at the cold, moonlit chamber. Alas, it was but a dream! She sighed; she did want so much to show him how she loved him. Yes, that was it. She had not understood it before, but she loved him. At the thought, she seemed to be lying in a stream of fire, and flames flickered before her eyes, while every pulse in her heart throbbed and throbbed and throbbed. She loved him. How wonderful it was to say it to herself! She loved him! How glorious the words were, how tremendously real, and yet how unreal! Good God, what was the use, even if she did love him? Tears of self-pity came into her eyes—and yet! She huddled comfortably under the soft, warm coverlet of down—after all it was delicious to lie quite still and think of him and of her great, great love.

When Marie met Ulrik Christian again, she no longer felt timid. Her secret buoyed her up with a sense of her own importance, and the fear of revealing it gave her manner a poise that made her seem almost a woman. They were happy days that followed, fantastic, wonderful days! Was it not joy enough when Ulrik Christian went, to throw a hundred kisses after him, unseen by him and all others, or when he came, to fancy how her beloved would take her in his arms and call her by every sweet name she could think of, how he would sit by her side while they looked long into each other's eyes, and how she would run her hand through his soft, wavy brown hair? What did it matter that none of these things happened? She blushed at the very thought that they might happen.

They were fair and happy days, but toward the end of November Ulrik Christian fell dangerously ill. His health, long undermined by debauchery of every conceivable kind, had perhaps been unable to endure the continued strain of night watches and hard work in connection with his post. Or possibly fresh dissipations had strung the bow too tightly. A wasting disease marked by intense pain, wild fever dreams, and constant restlessness, attacked him, and soon took such a turn that none could doubt the name of the sickness was death.

On the eleventh of December Pastor Hans Didrichsen Bartskjær, chaplain to the royal family, was walking uneasily up and down over the fine straw mattings that covered the floor in the large leather-brown room outside of Ulrik Christian's sick chamber. He stopped absentmindedly before the paintings on the walls and seemed to examine with intense interest the fat, naked nymphs outstretched under the trees, the bathing Susannas, and the simpering Judith with bare, muscular arms. They could not hold his attention long, however, and he went to the window, letting his gaze roam from the gray-white sky to the wet, glistening copper roofs and the long mounds of dirty, melting snow in the castle park below. Then he resumed his nervous pacing, murmuring, and gesticulating.

Was that the door opening? He stopped short to listen.

No! He drew a deep breath and sank down into a chair, where he sat sighing and rubbing the palms of his hands together until the door really opened. A middle-aged woman wearing a huge flounced cap of red-dotted stuff appeared and beckoned cautiously to him. The pastor pulled himself together, stuck his prayer book under his arm, smoothed his cassock, and entered the sick chamber.

The large oval room was wainscoted in dark wood from floor to ceiling. From the central panel, depressed below the surface of the wall, grinned a row of hideous, white-toothed heads of blackamoors and Turks painted in gaudy colors. The deep, narrow lattice window was partially veiled by a sash curtain of thin, blue-gray stuff, leaving the lower part of the room in deep twilight, while the sun-beams played freely on the painted ceiling, where horses, weapons, and naked limbs mingled in an inextricable tan-gle, and on the canopy of the four-poster bed, from which hung draperies of yellow damask fringed with silver.

The air that met the pastor as he entered was warm, and so heavy with the scent of salves and nostrums that for a moment he could hardly breathe. He clutched a chair for support, his head swam, and everything seemed to be whirling around him—the table covered with flasks and phials, the window, the nurse with her cap, the sick man on the bed, the sword rack, and the door opening into the adjoining room where a fire was blazing in the grate.

"The peace of God be with you, my lord!" he greeted in a trembling voice as soon as he recovered from his mo-mentary dizziness.

"What the devil d' ye want here?" roared the sick man, trying to lift himself in bed.

"*Gemach, gnädigster Herr, gemach!*" Shoemaker's Anne,

the nurse, hushed him and, coming close to the bed, gently stroked the coverlet. " 'Tis the venerable *Confessionarius* of his Majesty, who has been sent hither to give you the sacrament."

"Gracious Sir, noble Lord Gyldenlöve!" began the pastor as he approached the bed. "Though 'tis known to me that you have not been among the simple wise or the wisely simple who use the Word of the Lord as their rod and staff and who dwell in His courts and although that God whose cannon is the crashing thunderbolt likewise holds in His hand the golden palm of victory and the blood dripping cypresses of defeat, yet men may understand, though not justify, the circumstance that you, whose duty it has been to command and set a valiant example to your people, may for a moment have forgotten that we are but as nothing, as a reed in the wind, nay, as the puny grafted shoot in the hands of the mighty Creator. You may have thought foolishly, This I have done; this is a fruit that I have brought to maturity and perfection. Yet now, beloved lord, when you lie here on your bed of pain, now God who is the merciful God of love hath surely enlightened your understanding and turned your heart to Him in longing with fear and trembling to confess your uncleansed sins, that you may trustfully accept the grace and forgiveness which His loving hands are holding out to you. The sharp-toothed worm of remorse——"

"Cross me fore and cross me aft! Penitence, forgiveness of sins, and life eternal!" jeered Ulrik Christian and sat up in bed. "Do you suppose, you sour-faced baldpate, do you suppose because my bones are rotting out of my body in stumps and slivers that gives me more stomach for your parson-palaver?"

"Most gracious lord, you sadly misuse the privilege which your high rank and yet more your pitiable condition give you to berate a poor servant of the Church, who is but doing his duty in seeking to turn your thoughts toward that which is assuredly to you the one thing needful. Oh, honored lord, it avails but little to kick against the pricks! Has not the wasting disease that has struck your body taught you that none can escape the chastisements of the Lord God, and that the scourgings of heaven fall alike on high and low?"

Ulrik Christian interrupted him, laughing, "Hell consume me, but you talk like a witless school-boy! This sickness that's eating my marrow I've rightfully brought on myself, and if you suppose that heaven or hell sends it, I can tell you that a man gets it by drinking and wenching and revelling at night. You may depend on 't. And now take your scholastic legs out of this chamber with all speed, or else I 'll—"

Another attack seized him, and as he writhed and moaned with the intense pain, his oaths and curses were so blasphemous and so appalling in their inventiveness that the scandalized pastor stood pale and aghast. He prayed God for strength and power of persuasion, if mayhap he might be vouchsafed the privilege of opening this hardened soul to the truth and glorious consolation of religion. When the patient was quiet again, he began, "My lord, my lord, with tears and weeping I beg and beseech you to cease from such abominable cursing and swearing! Remember, the axe is laid unto the root of the tree, and it shall be hewn down and cast into the fire if it continues to be unfruitful and does not in the eleventh hour bring forth flowers and good fruit! Cease your baleful resistance, and

throw yourself with penitent prayers at the feet of our
Saviour—"

When the pastor began his speech, Ulrik Christian sat
up at the headboard of the bed. He pointed threateningly
to the door and cried again and again, "Begone, parson!
Begone, march! I can't abide you any longer!"

"Oh, my dear lord," continued the clergyman, "if
mayhap you are hardening yourself because you misdoubt
the possibility of finding grace, since the mountain of your
sins is overwhelming, then hear with rejoicing that the
fountain of God's grace is inexhaustible—"

"Mad dog of a parson, will you go!" hissed Ulrik Christian between clenched teeth; "one—two!"

"And if your sins were red as blood, ay, as Tyrian
purple—"

"Right about face!"

"He shall make them white as Lebanon's—"

"Now by St. Satan and all his angels!" roared Ulrik
Christian as he jumped out of bed, caught a rapier from
the sword rack, and made a furious lunge after the pastor,
who, however, escaped into the adjoining room, slamming
the door after him. In his rage Ulrik Christian flung himself at the door, but sank exhausted to the floor and had to
be lifted into bed, though he still held the sword.

The forenoon passed in a drowsy calm. He suffered
no pain, and the weakness that came over him seemed a
pleasant relief. He lay staring at the points of light pene-
trating the curtain and counted the black rings in the
iron lattice. A pleased smile flitted over his face when he
thought of his onslaught on the pastor, and he grew irritable only when Shoemaker's Anne would coax him to close
his eyes and try to sleep.

In the early afternoon a loud knock at the door announced the entrance of the pastor of Trinity Church, Dr. Jens Justesen. He was a tall, rather stout man with coarse, strong features, short black hair, and large, deep-set eyes. Stepping briskly up to the bed, he said simply, "Goodday!"

As soon as Ulrik Christian became aware that another clergyman was standing before him, he began to shake with rage, and let loose a broadside of oaths and railing against the pastor, against Shoemaker's Anne, who had not guarded his peace better, against God in heaven and all holy things.

"Silence, child of man!" thundered Pastor Jens. "Is this language meet for one who has even now one foot in the grave? 'Twere better you employed the flickering spark of life that still remains to you in making your peace with the Lord, instead of picking quarrels with men. You are like those criminals and disturbers of peace who, when their judgment is fallen and they can no longer escape the red-hot pincers and the axe, then in their miserable impotence curse and revile the Lord our God with filthy and wild words. They seek thereby courage to drag themselves out of that almost brutish despair, that craven fear and slavish remorse without hope, into which such fellows generally sink toward the last and which they fear more than death and the tortures of death."

Ulrik Christian listened quietly until he had managed to get his sword out from under the coverlet. Then he cried, "Guard yourself, priest-belly!" and made a sudden lunge after Pastor Jens, who coolly turned the weapon aside with his broad prayer book.

"Leave such tricks to pages!" he said contemptuously. "They 're scarce fitting for you or me. And now this woman "—turning to Shoemaker's Anne—"had best leave us private."

Anne quitted the room, and the pastor drew his chair up to the bed while Ulrik Christian laid his sword on the coverlet.

Pastor Jens spoke fair words about sin and the wages of sin, about God's love for the children of men, and about the death on the cross.

Ulrik Christian lay turning his sword in his hand, letting the light play on the bright steel. He swore, hummed bits of ribald songs, and tried to interrupt with blasphemous questions, but the pastor went on speaking about the seven words of the cross, about the holy sacrament of the altar, and the bliss of heaven.

Then Ulrik Christian sat up in bed and looked the pastor straight in the face.

" 'Tis naught but lies and old wives' tales," he said.

" May the devil take me where I stand, if it is n't true!" cried the pastor, "every blessed word!" He hit the table with his fist till the jars and glasses slid and rattled against one another while he rose to his feet and spoke in a stern voice, " 'Twere meet that I should shake the dust from my feet in righteous anger and leave you here alone, a sure prey to the devil and his realm, whither you are most certainly bound. You are one of those who daily nail our Lord Jesus to the gibbet of the cross, and for all such the courts of hell are prepared. Do not mock the terrible name of hell, for it is a name that contains a fire of torment and the wailing and gnashing of teeth of the damned! Alas, the anguish of hell is greater than any human mind can conceive, for if one were tortured to death and woke in hell, he would long for the wheel and the red-hot pincers as for Abraham's bosom. 'T is true that sickness and disease are bitter to the flesh of man when they pierce like a draught, inch by inch, through every fibre of the body and stretch the sinews till they crack, when they burn like salted fire in the vitals, and gnaw with dull teeth in the innermost marrow! But the sufferings of hell are a raging storm racking every limb and joint, a whirlwind of unthinkable woe, an eternal dance of anguish; for as one wave rolls upon another, and is followed by another and another in all eternity, so the scalding pangs and blows of hell follow one another ever and everlastingly, without end and without pause."

The sick man looked around bewildered. "I won't!" he said, "I won't! I've nothing to do with your heaven or hell. I would die, only die and nothing more!"

"You shall surely die," said the pastor, "but at the end of the dark valley of death are two doors, one leading to the bliss of heaven and one to the torments of hell. There is no other way, no other way at all."

"Yes, there is, pastor; there must be—tell me, is there not?—a deep, deep grave hard by for those who went their own way, a deep black grave leading down to nothing—to no earthly thing?"

"They who went their own way are headed for the realm of the devil. They are swarming at the gate of hell; high and low, old and young, they push and scramble to escape the yawning abyss and cry miserably to that God whose path they would not follow, begging Him to take them away. The cries of the pit are over their heads, and they writhe in fear and agony, but the gates of hell shall close over them as the waters close over the drowning."

"Is it the truth you're telling me? On your word as an honest man, is it anything but a tale?"

"It is."

"But I won't! I 'll do without your God! I don't want to go to heaven, only to die!"

"Then pass on to that horrible place of torment where those who are damned for all eternity are cast about on the boiling waves of an endless sea of sulphur, where their limbs are racked by agony, and their hot mouths gasp for air among the flames that flicker over the surface. I see their bodies drifting like white gulls on the sea, yea, like a frothing foam in a storm, and their shrieks are like the noise of the earth when the earthquake tears it, and their anguish is without a name. Oh, would that my prayers might save thee from it, miserable man! But grace has hidden its countenance, and the sun of mercy is set forever."

"Then help me, pastor, help me!" groaned Ulrik Christian. "What are you a parson for, if you can't help me? Pray, for God's sake, pray! Are there no prayers in your mouth? Or give me your wine and bread, if there 's salvation in 'em as they say! Or is it all a lie—a confounded lie? I 'll crawl to the feet of your God like a whipped boy, since He 's so strong—it is not fair—He 's so mighty, and we 're so helpless! Make Him kind, your God, make Him kind to me! I bow down—I bow down—I can do no more!"

"Pray!"

"Ay, I 'll pray, I 'll pray all you want—indeed!" he knelt in bed and folded his hands. "Is that right?" he asked, looking toward Pastor Jens. "Now, what shall I say?"

The pastor made no answer.

For a few moments Ulrik Christian knelt thus, his large, bright, feverish eyes turned upward. "There are no words, pastor," he whimpered. "Lord Jesu, they 're all gone," and he sank down, weeping.

Suddenly he sprang up, seized his sword, broke it, and cried, "Lord Jesu Christ, see, I break my sword!" and he lifted the shining pieces of the blade. "*Pardon*, Jesu, *pardon!*"

The pastor then spoke words of consolation to him and gave him the sacrament without delay, for he seemed not to have a long time left. After that Pastor Jens called Shoemaker's Anne and departed.

The disease was believed to be contagious; hence none of those who had been close to the dying man attended him in his illness, but in the room below a few of his family and friends, the physician in ordinary to the King, and two or three gentlemen of the court were assembled to receive the noblemen, foreign ministers, officers, courtiers, and city councilmen who called to inquire about him. So the peace of the sick chamber was not disturbed, and Ulrik Christian was again alone with Shoemaker's Anne.

Twilight fell. Anne threw more wood on the fire, lit two candles, took her prayer book, and settled herself comfortably. She pulled her cap down to shade her face and very soon was asleep. A barber-surgeon and a lackey had been posted in the ante-room to be within call, but they were both squatting on the floor near the window, playing dice on the straw matting to deaden the sound. They were so absorbed in their game that they did not notice someone stealing through the room until they heard the door of the sick-chamber close.

"It must have been the doctor," they said, looking at each other in fright.

It was Marie Grubbe. Noiselessly she stole up to the bed and bent over the patient, who was dozing quietly. In the dim, uncertain light he looked very pale and unlike himself, the forehead had a deathly whiteness, the eyelids were unnaturally large, and the thin wax-yellow hands were groping feebly and helplessly over the dark blue bolster.

Marie wept. "Art thou so ill?" she murmured. She knelt, supporting her elbows on the edge of the bed, and gazed at his face.

"Ulrik Christian," she called, and laid her hand on his shoulder.

"Is anyone else here?" he moaned weakly.

She shook her head. "Art thou very ill?" she asked.

"Yes, 'tis all over with me."

"No, no, it must not be! Whom have I if you go? No, no, how can I bear it!"

"To live?—'tis easy to live, but I have had the bread of death and the wine of death; I must die—yes, yes—bread and wine—body and blood—d' you believe they help? No, no, in the name of Jesus Christ, in the name of Jesus Christ! Say a prayer, child; make it a strong one!"

Marie folded her hands and prayed.

"Amen, amen! Pray again! I'm such a great sinner, child; it needs so much! Pray again, a long prayer with many words—many words! Oh, no, what's that? Why is the bed turning?—Hold fast, hold fast! 'T is turning —like a whirlwind of unthinkable woe, a dance of eternal anguish, and—ha, ha, ha! Am I drunk again? What devilry is this—what have I been drinking? Wine! Ay, of course, 't was wine I drank, ha, ha! We're gaily yet, we're gaily—Kiss me, my chick!

> Herzen und Küssen
> Ist Himmel auf Erd—

Kiss me again, sweetheart; I'm so cold, but you're round

and warm. Kiss me warm! You're white and soft, white and smooth—"

He had thrown his arms around Marie and pressed the terrified child close to him. At that moment Shoemaker's Anne woke and saw her patient sitting up and fondling a strange woman. She lifted her prayer book threateningly and cried, "*H'raus*, thou hell-born wench! To think of the shameless thing sitting here and wantoning with the poor dying gentleman before my very eyes! *H'raus*, whoever ye are—handmaid of the wicked one, sent by the living Satan!"

"Satan!" shrieked Ulrik Christian and flung away Marie Grubbe in horror. "Get thee behind me! Go, go!" he made the sign of the cross again and again. "Oh, thou cursed devil! You would lead me to sin in my last breath, in my last hour, when one should be so careful. Begone, begone in the blessed name of the Lord, thou demon!" His eyes wide open, fear in every feature, he stood up in bed and pointed to the door.

Speechless and beside herself with terror, Marie rushed out. The sick man threw himself down and prayed and prayed while Shoemaker's Anne read slowly and in a loud voice prayer after prayer from her book with the large print.

A few hours later Ulrik Christian was dead.

CHAPTER VI

AFTER the attempt to storm Copenhagen in February
of fifty-nine, the Swedes retired and contented
themselves with keeping the city isolated. The beleaguered
townspeople breathed more freely. The burdens of war
were lightened, and they had time to rejoice in the honors
they had won and the privileges that had been conferred
on them. It is true there were some who had found a zest
in the stirring scenes of war and felt their spirits flag, as
they saw dull peace unfold its tedious routine, but the great
mass of people were glad and light at heart. Their happiness found vent in merry routs, for weddings, christenings,
and betrothals, long postponed while the enemy was so
oppressively near, gathered gay crowds in every court and
alley of the city.

Furthermore, there was time to take note of the neighbors and make the mote in their eyes into a beam. There
was time to backbite, to envy and hate. Jealousies, whether
of business or love, shot a powerful growth again, and old
enmity bore fruit in new rancor and new vengeance. There
was one who had lately augmented the number of his enemies, until he had drawn well-nigh the hate of the whole
community upon his head. This man was Corfitz Ulfeldt.
He could not be reached, for he was safe in the camp of
the Swedes, but certain of his relatives and those of his
wife who were suspected of a friendly regard for him, were
subjected to constant espionage and annoyance while the
court knew them not.

There were but few such, but among them was Sofie
Urne, Ulrik Frederik's betrothed. The Queen, who hated
Ulfeldt's wife more than she hated Ulfeldt himself, had

from the first been opposed to Ulrik Frederik's alliance with
a gentlewoman so closely related to Eleonore Christine,
and since the recent actions of Ulfeldt had placed him in
a more sinister light than ever, she began to work upon
the King and others in order to have the engagement annulled.

Nor was it long before the King shared the Queen's
view. Sofie Urne, who was in fact given to intrigue, had
been painted as so wily and dangerous, and Ulrik Frederik
as so flighty and easily led, that the King clearly saw how
much trouble might come of such an alliance. Yet he had
given his consent and was too sensitive about his word
of honor to withdraw it. He therefore attempted to reason
with Ulrik Frederik, and pointed out how easily his present
friendly footing at court might be disturbed by a woman
who was so unacceptable to the King and Queen, and justly
so, as her sympathies were entirely with the foes of the
royal house. Moreover, he said, Ulrik Frederik was standing in his own light, since none could expect important
posts to be entrusted to one who was constantly under the
influence of the enemies of the court. Finally, he alluded
to the intriguing character of Mistress Sofie and even expressed doubt of the sincerity of her regard. True love, he
said, would have sacrificed itself rather than bring woe upon
its object, would have hidden its head in sorrow rather than
exulted from the housetops. But Mistress Sofie had shown
no scruples; indeed, she had used his youth and blind infatuation to serve her own ends.

The King talked long in this strain but could not pre-
vail upon Ulrik Frederik, who still had a lively recollection
of the pleading it had cost him to make Mistress Sofie reveal her affection. He left the King, more than ever resolved

that nothing should part them. His courtship of Mistress Sofie was the first serious step he had ever taken in his life, and it was a point of honor with him to take it fully. There had always been so many hands ready to lead and direct him, but he had outgrown all that; he was old enough to walk alone, and he meant to do it. What was the favor of the King and the court, what were honor and glory, compared to his love? For that alone he would strive and sacrifice; in that alone he would live.

The King, however, let it be known to Christoffer Urne that he was opposed to the match, and the house was closed to Ulrik Frederik, who henceforth could see Mistress Sofie only by stealth. At first this merely fed the flame, but soon his visits to his betrothed grew less frequent. He became more clear-sighted where she was concerned, and there were moments when he doubted her love and even wondered whether she had not led him on, that summer day, while she seemed to hold him off.

The court, which had hitherto met him with open arms, was cold as ice. The King, who had taken such a warm interest in his future, was indifference itself. There were no longer any hands stretched out to help him, and he began to miss them, for he was by no means man enough to go against the stream. When it merely ceased to waft him along, he lost heart instantly. At his birth a golden thread had been placed in his hand, and he had but to follow it upward to happiness and honor. He had dropped this thread to find his own way, but he still saw it glimmering. What if he were to grasp it again? He could neither stiffen his back to defy the King nor give up Sofie. He had to visit her in secret, and this was perhaps the hardest of all for his pride to stomach. Accustomed to move in pomp and display, to

take every step in princely style, he winced at crawling
through back alleys. Days passed and weeks passed, filled
with inactive brooding and still-born plans. He loathed his
own helplessness and began to despise himself for a lag-
gard. Then came the doubt: perhaps his dawdling had killed
her love, or had she never loved him? They said she was
clever, and no doubt she was, but—as clever as they said?
Oh, no! What was love, then, if she did not love, and yet
—and yet . . .

Behind Christoffer Urne's garden ran a passage just
wide enough for a man to squeeze through. This was the
way Ulrik Frederik had to take when he visited his mistress,
and he would usually have Hop-o'-my-Thumb mounted on
guard at the end of the passage, lest people in the street
should see him climbing the board fence.

On a balmy, moonlit summer night three or four hours
after bedtime, Daniel had wrapped himself in his cloak and
found a seat for himself on the remains of a pig's trough
which someone had thrown out from a neighboring house.
He was in a pleasant frame of mind, slightly drunk, and
chuckling to himself at his own merry conceits. Ulrik Frederik had already scaled the fence and was in the garden. It
was fragrant with elder blossoms. Linen laid out to bleach
made long white strips across the grass. There was a soft
rustling in the maples overhead and the rose bushes at his
side; their red blossoms looked almost white in the moon-
light. He went up to the house, which stood shining white,
the windows in a yellow glitter. How quiet everything
was—radiant and calm! Suddenly the glassy whirr of a
cricket shivered the stillness. The sharp, blue-black shadows of the hollyhocks seemed painted on the wall behind
them. A faint mist rose from the bleach-linen. There!—

he lifted the latch, and the next moment he was in the darkness within. Softly he groped his way up the rickety staircase until he felt the warm, spice-scented air of the attic. The rotten boards of the floor creaked under his step. The moon shone through a small window overhead, throwing a square of light on the flat top of a grain pile. Scramble over—the dust whirling in the column of light! Now—the gable-room at last! The door opened from within and threw a faint reddish glow that illuminated for a second the pile of grain, the smoke-yellowed, sloping chimney, and the roof beams. The next moment they were shut out, and he stood by Sofie's side in the family clothes-closet.

The small, low room was almost filled with large linen-presses. From the loft hung bags full of down and feathers. Old spinning wheels were flung into the corners, and the walls were festooned with red onions and silver-mounted harness. The window was closed with heavy wooden shutters, but on a brass-trimmed chest beneath it stood a small hand lantern. Sofie opened its tiny horn-pane to get a brighter light. Her loosened hair hung down over the fur-edged broadcloth robe she had thrown over her homespun dress. Her face was pale and grief worn, but she smiled gaily and poured out a stream of chatter. She was sitting on a low stool, her hands clasped around her knees, looking up merrily at Ulrik Frederik, who stood silent above her while she talked and talked, lashed on by the fear his ill humor had roused in her.

"How now, Sir Grumpy?" she said. "You've nothing to say? In all the hundred hours that have passed, have you not thought of a hundred things you wanted to whisper to me? Oh, then you have not longed as I have!" She trimmed the candle with her fingers and threw the bit of burning wick on the floor. Instinctively Ulrik Frederik took a step forward and put it out with his foot.

"That's right!" she went on. "Come here and sit by my side; but first you must kneel and sigh and plead with me to be fond again, for this is the third night I'm watching. Yester eve and the night before I waited in vain, till my eyes were dim." She lifted her hand threateningly. "To your knees, Sir Faithless, and pray as if for your life!" She spoke with mock solemnity, then smiled, half beseeching, half impatient. "Come here and kneel, come!"

Ulrik Frederik looked around almost grudgingly. It seemed too absurd to fall on his knees there in Christoffer Urne's attic. Yet he knelt down, put his arm around her waist, and hid his face in her lap, though without speaking.

She too was silent, oppressed with fear; for she had seen Ulrik Frederik's pale, tormented face and uneasy eyes. Her hand played carelessly with his hair, but her heart beat violently in apprehension and dread.

They sat thus for a long time.

Then Ulrik Frederik started up.

"No, no!" he cried. "This can't go on! God our Father in heaven is my witness that you're dear to me as the innermost blood of my heart, and I don't know how I'm to live without you. But what does it avail? What can come of it? They're all against us—every one. Not a tongue will speak a word of cheer, but all turn from me. When they see me, 'tis as though a cold shadow fell over them where before I brought a light. I stand so utterly alone, Sofie, 'tis bitter beyond words. True, I know you warned me, but I'm eaten up in this strife. It sucks my courage and my honor, and though I'm consumed with shame, I must ask you to set me free. Dearest girl, release me from my word!"

Sofie had risen and stood cold and unflinching like a statue, eyeing him gravely as he spoke.

"I am with child," she said quietly and firmly.

If she had consented, if she had given him his freedom, Ulrik Frederik felt that he would not have taken it. He would have thrown himself at her feet. Sure of her, he would have defied the King and all. But she did not. She but pulled his chain to show him how securely he was bound. Oh, she was clever as they said! His blood boiled; he could have fallen upon her, clutched her white throat to drag the truth out of her and force her to open every petal and lay bare every shadow and fold in the rose of her love that he might know the truth at last! But he mastered himself and said with a smile: "Yes, of course, I know —'t was nothing but a jest, you understand."

Sofie looked at him uneasily. No, it had not been a jest. If it had been, why did he not come close to her and kiss her? Why did he stand there in the shadow? If she could only see his eyes! No, it was no jest. He had asked as seriously as she had answered. Ah, that answer! She began to see what she had lost by it. If she had only said yes, he would never have left her! "Oh, Ulrik Frederik," she said, "I was but thinking of our child, but if you no longer love me, then go, go at once and build your own happiness! I will not hold you back."

"Did I not tell you that 't was but a jest? How can you think that I would ask you to release me from my word and sneak off in base shame and dishonor! Whenever I lifted my head again," he went on, "I must fear lest the eye that had seen my ignominy should meet mine and force it to the ground." And he meant what he said. If she had loved him as passionately as he loved her, then perhaps, but now—never.

Sofie went to him and laid her head on his shoulder, weeping.

"Farewell, Ulrik Frederik," she said. "Go, go! I would not hold you one hour after you longed to be gone, no, not if I could bind you with a hair."

He shook his head impatiently. "Dear Sofie," he said, winding himself out of her arms, "let us not play a comedy with each other. I owe it both to you and to myself that the pastor should join our hands; it cannot be too soon. Let it be in two or three days—but secretly, for it is of no use to set the world against us more than has been done already." Sofie dared not raise any objection. They agreed on the time and the place and parted with tender good-nights.

When Ulrik Frederik came down into the garden, it was dark, for the moon had veiled itself, and a few heavy raindrops fell from the inky sky. The early cocks were crowing in the mews, but Daniel had fallen asleep on his post.

A week later his best parlor was the scene of Mistress Sofie's and Ulrik Frederik's private marriage by an obscure clergyman. The secret was not so well guarded, however, but that the Queen could mention it to the King a few days later. The result was that in a month's time the contract was annulled by royal decree and Mistress Sofie was sent to the cloister for gentlewomen at Itzehoe.

Ulrik Frederik made no attempt to resist this step. Although he felt deeply hurt, he was weary and bowed in dull dejection to whatever had to be. He drank too much almost every day and when in his cups would weep and plaintively describe to two or three boon companions, who were his only constant associates, the sweet, peaceful, happy life he might have led. He always ended with mournful hints that his days were numbered and that his broken heart would soon be carried to that place of healing where the bolsters were of black earth and the worms were chirurgeon.

The King, to make an end of all this, ordered him to accompany the troops which the Dutch were transferring to Fyen, and thence he returned in November with the news of the victory at Nyborg. He resumed his place at the court and in the favor of the King and seemed to be quite his old self.

CHAPTER VII

MARIE GRUBBE was now seventeen.

On the afternoon when she fled in terror from the death-bed of Ulrik Christian Gyldenlöve, she had rushed up to her own chamber and paced the floor, wringing her hands and moaning as with intense bodily pain until Lucie had run to Mistress Rigitze and breathlessly begged her for God's sake to come to Miss Marie, for she thought something had gone to pieces inside of her. Mistress Rigitze came but could not get a word out of the child. She had thrown herself before a chair with face hidden in the cushions, and to all Mistress Rigitze's questions answered only that she wanted to go home, she wanted to go home, she would n't stay a moment longer, and she had wept and sobbed, rocking her head from side to side. Mistress Rigitze had finally given her a good beating and scolded Lucie, saying that between them they had nearly worried the life out of her with their nonsense, and therewith she left the two to themselves.

Marie took the beating with perfect indifference. Had anyone offered her blows in the happy days of her love, it would have seemed the blackest calamity, the deepest degradation, but now it no longer mattered. In one short hour her longings, her faith, and her hopes had all been withered, shrivelled up, and blown away. She remembered once at Tjele when she had seen the men stone to death a dog that had ventured within the high railing of the duck-park. The wretched animal swam back and forth, unable to get out, the blood running from many wounds, and she remembered how she had prayed to God at every stone that it might strike deep, since the dog was so miserable that to spare it would have been the greatest cruelty. She felt like poor Diana and welcomed every sorrow, only wishing that it would strike deep, for she was so unhappy that the death-blow was her only hope.

Oh, if that was the end of all greatness—slavish whimpering, lecherous raving, and craven terror!—then there was no such thing as greatness. The hero she had dreamed of, *he* rode through the portals of death with ringing spurs and shining mail, with head bared and lance at rest, not with fear in witless eyes and whining prayers on trembling lips. Then there was no shining figure that she could dream of in worshipping love, no sun that she could gaze on till the world swam in light and rays and color before her blinded eyes. It was all dull and flat and leaden, bottomless triviality, lukewarm commonplace, and nothing else.

Such were her first thoughts. She seemed to have been transported for a short time to a fairy-land where the warm, life-laden air had made her whole being unfold like an exotic flower, flashing sunlight from every petal, breathing fragrance in every vein, blissful in its own light and scent, growing and growing, leaf upon leaf and petal upon petal, in irresistible strength and fullness. But this was all past. Her life was barren and void again; she was poor and numb with cold. No doubt the whole world was like that and all the people likewise. And yet they went on living in their futile bustle. Oh, her heart was sick with disgust at seeing them flaunt their miserable rags and proudly listen for golden music in their empty clatter.

Eagerly she reached for those treasured old books of devotion that had so often been proffered her and as often rejected. There was dreary solace in their stern words on the misery of the world and the vanity of all earthly things, but the one book that she pored over and came back to again and again was the Revelation of St. John the Divine. She never tired of contemplating the glories of the heavenly Jerusalem; she pictured it to herself down to the smallest detail, walked through every by-way, peeped in at every door. She was blinded by the rays of sardonyx and chrysolyte, chrysoprasus and jacinth; she rested in the shadow of the gates of pearl and saw her own face mirrored in the streets of gold like transparent glass. Often she wondered what she and Lucie and Aunt Rigitze and all the other people of Copenhagen would do when the first angel poured out the vial of the wrath of God upon earth, and the second poured out his vial, and the third poured out his—she never got any farther, for she always had to begin over again.

When she sat at her work, she would sing one long passion hymn after another, in a loud, plaintive voice, and in her spare moments she would recite whole pages from "The Chain of Prayerful Souls" or "A Godly Voice for Each of the Twelve Months," for these two she knew almost by heart.

Underneath all this piety there lurked a veiled ambition. Though she really felt the fetters of sin and longed for communion with God, there mingled in her religious exercises a dim desire for power, a half-realized hope that she might become one of the first in the kingdom of heaven. This brooding worked a transformation in her whole being. She shunned people and withdrew within herself. Even her appearance was changed, the face pale and thin, the eyes burning with a hard flame—and no wonder; for the terrible visions of the Apocalypse rode life-size through her dreams at night, and all day long her thoughts dwelt on what was dark and dreary in life. When Lucie had gone to sleep in the evening, she would steal out of bed and find a mystic ascetic pleasure in falling on her knees and praying, till her bones ached and her feet were numb with cold.

Then came the time when the Swedes raised the siege, and all Copenhagen divided its time between filling glasses as host and draining them as guest. Marie's nature, too, rebounded from the strain, and a new life began for her, on a certain day when Mistress Rigitze, followed by a seamstress, came up to her room and piled the tables and chairs high with the wealth of sacks, gowns, and pearl-embroidered caps that Marie had inherited from her mother. It was considered time that she should wear grown-up clothes.

She was in raptures at being the centre of all the bustle that broke in on her quiet chamber, all this ripping and measuring, cutting and basting. How perfectly dear that pounce-red satin glowing richly where it fell in long, heavy folds or shining brightly where it fitted smoothly over her form! How fascinating the eager parley about whether this silk chamelot was too thick to show the lines of her figure or that Turkish green too crude for her complexion! No scruples, no dismal broodings could stand before this joyous, bright reality. Ah, if she could but once sit at the festive board—for she had begun to go to assemblies—wearing this snow-white, crisp ruff among other young maidens in just as crisp ruffs, all the past would become as strange to her as the dreams of yesternight; and if she could but once tread the saraband and pavan in sweeping cloth of gold and lace mitts and broidered linen, those spiritual excesses would make her cheeks burn with shame.

It all came about: she was ashamed, and she did tread the saraband and pavan; for she was sent twice a week

with other young persons of quality to dancing school in
Christen Skeel's great parlor, where an old Mecklenburger
taught them steps and figures and a gracious carriage according to the latest Spanish mode. She learned to play on
the lute and was perfected in French; for Mistress Rigitze
had her own plans.

Marie was happy. As a young prince who has been held
captive is taken straight from the gloomy prison and harsh
jailer to be lifted to the throne by an exultant people, to
feel the golden emblem of power and glory pressed firmly
upon his curls, and see all bowing before him in smiling
homage, so she had stepped from her quiet chamber into
the world, and all had hailed her as a queen indeed; all
had bowed, smiling, before the might of her beauty.

There is a flower called the pearl hyacinth; as that is
blue, so were her eyes in color, but their lustre was that of
the falling dewdrop, and they were deep as a sapphire resting in shadow. They could fall as softly as sweet music that
dies, and glance up exultant as a fanfare. Wistful — ay, as
the stars pale at daybreak with a veiled, tremulous light,
so was her look when it was wistful. It could rest with such
smiling intimacy that many a man felt it like a voice in a
dream, far away but insistent, calling his name; but when
it darkened with grief, it was full of such hopeless woe
that one could almost hear the heavy dripping of blood.

Such was the impression she made, and she knew it,
but not wholly. Had she been older and fully conscious of
her beauty, it might have turned her to stone. She might
have come to look upon it as a jewel to be kept burnished
and in a rich setting that it might be the desire of all; she
might have suffered admiration coldly and quietly. Yet it
was not so. Her beauty was so much older than herself

and she had so suddenly come into the knowledge of its power, that she had not learned to rest upon it and let herself be borne along by it serene and self-possessed. Rather, she made efforts to please, grew coquettish and very fond of dress, while her ears drank in every word of praise, her eyes absorbed every admiring look, and her heart treasured it all.

She was seventeen, and it was Sunday, the first Sunday after peace had been declared. In the morning she had attended the thanksgiving service, and in the afternoon she was dressing for a walk with Mistress Rigitze.

The whole town was astir with excitement, for peace had opened the city gates, which had been closed for twenty-two long months. All were rushing to see where the suburb had stood, where the enemy had been encamped, and where "ours" had fought. They had to go down into the trenches, climb the barricades, peep into the necks of the mines, and pluck at the gabions. This was the spot where such a one had been posted, and here so-and-so had fallen, and over there another had rushed forward and been surrounded. Everything was remarkable, from the wheel tracks of the cannon carriages and the cinders of the watch fires to the bullet-pierced board fences and the sun-bleached skull of a horse. And so the narrating and explaining, the supposing and debating, went on, up the ramparts and down the barricades.

Gert Pyper was strutting about with his whole family. He stamped the ground at least a hundred times and generally thought he noticed a strangely hollow sound while his rotund spouse pulled him anxiously by the sleeve and begged him not to be too foolhardy, but Master Gert only stamped the harder. The grown-up son showed his little betrothed where he had been standing on the night when he got a bullet hole through his duffel great-coat, and where the turner's boy had had his head shot off. The smaller children cried because they were not allowed to keep the rifle ball they had found, for Erik Lauritzen, who was also there, said it might be poisoned. He was poking the half-rotten straw where the barracks had stood, for he remembered a story of a soldier who had been hanged outside of Magdeburg and under whose pillow seven of his comrades had found so much money that they had deserted before the official looting of the city began.

The green fields and grayish white roads were dotted black with people coming and going. They walked about examining the well-known spots like a newly discovered world or an island suddenly shot up from the bottom of the sea, and there were many who, when they saw the country stretching out before them field behind field and meadow behind meadow, were seized with *wanderlust* and began to walk on and on as though intoxicated with the sense of space, of boundless space.

Toward supper time, however, the crowds turned homeward and, as moved by one impulse, sought the North Quarter, where the graveyard of St. Peter's Church lay surrounded by spacious gardens, for it was an old-time custom to take the air under the green trees after vespers on summer Sundays. While the enemy was encamped before the ramparts, the custom naturally fell into disuse, and the churchyard had been as empty on Sundays as on week days; but this day old habits were revived, and people streamed in through both entrances from Nörregade: nobles and citizens, high and low, all had remembered the full-crowned linden trees of St. Peter's churchyard.

On the grassy mounds and the broad tombstones sat
merry groups of townspeople, man and wife, children and
neighbors, eating their supper, while in the outskirts of the
party stood the 'prentice boy munching the delicious Sunday sandwich as he waited for the basket. Tiny children
tripped with hands full of broken food for the beggar young-
sters that hung on the wall. Lads thirsting for knowledge
spelled their way through the lengthy epitaphs while father
listened full of admiration, and mother and the girls scanned
the dresses of the passers-by, for by this time the gentlefolk were walking up and down in the broad paths. They
usually came a little later than the others and either supped
at home or in one of the eating-houses in the gardens round
about.

Stately matrons and dainty maids, old councillors and
young officers, stout noblemen and foreign ministers passed
in review. There went bustling, gray-haired Hans Nansen,
shortening his steps to the pace of the wealthy Villem
Fiuren and listening to his piping voice. There came Cor-
fits Trolle and the stiff Otto Krag. Mistress Ide Daa,
famed for her lovely eyes, stood talking to old Axel Urup,
who showed his huge teeth in an everlasting smile, while
the shrunken form of his lady, Mistress Sidsel Grubbe,
tripped slowly by the side of Sister Rigitze and the impatient Marie. There were Gersdorf and Schack and Thuresen of the tow-colored mane and Peder Retz with Spanish
dress and Spanish manners.

Ulrik Frederik was among the rest, walking with Niels
Rosenkrands, the bold young lieutenant-colonel whose
French breeding showed in his lively gestures. When they
met Mistress Rigitze and her companions, Ulrik Frederik would have passed them with a cold, formal greeting,

for ever since his separation from Sofie Urne he had nursed
a spite against Mistress Rigitze, whom he suspected, as one
of the Queen's warmest adherents, of having had a finger
in the matter. But Rosenkrands stopped, and Axel Urup
urged them so cordially to sup with the party in Johan
Adolph's garden that they could not well refuse.

A few minutes later they were all sitting in the little
brick summer house eating the simple country dishes that
the gardener set before them.

"Is it true, I wonder," asked Mistress Ide Daa, "that the
Swedish officers have so bewitched the maidens of Sjælland with their pretty manners that they have followed
them in swarms out of land and kingdom?"

"Marry, it's true enough at least of that minx Mistress
Dyre," replied Mistress Sidsel Grubbe.

"Of what Dyres is she?" asked Mistress Rigitze.

"The Dyres of Skaaneland, you know, sister, those
who have such light hair. They're all intermarried with the
Powitzes. The one who fled the country, she's a daughter
of Henning Dyre of West Neergaard, he who married Sido-
nie, the eldest of the Ove Powitzes, and she went bag and
baggage—took sheets, bolsters, plate, and ready money
from her father."

"Ay," smiled Axel Urup, "strong love draws a heavy
load."

"Faith," agreed Oluf Daa, who always struck out with
his left hand when he talked, "love—as a man may say
—love is strong."

"Lo-ove," drawled Rosenkrands, daintily stroking his
moustache with the back of his little finger, "is like Hercules in female dress; gentle and charming in appearance and seeming all weak-ness and mild-ness, yet it has

stre-ength and craftiness to complete all the twelve labors of Hercules."

"Indeed," broke in Mistress Ide Daa, "that is plainly to be seen from the love of Mistress Dyre, which at least completed one of the labors of Hercules, inasmuch as it cleaned out chests and presses, even as he cleaned the stable of Uriah—or whatever his name was—you know."

"I would rather say"—Ulrik Frederik turned to Marie Grubbe—"that love is like falling asleep in a desert and waking in a balmy pleasure garden, for such is the virtue of love that it changes the soul of man and that which was barren now seems a very wonder of delight. But what are your thoughts about love, fair Mistress Marie?"

"Mine?" she asked. "I think love is like a diamond, for as a diamond is beautiful to look upon, so is love fair, but as the diamond is poison to anyone who swallows it, in the same manner love is a kind of poison and produces a baneful raging distemper in those who are infected by it—at least if one is to judge by the strange antics one may observe in amorous persons and by their curious conversation."

"Ay," whispered Ulrik Frederik gallantly, "the candle may well talk reason to the poor moth that is crazed by its light!"

"Forsooth, I think you are right, Marie," began Axel Urup, pausing to smile and nod to her. "Yes, yes, we may well believe that love is but a poison, else how can we explain that coldblooded persons may be fired with the most burning passion merely by giving them miracle-philtres and love-potions?"

"Fie!" cried Mistress Sidsel; "don't speak of such terrible godless business—and on a Sunday, too!"

" My dear Sidse," he replied, "there 's no sin in that—none at all. Would you call it a sin, Colonel Gyldenlöve? No? Surely not. Does not even Holy Writ tell of witches and evil sorceries? Indeed and indeed it does. What I was about to say is that all our humors have their seat in the blood. If a man is fired with anger, can't he feel the blood rushing up through his body and flooding his eyes and ears? And if he 's frightened o' the sudden, does not the blood seem to sink down into his feet and grow cold all in a trice? Is it for nothing, do you think, that grief is pale and joy red as a rose? And as for love, it comes only after the blood has ripened in the summers and winters of seventeen or eighteen years; then it begins to ferment like good grape wine; it seethes and bubbles. In later years it clears and settles as do other fermenting juices; it grows less hot and fierce. But as good wine begins to effervesce again when the grape-vine is in bloom, so the disposition of man, even of the old, is more than ordinarily inclined to love at certain seasons of the year when the blood, as it were, remembers the springtime of life."

"Ay, the blood," added Oluf Daa, "as a man may say, the blood—'t is a subtle matter to understand—as a man may say."

"Indeed," nodded Mistress Rigitze, "everything acts on the blood, both sun and moon and approaching storm; that's as sure as if 't were printed."

"And likewise the thoughts of other people," said Mistress Ide. "I saw it in my eldest sister. We lay in one bed together, and every night as soon as her eyes were closed, she would begin to sigh and stretch her arms and legs and try to get out of bed as someone were calling her. And 'twas but her betrothed, who was in Holland, and was so full of longing for her that he would do nothing day and night but think of her until she never knew an hour's peace, and her health—don't you remember, dear Mistress Sidsel, how weak her eyesight was all the time Jörgen Bille was from home?"

"Do I remember? Ah, the dear soul! But she bloomed again like a rosebud. Bless me, her first lying-in—" and she continued the subject in a whisper.

Rosenkrands turned to Axel Urup. "Then you believe," he said, "that an *elixir d'am-our* is a fermenting juice poured into the blood? That tallies well with a tale the late Mr. Ulrik Christian told me one day we were on the ramparts together. 'T was in Antwerp it happened—in the Hotellerie des Trois Brochets, where he had lodgings. That morning at ma-ass he had seen a fair, fair maid-en, and she had looked quite kind-ly at him. All day long she was not in his thoughts, but at night when he entered his chamber, there was a rose at the head of the bed. He picked it up and smelled it, and in the same mo-ment the coun-ter-feit of the maiden stood before him as painted on the wall, and he was seized with such sudden and fu-rious longing for her that he could have cried aloud. He rushed out of the house and into the street, and there he ran up and down, wail-ing like one be-witched. Something seemed to draw and draw him and burn like fire, and he never stopped till day dawned."

So they talked until the sun went down, and they parted to go home through the darkening streets. Ulrik Frederik joined but little in the general conversation, for he was afraid that if he said anything about love, it might be taken for reminiscences of his relation with Sofie Urne. Nor was he in the mood for talking, and when he and Rosenkrands were alone, he made such brief, absentminded replies that his companion soon wearied of him and left him to himself.

Ulrik Frederik turned homeward to his own apartments, which this time were at Rosenborg. His valet being out, there was no light in the large parlor, and he sat alone there in the dark till almost midnight.

He was in a strange mood, divided between regret and foreboding. It was one of those moods when the soul seems to drift as in a light sleep, without will or purpose, on a slowly gliding stream while mist-like pictures pass on the background of dark trees, and half-formed thoughts rise from the sombre stream like great dimly-lit bubbles that glide—glide onward and burst. Bits of the conversation that afternoon, the motley crowds in the churchyard, Marie Grubbe's smile, Mistress Rigitze, the Queen, the King's favor, the King's anger that other time . . . the way Marie moved her hands, Sofie Urne, pale and far away — yet paler and yet farther away —the rose at the head of the bed and Marie Grubbe's voice, the cadence of some word—he sat listening and heard it again and again winging through the silence.

He rose and went to the window, opened it, and leaned his elbows on the wide casement. How fresh it all was — so cool and quiet! The bittersweet smell of roses cooled with dew, the fresh, pungent scent of new-mown hay, and the spicy fragrance of the flowering maple were wafted in. A mist-like rain spread a blue, tremulous dusk over the garden. The black boughs of the larch, the drooping leafy veil of the birch, and the rounded crowns of the beech stood like shadows breathed on a background of gliding mist, while the clipped yew trees shot upward like the black columns of a roofless temple.

The stillness was that of a deep grave, save for the raindrops falling light as thistledown, with a faint, monotonous sound like a whisper that dies and begins again and dies there behind the wet, glistening trunks.

What a strange whisper it was when one listened! How wistful!—like the beating of soft wings when old memories flock. Or was it a low rustle in the dry leaves of lost illusions? He felt lonely, drearily alone and forsaken. Among all the thousands of hearts that beat round about in the stillness of the night, not one turned in longing to him! Over all the earth there was a net of invisible threads binding soul to soul, threads stronger than life, stronger than death; but in all that net not one tendril stretched out to him. Homeless, forsaken! Forsaken? Was that a sound of goblets and kisses out there? Was there a gleam of white shoulders and dark eyes? Was that a laugh ringing through the stillness?—What then? Better the slow-dripping bitterness of solitude than that poisonous, sickly sweetness. . . . Oh, curses on it! I shake your dust from my thoughts, slothful life, life for dogs, for blind men, for weaklings. . . . As a rose! O God, watch over her and keep her through the dark night! Oh, that I might be her guard and protector, smooth every path, shelter her against every wind—so beautiful—listening like a child—as a rose! . . .

CHAPTER VIII

ADMIRED and courted though she was, Marie Grubbe soon found that while she had escaped from the nursery, she was not fully admitted to the circles of the grown up. For all the flatteries lavished on them, such young maidens were kept in their own place in society. They were made to feel it by a hundred trifles that in themselves meant nothing but when taken together meant a great deal. First of all, the children were insufferably familiar, quite like their equals. And then the servants—there was a well-defined difference in the manner of the old footman when he took the cloak of a maid or a matron, and the faintest shade in the obliging smile of the chambermaid showed her sense of whether she was waiting on a married or an unmarried woman. The free-and-easy tone which the half-grown younkers permitted themselves was most unpleasant, and the way in which snubbings and icy looks simply slid off from them was enough to make one despair.

She liked best the society of the younger men, for even when they were not in love with her, they would show her the most delicate attention and say the prettiest things with a courtly deference that quite raised her in her own estimation —though to be sure it was tiresome when she found that they did it chiefly to keep in practice. Some of the older gentlemen were simply intolerable with their fulsome compliments and their mock gallantry, but the married women were worst of all, especially the brides. The encouraging, though a bit preoccupied, glance, the slight condescending nod with head to one side, and the smile— half pitying, half jeering —with which they would listen to her—it was insulting! Moreover, the conduct of the girls themselves was not of a kind to raise their position. They would never stand together, but if one could humiliate another, she was only too glad to do so. They had no idea of surrounding themselves with an air of dignity by attending to the forms of polite society the way the young married women did.

Her position was not enviable, and when Mistress Rigitze let fall a few words to the effect that she and other members of the family had been considering a match between Marie and Ulrik Frederik, she received the news with joy. Though Ulrik Frederik had not taken her fancy captive, a marriage with him opened a wide vista of pleasant possibilities. When all the honors and advantages had been described to her—how she would be admitted into the inner court circle, the splendor in which she would live, the beaten track to fame and high position that lay before Ulrik Frederik as the natural son and even more as the especial favorite of the King—while she made a mental note of how handsome he was, how courtly, and how much in love—it seemed that such happiness was almost too great to be possible, and her heart sank at the thought that after all, it was nothing but loose talk, schemes, and hopes.

Yet Mistress Rigitze was building on firm ground, for not only had Ulrik Frederik confided in her and begged her to be his spokesman with Marie, but he had induced her to sound the gracious pleasure of the King and Queen, and they had both received the idea very kindly and had given their consent, although the King had felt some hesitation to begin with. The match had, in fact, been settled long since by the Queen and her trusted friend and chief gentlewoman, Mistress Rigitze, but the King was not moved only by the persuasions of his consort. He knew

that Marie Grubbe would bring her husband a consider-
able fortune, and although Ulrik Frederik held Vording-
borg in fief, his love of pomp and luxury made constant
demands upon the King, who was always hard pressed
for money. Upon her marriage Marie would come into
possession of her inheritance from her dead mother, Mistress Marie Juul, while her father, Erik Grubbe, was at
that time owner of the manors of Tjele, Vinge, Gammel-
gaard, Bigum, Trinderup, and Nörbæk, besides various
scattered holdings. He was known as a shrewd manager
who wasted nothing and would no doubt leave his daughter a large fortune. So all was well. Ulrik Frederik could
go courting without more ado, and a week after midsummer their betrothal was solemnized.

Ulrik Frederik was very much in love, but not with the
stormy infatuation he had felt when Sofie Urne ruled his
heart. It was a pensive, amorous, almost wistful sentiment, rather than a fresh, ruddy passion. Marie had told
him the story of her dreary childhood, and he liked to picture to himself her sufferings with something of the voluptuous pity that thrills a young monk when he fancies the
beautiful white body of the female martyr bleeding on the
sharp spikes of the torture wheel. Sometimes he would be
troubled with dark forebodings that an early death might
tear her from his arms. Then he would vow to himself
with great oaths that he would bear her in his hands and
keep every poisonous breath from her, that he would lead
the light of every gold-shining mood into her young heart
and never, never grieve her.

Yet there were other times when he exulted at the
thought that all this rich beauty, this strange, wonderful
soul were given into his power as the soul of a dead man

into the hands of God to grind in the dust if he liked, to
raise up when he pleased, to crush down, to bend.

It was partly Marie's own fault that such thoughts could
rise in him, for her love, if she did love, was of a strangely
proud, almost insolent nature. It would be but a halting
image to say that her love for the late Ulrik Christian had
been like a lake whipped and tumbled by a storm while
her love for Ulrik Frederik was the same water in the evening, becalmed, cold, and glassy, stirred but by the breaking of frothy bubbles among the dark reeds of the shore.
Yet the simile would have some truth, for not only was she
cold and calm toward her lover, but the bright myriad
dreams of life that thronged in the wake of her first passion
had paled and dissolved in the drowsy calm of her present
feeling.

She loved Ulrik Frederik after a fashion, but might it
not be chiefly as the magic wand opening the portals to the
magnificent pageant of life, and might it not be the pageant
that she really loved? Sometimes it would seem otherwise.
When she sat on his knee in the twilight and sang little
airs about Daphne and Amaryllis to her own accompaniment, the song would die away, and while her fingers played
with the strings of the cithern, she would whisper in his
waiting ear words so sweet and warm that no true love owns
them sweeter, and there were tender tears in her eyes that
could be only the dew of love's timid unrest. And yet—
might it not be that her longing was conjuring up a mere
mood rooted in the memories of her past feeling, sheltered
by the brooding darkness, fed by hot blood and soft music,
—a mood that deceived herself and made him happy? Or
was it nothing but maidenly shyness that made her chary
of endearments by the light of day, and was it nothing but

girlish fear of showing a girl's weakness that made her eyes
mock and her lips jeer many a time when he asked for a
kiss or, vowing love, would draw from her the words all
lovers long to hear? Why was it, then, that when she was
alone and her imagination had wearied of picturing for the
thousandth time the glories of the future, she would often
sit gazing straight before her hopelessly and feel unutter-
ably lonely and forsaken?

In the early afternoon of an August day Marie and Ulrik
Frederik were riding, as often before, along the sandy road
that skirted the Sound beyond East Gate. The air was fresh
after a morning shower, the sun stood mirrored in the water,
and blue thunder clouds were rolling away in the distance.
    They cantered as quickly as the road would allow them,
a lackey in a long crimson coat following closely. They rode
past the gardens where green apples shone under dark
leaves, past fish nets hung to dry with the raindrops still
glistening in their meshes, past the King's fisheries with
red-tiled roof, and past the glue-boiler's house, where the
smoke rose straight as a column out of a chimney. They
jested and laughed, smiled and laughed, and galloped on.
    At the sign of the Golden Grove they turned and rode
through the woods toward Overdrup, then walked their
horses through the underbrush down to the bright surface
of the lake. Tall beeches leaned to mirror their green vault
in the clear water. Succulent marsh grass and pale pink
feather-foil made a wide motley border where the slope,
brown with autumn leaves, met the water. High in the
shelter of the foliage in a ray of light that pierced the cool
shadow, mosquitoes whirled in a noiseless swarm. A red
butterfly gleamed there for a second, then flew out into the

sunlight over the lake. Steel-blue dragonflies made bright streaks through the air, and the darting pike drew swift wavy lines over the surface of the water. Hens were cackling in the farmyard beyond the brushwood, and from the other side of the lake came a note of wood doves cooing under the domes of the beech trees in Dyrehaven.

They slackened their speed and rode out into the water to let their horses dabble their dusty hoofs and quench their thirst. Marie had stopped a little farther out than Ulrik Frederik and sat with reins hanging in order to let her mare lower its head freely. She was tearing the leaves from a long branch in her hand and sent them fluttering down over the water, which was beginning to stir in soft ripples.

"I think we may get a thunderstorm," she said, her eyes following the course of a light wind that went whirling over the lake raising round, dark, roughened spots on the surface.

"Perhaps we had better turn back," suggested Ulrik Frederik.

"Not for gold!" she answered and suddenly drove her mare to the shore. They walked their horses round the lake to the road and entered the tall woods.

"I would I knew," said Marie, when she felt the cool air of the forest fan her cheeks and drew in its freshness in long, deep breaths. "I would I knew—" She got no further but stopped and looked up into the green vault with shining eyes.

"What wouldst thou know, dear heart?"

"I'm thinking there's something in the forest air that makes sensible folks mad. Many's the time I have been walking in Bigum woods when I would keep on running and running till I got into the very thickest of it. I'd be

wild with glee and sing at the top of my voice and walk
and pick flowers and throw them away again and call to
the birds when they flew up—and then, on the sudden,
a strange fright would come over me, and I would feel, oh!
so wretched and so small! Whenever a branch broke, I'd
start, and the sound of my own voice gave me more fright
than anything else. Hast thou never felt it?"

Before Ulrik Frederik could answer her song rang out:

"Right merrily in the woods I go
  Where elm and apple grow,
  And I pluck me there sweet roses two
  And deck my silken shoe.
  Oh, the dance,
  Oh, the dance,
  Oh, tra-la-la!
  Oh, the red, red berries on the dogrose bush!"

and as she sang, the whip flew down over her horse, she
laughed, hallooed, and galloped at top speed along a narrow
forest path where the branches swept her shoulders. Her
eyes sparkled; her cheeks burned; she did not heed Ulrik
Frederik calling after her. The whip whizzed through the
air again, and off she went with reins slack! Her fluttering habit was flecked with foam. The soft earth flew up
around her horse. She laughed and cut the tall ferns with
her whip.

Suddenly the light seemed to be lifted from leaf and
branch and to flee from the rain-heavy darkness. The
rustling of the bushes had ceased, and the hoofbeats were
silent as she rode across a stretch of forest glade. On
either side the trees stood like a dark encircling wall.
Ragged gray clouds were scudding over the black, lower-

ing heavens. Before her rolled the murky blue waters of the Sound, and beyond rose banks of fog. She drew rein, and her tired mount stopped willingly. Ulrik Frederik galloped past, swung back in a wide circle, and halted at her side.

At that moment a shower fell like a gray, heavy, wet curtain drawn slantwise over the Sound. An icy wind flattened the grass, whizzed in their ears, and made a noise like foaming waves in the distant treetops. Large flat hail stones rattled down over them in white sheets, settled like bead strings in the folds of her dress, fell in a spray from the horses' manes, and skipped and rolled in the grass as though swarming out of the earth.

They sought shelter under the trees, rode down to the beach, and presently halted before the low door of the Bide-a-Wee Tavern. A stableboy took the horses, and the tall, bareheaded innkeeper showed them into his parlor, where, he said, there was another guest before them. It proved to be Hop-o'-my-Thumb, who rose at their entrance, offering to give up the room to their highnesses, but Ulrik Frederik graciously bade him remain.

"Stay here, my man," he said, "and entertain us in this confounded weather. I must tell you, my dear"—turning to Marie—"that this insignificant mannikin is the renowned comedian and merry-andrew of alehouses, Daniel Knopf, well learned in all the liberal arts such as dicing, fencing, drinking, shrovetide sports, and such matters, otherwise in fair repute as an honorable merchant in the good city of Copenhagen."

Daniel scarcely heard this eulogy. He was absorbed in looking at Marie Grubbe and formulating some graceful words of felicitation, but when Ulrik Frederik roused him with a sounding blow on his broad back, his face flushed with resentment and embarrassment. He turned to him angrily but mastered himself and said with his coldest smile, "We're scarce tipsy enough, Colonel."

Ulrik Frederik laughed and poked his side crying, "Oh, you sacred knave! Would you put me to confusion, you plaguy devil, and make me out a wretched braggart who lacks parchments to prove his boasting? Fie, fie, out upon you! Is that just? Have I not a score of times praised your wit before this noble lady till she has time and again expressed the greatest longing to see and hear your far-famed drolleries? You might at least give us the blind Cornelius Fowler and his whistling birds or play the trick—you know—with the sick cock and the clucking hens!"

Marie now added her persuasions, saying that Colonel Gyldenlöve was quite right, she had often wondered what pastime, what fine and particular sport, could keep young gentlemen in filthy alehouses for half days and whole nights together, and she begged that Daniel would oblige them without further urging.

Daniel bowed with perfect grace and replied that his poor pranks were rather of a kind to give fuddled young sparks added occasion for roaring and bawling than to amuse a dainty and highborn young maiden. Nevertheless, he would put on his best speed to do her pleasure, for none should ever say it of him that any command from her fair ladyship had failed of instant obedience and execution.

"Look 'ee!" he began, throwing himself down by the table and sticking out his elbows. "Now I'm a whole assembly of your betrothed's honorable companions and especial good friends."

He took a handful of silver dollars from his pocket and

laid them on the table, pulled his hair down over his eyes, and dropped his lower lip stupidly.

"Devil melt me!" he drawled, rattling the coins like dice. "I'm not the eldest son of the honorable Erik Kaase for nothing! What! you'd doubt my word, you muckworm? I flung ten, hell consume me, ten with a jingle! Can't you see, you dog? I'm asking if you can't see?— you blind lamprey, you! Or d' ye want me to rip your guts with my stinger and give your liver and lungs a chance to see too? Shall I—huh? You ass!"

Daniel jumped up and pulled a long face.

"You'd challenge me, would you?" he said hoarsely with a strong North Skaane accent, "you stinkard, you! D' you know whom you're challenging? So take me king o' hell, I'll strike your — Nay, nay," he dropped into his natural voice, "that's perhaps too strong a jest to begin with. Try another!"

He sat down, folded his hands on the edge of his knees as though to make room for his stomach, puffed himself up fat and heavy jowled, then whistled firmly and thoughtfully but in an altogether too slow tempo the ballad of Roselil and Sir Peter. Then he stopped, rolled his eyes amorously, and called in fond tones:

"Cockatoo—cockadoodle-doo!" He began to whistle again, but had some difficulty in combining it with an ingratiating smile. "Little sugar-top!" he called, "little honeydew, come to me, little chuck! P'st! Will it lap wine, little kitty? Lap nice sweet wine from little cruse?"

Again he changed his voice, leaned forward in his chair, winked with one eye, and crooked his fingers to comb an imaginary beard.

"Now stay here," he said coaxingly, "stay here, fair

Karen; I'll never forsake you, and you must never forsake me,"—his voice grew weepy,—"we'll never part, my dear, dear heart, never in the world! Silver and gold and honor and glory and precious noble blood—begone! I curse you! Begone! I say. You're a hundred heavens high above them, the thing of beauty you are! Though they've scutcheons and emblems—would that make 'em any better? You've got an emblem too—the red mark on your white shoulder that Master Anders burned with his hot iron, that's your coat-of-arms! I spit on my scutcheon to kiss that mark—that's all I think of scutcheons— that's all! For there isn't in all the land of Sjælland a high-born lady as lovely as you are—is there, huh? No, there isn't—not a bit of one!"

"That's—that's a lie!" he cried in a new voice, jumped up, and shook his fist over the table. "My Mistress Ide, you blockhead, she's got a shape—as a man may say—she's got limbs—as a man may say—limbs, I tell you, you slubberdegulleon!"

At this point Daniel was about to let himself fall into the chair again, but at that moment Ulrik Frederik pulled it away, and he rolled on the floor. Ulrik Frederik laughed uproariously, but Marie ran to him with hands outstretched as though to help him up. The little man, half rising on his knees, caught her hand and gazed at her with an expression so full of gratitude and devotion that it haunted her for a long time. Presently they rode home, and none of them thought that this chance meeting in the Bide-a-Wee Tavern would lead to anything further.

CHAPTER IX

THE States-General that convened in Copenhagen in the late autumn brought to town many of the nobility, all anxious to guard their ancient rights against encroachment but none the less eager for a little frolic after the busy summer. Nor were they averse to flaunting their wealth and magnificence in the faces of the townspeople, who had grown somewhat loud-voiced since the war, and to reminding them that the line between gentlemen of the realm and the unfree mob was still firm and immutable in spite of the privileges conferred by royalty, in spite of citizen valor and the glamor of victory, in spite of the teeming ducats in the strong boxes of the hucksters.

The streets were bright with throngs of noblemen and their ladies, bedizened lackeys, and richly caparisoned horses in silver-mounted harness. There was feasting and open house in the homes of the nobility. Far into the night the violin sounded from well-lit halls, telling the sleepy citizens that the best blood of the realm was warming to a stately dance over parquet floors while the wine sparkled in ancestral goblets.

All these festivities passed Marie Grubbe by; none invited her. Because of their ties to the royal family, some of the Grubbes were suspected of siding with the King against the Estate, and moreover the good old nobility cordially hated that rather numerous upper aristocracy formed by the natural children of the kings and their relatives. Marie was therefore slighted for a twofold reason, and as the court lived in retirement during the session of the States-General, it offered her no compensation.

It seemed hard at first, but soon it woke the latent

defiance of her nature and made her draw closer to Ulrik
Frederik. She loved him more tenderly for the very reason
that she felt herself being wronged for his sake. So when
the two were quietly married on the sixteenth of December, sixteen hundred and sixty, there was the best reason
to believe that she would live happily with the Master
of the King's Hunt, which was the title and office Ulrik
Frederik had won as his share of the favors distributed by
triumphant royalty.

This private ceremony was not in accordance with the
original plan, for it had long been the intention of the
King to celebrate their wedding in the castle, as Christian the Fourth had done that of Hans Ulrik and Mistress
Rigitze, but at the eleventh hour he had scruples and decided, in consideration of Ulrik Frederik's former marriage and divorce to refrain from public display.

So now they are married and settled, and time passes, and
time flies, and all is well—and time slackened its speed,
and time crawled; for it is true, alas! that when Leander
and Leonora have lived together for half a year, the glory is
often departed from Leander's love, though Leonora usually
loves him much more tenderly than in the days of their betrothal. She is like the small children who find the old story
new no matter how often it is told with the very same
words, the same surprises, and the self-same "Snip, snap,
snout, my tale's out," while Leander is more exacting and
grows weary as soon as his feeling no longer makes him
new to himself. When he ceases to be intoxicated, he suddenly becomes more than sober. The flush and glamor of
his ecstasy, which for a while gave him the assurance of a
demigod, suddenly departs: he hesitates, he thinks and be-

gins to doubt. He looks back at the chequered course of his
passion, heaves a sigh, and yawns. He is beset with longing,
like one who has come home after a lengthy sojourn in foreign parts and sees the altogether too familiar though long-
forgotten spots before him; as he looks at them, he wonders
idly whether he has really been gone from this well-known
part of the world so long.

In such a mood Ulrik Frederik sat at home one rainy
day in September. He had called in his dogs and had frol-
icked with them for a while, had tried to read, and had
played a game of backgammon with Marie. The rain was
pouring. It was impossible to go walking or riding, and so
he had sought his armory, as he called it, thinking he would
polish and take stock of his treasures — this was just the
day for it! It occurred to him that he had inherited a chest
of weapons from Ulrik Christian; he had ordered it brought
down from the attic and sat lifting out one piece after
another.

There were splendid rapiers of bluish steel inlaid with
gold or silvery bright with dull engraving. There were
hunting knives, some heavy and one-edged, some long and
flexible like tongues of flame, some three-edged and sharp
as needles. There were toledo blades, many toledos, light
as reeds and flexible as willows, with hilts of silver and jasper agate or of chased gold or gold and carbuncles. One
had nothing but a hilt of etched steel and for a sword-knot
a little silk ribbon embroidered in roses and vines with red
glass beads and green floss. It must be either a bracelet, a
cheap bracelet, or — Ulrik Frederik thought — more likely
a garter, and the rapier was stuck through it.

It comes from Spain, said Ulrik Frederik to himself,
for the late owner had served in the Spanish army for nine

years. Alack-a-day! He too was to have entered foreign
service with Carl Gustaf; but then came the war, and now
he supposed he would never have a chance to get out and
try his strength, and yet he was but three and twenty. To
live forever here at this tiresome little court—doubly tiresome since the nobility stayed at home—to hunt a little,
look to his estate once in a while, some time in the future
by the grace of the King to be made Privy Councillor of
the Realm and be knighted, keep on the right side of Prince
Christian and retain his office, now and then be sent on a
tedious embassy to Holland, grow old, get the rheumatism,
die, and be buried in Vor Frue Church—such was the brilliant career that stretched before him. And now they were
fighting down in Spain! There was glory to be won, a life
to be lived—that was where the rapier and the sword-knot
came from. No, he must speak to the King. It was still
raining, and it was a long way to Frederiksborg, but there
was no help for it. He could not wait; the matter must be
settled.

The King liked his scheme. Contrary to his custom he
assented at once, much to the surprise of Ulrik Frederik,
who during his whole ride had debated with himself all the
reasons that made his plan difficult, unreasonable, impossible. But the King said, Yes, he might leave before
Christmas. By that time the preparations could be completed and an answer received from the King of Spain.

The reply came in the beginning of December, but
Ulrik Frederik did not start until the middle of April, for
there was much to be done. Money had to be raised, re-
tainers equipped, letters written. Finally he departed.

Marie Grubbe was ill pleased with this trip to Spain. It
is true she saw the justice of Mistress Rigitze's argument

that it was necessary for Ulrik Frederik to go abroad and win honor and glory in order that the King might do something handsome for him; for although his Majesty had been made an absolute monarch, he was sensitive to what people said, and the noblemen had grown so captious and perverse that they would be sure to put the very worst construction on anything the King might do. Yet women have an inborn dread of all farewells, and in this case there was much to fear. Even if she could forget the chances of war and the long, dangerous journey and tell herself that a king's son would be well taken care of, yet she could not help her foreboding that their life together might suffer such a break by a separation of perhaps more than a year that it would never be the same again. Their love was yet so lightly rooted, and just as it had begun to grow, it was to be mercilessly exposed to ill winds and danger. Was it not almost like going out deliberately to lay it waste? And one thing she had learned in her brief married life: the kind of marriage she had thought so easy in the days of her betrothal, that in which man and wife go each their own way, could mean only misery with all darkness and no dawn. The wedge had entered their outward life; God forbid that it should pierce to their hearts! Yet it was surely tempting fate to open the door by such a parting.

Moreover, she was sadly jealous of all the light papistical feminine rabble in the land and dominions of Spain.

Frederik the Third, who, like many sovereigns of his time, was much interested in the art of transmuting baser metals into gold, had charged Ulrik Frederik when he came to Amsterdam to call on a renowned alchemist, the Italian Burrhi, and to drop a hint that if he should think of visit-

ing Denmark, the King and the wealthy Christian Skeel
of Sostrup would make it worth his while.

When Ulrik Frederik arrived in Amsterdam, he therefore
asked Ole Borch, who was studying there and knew Burrhi well, to conduct him to the alchemist. They found him a
man in the fifties, below middle height, and with a tendency
to fat, but erect and springy in his movements. His hair and
his narrow moustache were black, his nose was hooked and
rather thick, his face full and yellow in color; from the corners of his small, glittering black eyes innumerable furrows
and lines spread out like a fan, giving him an expression at
once sly and goodhumored. He wore a black velvet coat
with wide collar and cuffs and crape-covered silver buttons,
black knee-breeches and silk stockings, and shoes with
large black rosettes. His taste for fine lace appeared in the
edging on his cravat and shirt bosom and in the ruffles that
hung in thick folds around his wrists and knees. His hands
were small, white, and chubby and were loaded with rings
of such strange, clumsy shapes that he could not bring the
tips of his fingers together. Large brilliants glittered even
on his thumbs. As soon as they were seated, he remarked
that he was troubled with cold hands and stuck them in
a large fur muff, although it was summer.

The room into which he conducted Ulrik Frederik was
large and spacious with a vaulted ceiling and narrow Gothic
windows set high in the walls. Chairs were ranged around
a large centre table, their wooden seats covered with soft
cushions of red silk from which hung long, heavy tassels.
The top of the table was inlaid with a silver plate on which
the twelve signs of the zodiac, the planets, and some of the
more important constellations were done in niello. Above
it, a string of ostrich eggs hung from the ceiling. The floor

had been painted in a chequered design of red and gray, and
near the door a triangle was formed by old horseshoes that
had been fitted into the boards. A large coral tree stood under
one window, and a cupboard of dark carved wood with
brass mountings was placed under the other. A life-size
doll representing a Moor was set in one corner, and along
the walls lay blocks of tin and copper ore. The blackamoor
held a dried palm leaf in his hand.

When they were seated and the first interchange of
amenities was over, Ulrik Frederik — they were speaking in French — asked whether Burrhi would not with his
learning and experience come to the aid of the searchers
after wisdom in the land of Denmark.

Burrhi shook his head.

"'T is known to me," he replied, "that the secret art
has many great and powerful votaries in Denmark, but I
have imparted instruction to so many royal gentlemen and
church dignitaries and, while I will not say that ingratitude
or meagre appreciation have always been my appointed portion, yet have I encountered so much captiousness and
lack of understanding that I am unwilling to assume again
the duties of a master to such distinguished scholars. I
do not know what rule or method the King of Denmark
employs in his investigations, and my remarks can therefore contain no disparagement of him, but I can assure you
in confidence that I have known gentlemen of the highest nobility in the land, nay, anointed rulers and hereditary
kings who have been so ignorant of their *historia naturalis*
and *materia magica* that the most lowborn quacksalver could
not entertain such vulgar superstitions as they do. They
even put their faith in that widely disseminated though
shameful delusion that making gold is like concocting a

sleeping potion or a healing pillula, that if one has the cor-
rect ingredients, 't is but to mix them together, set them
over the fire, and lo! the gold is there. Such lies are circu-
lated by catch-pennies and ignoramuses—whom may the
devil take! Cannot the fools understand that if 't were so
simple a process, the world would be swimming in gold?
For although learned authors have held, and surely with
reason, that only a certain part of matter can be clarified
in the form of gold, yet even so we should be flooded. Nay,
the art of the gold maker is costly and exacting. It requires
a fortunate hand, and there must be certain constellations
and conjunctions in the ascendant if the gold is to flow
properly. 'T is not every year that matter is equally gold-
yielding. You have but to remember that it is no mere dis-
tillation nor sublimation but a very re-creating of nature
that is to take place. Nay, I will dare to say that a tremor
passes over the abodes of the spirits of nature whenever
a portion of the pure, bright metal is freed from the thou-
sand-year-old embrace of *materia vilis*."

"Forgive my question," said Ulrik Frederik, "but do
not these occult arts imperil the soul of him who prac-
tises them?"

"Indeed no," said Burrhi; "how can you harbor such
a thought? What magician was greater than Solomon,
whose seal, the great as well as the small, has been wondrously preserved to us unto this day? And who imparted
to Moses the power of conjuring? Was it not Sabaoth, the
spirit of the storm, the terrible one?" He pressed the stone
in one of his rings to his lips. " 'Tis true," he continued,
"that we know great names of darkness and awful words,
yea, fearful mystic signs which if they be used for evil,
as many witches and warlocks and vulgar soothsayers use

them, instantly bind the soul of him who names them in the fetters of Gehenna; but we call upon them only to free the sacred primordial element from its admixture of and pollution by dust and earthly ashes; for that is the true nature of gold; it is the original matter that was in the beginning and gave light before the sun and the moon had been set in their appointed places in the vault of heaven."

They talked thus at length about alchemy and other occult arts until Ulrik Frederik asked whether Burrhi had been able to cast his horoscope by the aid of the paper he had sent him through Ole Borch a few days earlier.

"In its larger aspects," replied Burrhi, "I might prognosticate your fate, but when the nativity is not cast in the very hour a child is born, we fail to get all the more subtle phenomena, and the result is but little to be depended upon. Yet some things I know. Had you been of citizen birth and in the position of a humble physician, then I should have had but joyful tidings for you. As it is, your path through the world is not so clear. Indeed, the custom is in many ways to be deplored by which the son of an artisan becomes an artisan, the merchant's son a merchant, the farmer's son a farmer, and so on throughout all classes. The misfortune of many men is due to nothing else but their following another career than that which the stars in the ascendant at the time of their birth would indicate. Thus if a man born under the sign of the ram in the first section becomes a soldier, success will never attend him, but wounds, slow advancement, and early death will be his assured portion, whereas, if he had chosen a handicraft, such as working in stone or wrought metals, his course would have run smooth. One who is born under the sign of the fishes, if in the first section, should till the soil, or if he be a man of fortune, should acquire a landed estate, while he who is born in the latter part should follow the sea, whether it be as the skipper of a smack or as an admiral. The sign of the bull in the first part is for warriors, in the second part, for lawyers. The twins, which were in the ascendant at the time of your birth, are, as I have said before, for physicians in the first part and for merchants in the second. But now let me see your palm."

Ulrik Frederik held out his hand, and Burrhi went to the triangle of horseshoes, touching them with his shoes as a tight-rope dancer rubs his soles over the waxed board before venturing out on the line. Then he looked at the palm.

"Ay," said he, "the honor line is long and unbroken; it goes as far as it may go without reaching a crown. The luck line is somewhat blurred for a time, but farther on it grows more distinct. There is the life line; it seems but poor, I grieve to say. Take great care until you have passed the age of seven and twenty, for at that time your life is threatened in some sinister and secret fashion, but after that the line becomes clear and strong and reaches to a good old age. There is but one offshoot—ah, no, there is a smaller one hard by. You will have issue of two beds, but few in each."

He dropped the hand.

"Hark," he said gravely, "there is danger before you, but where it lurks is hidden from me. Yet it is in no wise the open danger of war. If it should be a fall or other accident of travel, I would have you take these triangular malachites; they are of a particular nature. See, I myself carry one of them in this ring; they guard against falling from horse or coach. Take them with you and carry them

ever on your breast, or if you have them set in a ring,
cut away the gold behind them, for the stone must touch
if it is to protect you. And here is a jasper. Do you see
the design like a tree? It is very rare and most precious
and good against stabbing in the dark and liquid poisons.
Once more I pray you, my dear young gentleman, that
you have a care, especially where women are concerned.
Nothing definite is revealed to me, but there are signs
of danger gleaming in the hand of a woman, yet I know
nothing for a certainty, and it were well to guard also
against false friends and traitorous servants, against cold
waters and long nights."

Ulrik Frederik accepted the gifts graciously and did not
neglect the following day to send the alchemist a costly
necklace as a token of his gratitude for his wise counsel
and protecting stones. After that he proceeded directly to
Spain without further interruption.

CHAPTER X

THE house seemed very quiet that spring day when the
sound of horses' hoofs had died away in the distance.
In the flurry of leave-taking the doors had been left open;
the table was still set after Ulrik Frederik's breakfast, with
his napkin just as he had crumpled it at his plate, and the
tracks of his great riding boots were still wet on the floor.
Over there by the tall pier glass he had pressed her to his
heart and kissed and kissed her in farewell, trying to comfort her with oaths and vows of a speedy return. Involun-
tarily she moved to the mirror as though to see whether it
did not hold something of his image as she had glimpsed it
a moment ago while locked in his arms. Her own lonely,
drooping figure and pale, tear-stained face met her searching glance from behind the smooth, glittering surface.

She heard the street door close, and the lackey cleared
the table. Ulrik Frederik's favorite dogs, Nero, Passando,
Rumor, and Delphine, had been locked in and ran about
the room whimpering and sniffing his tracks. She tried
to call them but could not for weeping. Passando, the tall
red foxhound, came to her; she knelt down to stroke and
caress the dog, but he wagged his tail in an absentminded
way, looked up into her face, and went on howling.

Those first days—how empty everything was and dreary!
The time dragged slowly, and the solitude seemed to hang
over her, heavy and oppressive, while her longing would
sometimes burn like salt in an open wound. Ay, it was
so at first, but presently all this was no longer new, and
the darkness and emptiness, the longing and grief came
again and again like snow that falls flake upon flake,
until it seemed to wrap her in a strange, dull hopelessness,

almost a numbness that made a comfortable shelter of her sorrow.

Suddenly all was changed. Every nerve was strung to the most acute sensitiveness, every vein throbbing with blood athirst for life, and her fancy teemed like the desert air with colorful images and luring forms. On such days she was like a prisoner who sees youth slip by, spring after spring, barren, without bloom, dull and empty, always passing, never coming. The sum of time seemed to be counted out with hours for pennies; at every stroke of the clock one fell rattling at her feet, crumbled, and was dust while she would wring her hands in agonized life-hunger and scream with pain.

She appeared but seldom at court or in the homes of her family, for etiquette demanded that she should keep to the house. Nor was she in the mood to welcome visitors, and as they soon ceased coming, she was left entirely to herself. This lonely brooding and fretting soon brought on an indolent torpor, and she would sometimes lie in bed for days and nights at a stretch, trying to keep in a state betwixt waking and sleeping which gave rise to fantastic visions. Far clearer than the misty dream pictures of healthy sleep, these images filled the place of the life she was missing.

Her irritability grew with every day, and the slightest noise was torture. Sometimes she would be seized with the strangest notions and with sudden mad impulses that might almost raise a doubt of her sanity. Indeed, there was perhaps but the width of a straw between madness and that curious longing to do some desperate deed merely for the sake of doing it without the least reason or even real desire for it.

Sometimes when she stood at the open window leaning against the casement and looking down into the paved court below, she would feel an overmastering impulse to throw herself down, merely to do it. But in that very second she seemed to have actually made the leap in her imagination and to have felt the cool, incisive tingling that accompanies a jump from a height. She darted back from the window to the inmost corner of the room, shaking with horror, the image of herself lying in her own blood on the hard stones so vivid in her mind that she had to go back to the window again and look down in order to drive it away.

Less dangerous and of a somewhat different nature was the fancy that would seize her when she looked at her own bare arm and traced, in a kind of fascination, the course of the blue and deep violet veins under the white skin. She wanted to set her teeth in that white roundness, and she actually followed her impulse, biting like a fierce little animal mark upon mark till she felt the pain and would stop and begin to fondle the poor maltreated arm.

At other times when she was sitting quietly, she would be suddenly moved to go in and undress, only that she might wrap herself in a thick quilt of red silk and feel the smooth, cool surface against her skin, or put an ice-cold steel blade down her naked back. She had many such whims.

Finally, after an absence of fourteen months, Ulrik Frederik returned. It was a July night, and Marie lay sleepless, listening to the slow soughing of the wind, restless with anxious thoughts. For the last week she had been expecting Ulrik Frederik every hour of the day and night, longing for his arrival and fearing it. Would everything be as in olden times—fourteen months ago? Sometimes she thought no, then again yes. The truth was, she could not quite forgive him for that trip to Spain. She felt that she had aged in this long time, had grown timid and listless, while he would come fresh from the glamor and stir, full of youth and high spirits, finding her pale and faded, heavy of step and of mind, nothing like her old self. At first he would be strange and cold to her; she would feel all the more cast down, and he would turn from her, but she would never forsake him. No, no, she would watch over him like a mother, and when the world went against him, he would come back to her, and she would comfort him and be kind to him, bear want for his sake, suffer and weep, do everything for him. At other times she thought that as soon as she saw him all must be as before; yes, they romped through the rooms like madcap pages; the walls echoed their laughter and revelry, the corners whispered of their kisses—

With this fancy in her mind she fell into a light sleep. Her dreams were of noisy frolic, and when she awoke, the noise was still there. Quick steps sounded on the stairs, the street door was thrown open, doors slammed, coaches rumbled, and horses' hoofs scraped the cobblestones.

There he is! she thought, sprang up, caught the large quilt, and wrapping it round her, ran through the rooms. In the large parlor she stopped. A tallow dip was burning in a wooden candlestick on the floor, and a few of the tapers had been lit in the sconces, but the servant in his flurry had run away in the midst of his preparations. Someone was speaking outside. It was Ulrik Frederik's voice, and she trembled with emotion.

The door was opened, and he rushed in still wearing his hat and cloak. He would have caught her in his arms but got only her hand, as she darted back. He looked so strange in his unfamiliar garb. He was tanned and stouter than of

old, and under his cloak he wore a queer dress, the like of
which she had never seen. It was the new fashion of long
waistcoat and fur-bordered coat, which quite changed his
figure and made him still more unlike his old self.

"Marie!" he cried, "dear girl!" and he drew her to him,
wrenching her wrist till she moaned with pain. He heard
nothing. He was flustered with drink, for the night was
not warm and they had baited well in the last tavern.
Marie's struggles were of no avail; he kissed and fondled
her wildly, immoderately. At last she tore herself away
and ran into the next room, her cheeks flushed, her bosom
heaving, but thinking that perhaps this was rather a
queer welcome, she came back to him.

Ulrik Frederik was standing in the same spot, quite bewildered between his efforts to make his fuddled brain comprehend what was happening and his struggles to unhook
the clasps of his cloak. His thoughts and his hands were
equally helpless. When Marie went to him and unfastened
his cloak, it occurred to him that perhaps it was all a joke,
and he burst into a loud laugh, slapped his thigh, writhed and
staggered, threatened Marie archly, and laughed with maud-
lin good nature. He was plainly trying to express something
funny that had caught his fancy, started but could not find
the words, and at last sank down on a chair, groaning and
gasping, while a broad, fatuous smile spread over his face.

Gradually the smile gave place to a sottish gravity. He
rose and stalked up and down in silent, displeased majesty,
planted himself by the grate in front of Marie, one arm
akimbo, the other resting on the mantel, and—still in his
cups—looked down at her condescendingly. He made a
long, potvaliant speech about his own greatness and the
honor that had been shown him abroad, about the good for-

tune that had befallen Marie when she, a common nobleman's daughter, had become the bride of a man who might
have brought home a princess of the blood. Without the
slightest provocation he went on to impress upon Marie
that he meant to be master of his own house, and she must
obey his lightest nod; he would brook no gainsaying, no,
not a word, not one. However high he might raise her, she
would always be his slave, his little slave, his sweet little
slave, and at that he became as gentle as a sportive lynx,
wept and wheedled. With all the importunity of a drunken
man he forced upon her gross caresses and vulgar endearments, unavoidable, inescapable.

The next morning Marie awoke long before Ulrik Frederik. She looked almost with hatred on the sleeping figure
at her side. Her wrist was swollen and ached from his violent greeting of the night before. He lay with muscular arms
thrown back under his powerful, hairy neck. His broad
chest rose and fell, breathing, it seemed to her, a careless
defiance, and there was a vacant smile of satiety on his
dull, moist lips.

She paled with anger and reddened with shame as she
looked at him. Almost a stranger to her after their long
parting, he had forced himself upon her, demanding her
love as his right, cocksure that all the devotion and passion
of her soul were his, just as he would be sure of finding
his furniture standing where he left it when he went out.
Confident of being missed, he had supposed that all her
longings had taken wing from her trembling lips to him
in the distance and that the goal of all her desire was his
own broad breast.

When Ulrik Frederik came out, he found her half sitting,
half reclining on a couch in the blue room. She was pale,

her features relaxed, her eyes downcast, and the injured
hand lay listlessly in her lap wrapped in a lace handkerchief. He would have taken it, but she languidly held out
her left hand to him and leaned her head back with a pained
smile.

Ulrik Frederik kissed the hand she gave him and made
a joking excuse for his condition the night before, saying
that he had never been decently drunk all the time he had
been in Spain, for the Spaniards knew nothing about drinking. Besides, if the truth were told, he liked the homemade
alicant and malaga wine from Johan Lehn's dram-shop
and Bryhans' cellar better than the genuine sweet devilry
they served down there.

Marie made no reply.

The breakfast table was set, and Ulrik Frederik asked
if they should not fall to, but she begged him to pardon
her letting him eat alone. She wanted nothing, and her
hand hurt; he had quite bruised it. When his guilt was thus
brought home to him, he was bound to look at the injured
hand and kiss it, but Marie quickly hid it in a fold of her
dress with a glance — he said — like a tigress defending
her helpless cub. He begged long, but it was of no use, and
at last he sat down to the table laughing and ate with an
appetite that roused a lively displeasure in Marie. Yet he
could not sit still. Every few minutes he would jump up
and run to the window to look out, for the familiar street
scenes seemed to him new and curious. With all this running his breakfast was soon scattered about the room, his
beer in one window, the bread knife in another, his napkin slung over the vase of the gilded Gueridon, and a bun
on the little table in the corner.

At last he had done eating and settled down at the window. As he looked out, he kept talking to Marie, who from her couch made brief answers or none at all. This went on for a little while until she came over to the window where he sat, sighed, and gazed out drearily.

Ulrik Frederik smiled and assiduously turned his signet ring round on his finger. "Shall I breathe on the sick hand?" he asked in a plaintive, pitying tone.

Marie tore the handkerchief from her hand and continued to look out without a word.

"'T will take cold, the poor darling," he said glancing up.

Marie stood resting the injured hand carelessly on the windowsill. Presently she began drumming with her fingers as on a keyboard, back and forth, from the sunshine into the shadow of the casement, then from the shadow to the sunlight again.

Ulrik Frederik looked on with a smile of pleasure at the beautiful pale hand as it toyed on the casement, gamboled like a frisky kitten, crouched as for a spring, set its back, darted toward the bread knife, turned the handle round and round, crawled back, lay flat on the windowsill, then stole softly toward the knife again, wound itself round the hilt, lifted the blade to let it play in the sunlight, flew up with the knife—

In a flash the knife descended on his breast, but he warded it off, and it simply cut through his long lace cuff into his sleeve as he hurled it to the floor and sprang up with a cry of horror, upsetting his chair, all in a second as with a single motion.

Marie was pale as death. She pressed her hands against her breast, and her eyes were fixed in terror on the spot where Ulrik Frederik had been sitting. A harsh, lifeless

laughter forced itself between her lips, and she sank down
on the floor noiselessly and slowly, as if supported by invisible hands. While she stood playing with the knife, she
had suddenly noticed that the lace of Ulrik Frederik's shirt
had slipped aside revealing his chest, and a senseless impulse
had come over her to plunge the bright blade into that white
breast, not from any desire to kill or wound but only because the knife was cold and the breast warm, or perhaps
because her hand was weak and aching while the breast was
strong and sound, but first and last because she could not
help it, because her will had no power over her brain and
her brain no power over her will.

Ulrik Frederik stood pale, supporting his palms on the
table which shook under his trembling till the dishes slid and
rattled. As a rule he was not given to fear nor wanting in
courage, but this thing had come like a bolt out of the blue,
so utterly senseless and incomprehensible that he could
only look on the unconscious form stretched on the floor
by the window with the same terror that he would have felt
for a ghost. Burrhi's words about the danger that gleamed in
the hand of a woman rang in his ears, and he sank to his
knees praying, for all reasonable security, all common-sense
safeguards seemed gone from this earthly life together with
all human foresight. Clearly the heavens themselves were
taking sides; unknown spirits ruled, and fate was determined by supernatural powers and signs. Why else should
she have tried to kill him? Why? Almighty God, why, why?
Because it must be—must be.

He picked up the knife almost furtively, broke the blade,
and threw the pieces into the empty grate. Still Marie
did not stir. Surely she was not wounded? No, the knife
was bright, and there was no blood on his cuffs, but she lay

there as quiet as death itself. He hurried to her and lifted her in his arms.

Marie sighed, opened her eyes, and gazed straight out before her with a lifeless expression, then, seeing Ulrik Frederik, threw her arms around him, kissed and fondled him still without a word. Her smile was pleased and happy, but a questioning fear lurked in her eyes. Her glance seemed to seek something on the floor. She caught Ulrik Frederik's wrist, passed her hand over his sleeve, and when she saw that it was torn and the cuff slashed, she shrieked with horror.

"Then I really did it!" she cried in despair. "O God in highest heaven, preserve my mind, I humbly beseech Thee! But why don't you ask questions? Why don't you fling me away from you like a venomous serpent? And yet, God knows, I have no part nor fault in what I did. It simply came over me. There was something that forced me. I swear to you by my hope of eternal salvation there was something that moved my hand. Ah, you don't believe it! How can you?" And she wept and moaned.

But Ulrik Frederik believed her implicitly, for this fully bore out his own thoughts. He comforted her with tender words and caresses, though he felt a secret horror of her as a poor helpless tool under the baleful spell of evil powers. Nor could he get over this fear, though Marie day after day used every art of a clever woman to win back his confidence. She had indeed sworn that first morning that she would make Ulrik Frederik put forth all his charms and exercise all his patience in wooing her over again, but now her behavior said exactly the reverse. Every look implored; every word was a meek vow. In a thousand trifles of dress and manner, in crafty surprises and delicate attentions, she confessed her tender, clinging love every hour of the day, and if she had merely had the memory of that morning's incident to overcome, she would certainly have won, but greater forces were arrayed against her.

Ulrik Frederik had gone away an impecunious prince from a land where the powerful nobility by no means looked upon the natural son of a king as more than their equal. Absolute monarchy was yet young, and the principle that a king was a man who bought his power by paying in kind was very old. The light of demi-godhead, which in later days cast a halo about the hereditary monarch, had barely been lit, and was yet too faint to dazzle anyone who did not stand very near it.

From this land Ulrik Frederik had gone to the army and court of Philip the Fourth, and there he had been showered with gifts and honors, had been made Grand d'Espagne and put on the same footing as Don Juan of Austria. The king made it a point to do homage in his person to Frederik the Third, and in bestowing on him every possible favor, he sought to express his satisfaction with the change of government in Denmark and his appreciation of King Frederik's triumphant efforts to enter the ranks of absolute monarchs.

Intoxicated and elated with all this glory, which quite changed his conception of his own importance, Ulrik Frederik soon saw that he had acted with unpardonable folly in making the daughter of a common nobleman his wife. Thoughts of making her pay for his mistake, confused plans for raising her to his rank and for divorcing her chased one another through his brain during his trip homeward. On top of this came his superstitious fear that his life was in danger from her, and he made up his mind that until he could see his course more clearly, he would be cold and

ceremonious in his manner to her and repel every attempt
to revive the old idyllic relation between them.

Frederik the Third, who was by no means lacking in
power of shrewd observation, soon noticed that Ulrik Frederik was not pleased with his marriage, and he divined the
reason. Thinking to raise Marie Grubbe in Ulrik Frederik's eyes, he distinguished her whenever he could and
showered upon her every mark of royal grace, but it was of
no avail. It merely raised an army of suspicious and jealous
enemies around the favorite.

The Royal Family spent the summer, as often before, at
Frederiksborg. Ulrik Frederik and Marie moved out there
to help plan the junketings and pageants that were to be
held in September and October, when the Elector of Saxony was coming to celebrate his betrothal with the Princess Anne Sofie. The court was small as yet, but the circle
was to be enlarged in the latter part of August, when the
rehearsals of ballets and other diversions were to begin. It
was very quiet, and they had to pass the time as best they
could. Ulrik Frederik took long hunting and fishing trips
almost every day. The King was busy at his turning lathe
or in the laboratory which he had fitted up in one of the
small towers. The Queen and the princesses were embroi-
dering for the coming festivities.

In the shady lane that led from the woods up to the
wicket of the little park, Marie Grubbe was wont to take
her morning walk. She was there today. Up in the lane
her dress of madder-red shone against the black earth of
the walk and the green leaves. Slowly she came nearer. A
jaunty black felt hat trimmed only with a narrow pearl
braid rested lightly on her hair, which was piled up in

heavy ringlets. A silver-mounted solitaire gleamed on the
rim where it was turned up on the side. Her bodice fitted smoothly, and her sleeves were tight to the elbow,
whence they hung, deeply slashed, held together by clasps
of mother-of-pearl and lined with flesh-colored silk. Wide,
close-meshed lace covered her bare arms. The robe trailed
a little behind but was caught up high on the sides, falling
in rounded folds across the front and revealing a black and
white diagonally striped skirt which was just long enough
to give a glimpse of black-clocked stockings and pearl-
buckled shoes. She carried a fan of swan's feathers and
raven's quills.

Near the wicket she stopped, breathed in her hollow
hand, held it first to one eye then to the other, tore off a
branch, and laid the cool leaves on her hot eyelids. Still
the signs of weeping were plainly to be seen. She went in
at the wicket and started up toward the castle, but turned
back and struck into a side path.

Her figure had scarcely vanished between the dark green
box hedges when a strange and sorry couple appeared in
the lane: a man who walked slowly and unsteadily as though
he had just risen from a severe illness leaning on a woman
in an old-fashioned cloth coat and with a wide green shade
over her eyes. The man was trying to go faster than his
strength would allow, and the woman was holding him
back, while she tripped along, remonstrating querulously.

"Hold, hold!" she said. "Wait a bit and take your feet
with you! You're running on like a loose wheel going down
hill. Weak limbs must be weakly borne. Gently now! Isn't
that what she told you, the wise woman in Lynge? What
sense is there in limping along on legs that have no more
starch nor strength than an old rotten thread!"

"Alack, good Lord, what legs they are!" whimpered the sick man and stopped, for his knees shook under him. "Now she's all out of sight"—he looked longingly at the wicket—"all out of sight! And there will be no promenade today, the harbinger says, and it's so long till tomorrow!"

"There, there, Daniel dear, the time will pass, and you can rest to-day and be stronger tomorrow, and then we shall follow her all through the woods way down to the wicket, indeed we shall. But now we must go home, and you shall rest on the soft couch and drink a good pot of ale, and then we shall play a game of reversis, and later on, when their highnesses have supped, Reinholdt Vintner will come, and then you shall ask him the news, and we'll have a good honest lanterloo till the sun sinks in the mountains, indeed we shall, Daniel dear, indeed we shall."

"'Ndeed we shall, 'ndeed we shall!" jeered Daniel. "You with your lanterloo and games and reversis! When my brain is burning like molten lead, and my mind's in a frenzy, and—Help me to the edge of the road and let me sit down a moment—there! Am I in my right mind, Magnille? Huh? I'm mad as a fly in a flask, that's what I am. 'T is sensible in a lowborn lout, a miserable, mangy, rickety wretch, to be eaten up with frantic love of a prince's consort! Oh ay, it's sensible, Magnille, to long for her till my eyes pop out of my head and to gasp like a fish on dry land only to see a glimpse of her form and to touch with my mouth the dust she has trodden—'t is sensible, I'm saying. Oh, if it were not for the dreams when she comes and bends over me and lays her white hand on my tortured breast—or lies there so still and breathes so softly and is so cold and forlorn and has none to guard her but only me

—or she flits by white as a naked lily!—but it's empty dreams, vapor and moonshine only, and frothy air-bubbles."

They walked on again. At the wicket they stopped, and Daniel supported his arms on it while his gaze followed the hedges.

"In there," he said.

Fair and calm the park spread out under the sunlight that bathed air and leaves. The crystals in the gravel walk threw back the light in quivering rays. Hanging cobwebs gleamed through the air, and the dry sheaths of the beech buds fluttered slowly to the ground, while high against the blue sky the white doves of the castle circled with sungold on swift wings. A merry dance-tune sounded faintly from a lute in the distance.

"What a fool!" murmured Daniel. "Should you think, Magnille, that one who owned the most precious pearl of all the Indies would hold it as naught and run after bits of painted glass? Marie Grubbe and—Karen Fiol! Is *he* in his right mind? And now they think he's hunting because forsooth, he lets the gamekeeper shoot for him, and comes back with godwits and woodcocks by the brace and bagful, and all the while he's fooling and brawling down at Lynge with a town woman, a strumpet. Faugh, faugh! Lake of brimstone, such filthy business! And he's so jealous of that spring ewe-lambkin he's afraid to trust her out of his sight for a day, while—"

The leaves rustled, and Marie Grubbe stood before him on the other side of the wicket. After she turned into the side path, she had gone down to the place where the elks and Esrom camels were kept and thence back to a little arbor near the gate. There she had overheard what Daniel said to Magnille, and now—

"Who are you?" she asked, "and were they true, the words you spoke?"

Daniel grasped the wicket and could hardly stand for trembling.

"Daniel Knopf, your ladyship, mad Daniel," he replied. "Pay no heed to his talk, it runs from his tongue, sense and nonsense, as it happens, brain-chaff and tongue-threshing, tongue-threshing and naught else."

"You lie, Daniel."

"Ay, ay, good Lord, I lie; I make no doubt I do, for in here, your ladyship"—he pointed to his forehead—"'tis like the destruction of Jerusalem. Courtesy, Magnille, and tell her ladyship, Madam Gyldenlöve, how daft I am. Don't let that put you out of countenance. Speak up, Magnille! After all we're no more cracked than the Lord made us."

"Is he truly mad?" Marie asked Magnille.

Magnille in her confusion bent down, caught a fold of Marie's dress through the bars of the wicket, kissed it, and looked quite frightened. "Oh, no, no, indeed he is not, God be thanked."

"She too," said Daniel, waving his arm. "We take care of each other, we two mad folks, as well as we can. 'Tis not the best of luck, but good Lord, though mad we be, still we see, we walk abroad and help each other get under the sod. But no one rings over our graves, for that's not allowed. I thank you kindly for asking. Thank you, and God be with you."

"Stay," said Marie Grubbe. "You are no more mad than you make yourself. You must speak, Daniel. Would you have me think so ill of you as to take you for a go-between of my lord and her you mentioned? Would you?"

"A poor addle-pated fellow!" whimpered Daniel waving his arm apologetically.

"God forgive you, Daniel! 'Tis a shameful game you are playing; and I believed so much better of you — so very much better."

"Did you? Did you truly?" he cried eagerly, his eyes shining with joy. "Then I'm in my right mind again. You've but to ask."

"Was it the truth what you said?"

"As the gospel, but —"

"You are sure? There is no mistake?"

Daniel smiled.

"Is — he there today?"

"Is he gone hunting?"

"Yes."

"Then yes."

"What manner" — Marie began after a short pause — "what manner of woman is she, do you know?"

"Small, your ladyship, quite small, round and red as a pippin, merry and prattling, laughing mouth and tongue loose at both ends."

"But what kind of people does she come from?"

"'Tis now two years ago or two and a half since she was the wife of a French *valet de chambre* who fled the country and deserted her, but she didn't grieve long for him; she joined her fate with an out-at-elbows harp player, went to Paris with him, and remained there and at Brussels, until she returned here last Whitsun. In truth, she has a natural good understanding and a pleasing manner, except at times when she is tipsy. This is all the knowledge I have."

"Daniel!" she said and stopped uncertainly.

"Daniel," he replied with a subtle smile, "is as faithful to you now and forever as your own right hand."

"Then will you help me? Can you get me a—a coach and coachman who is to be trusted the instant I give the word?"

"Indeed and indeed I can. In less than an hour from the moment you give the word the coach shall hold in Herman Plumber's meadow hard by the old shed. You may depend on me, your ladyship."

Marie stood still a moment and seemed to consider. "I will see you again," she said, nodded kindly to Magnille, and left them.

"Is she not the treasure house of all beauties, Magnille?" cried Daniel gazing rapturously up the walk where she had vanished. "And so peerless in her pride!" he went on triumphantly. "Ah, she would spurn me with her foot, scornfully set her foot on my neck, and softly tread me down in the deepest dust if she knew how boldly Daniel dares dream of her person—So consuming beautiful and glorious! My heart burned in me with pity to think that she had to confide in me, to bend the majestic palm of her pride— But there's ecstasy in that sentiment, Magnille, heavenly bliss, Magnilchen!"

And they tottered off together.

The coming of Daniel and his sister to Frederiksborg had happened in this wise. After the meeting in the Bide-a-Wee Tavern, poor Hop-o'-my-Thumb had been seized with an insane passion for Marie. It was a pathetic, fantastic love that hoped nothing, asked nothing, and craved nothing but barren dreams. No more at all. The bit of reality that he needed to give his dreams a faint color of life he found fully in occasional glimpses of her near by or flitting

past in the distance. When Gyldenlöve departed and Marie
never went out his longing grew apace, until it made him
almost insane and at last threw him on a sick-bed.

When he rose again, weak and wasted, Gyldenlöve had
returned. Through one of Marie's maids who was in his
pay, he learned that the relation between Marie and her husband was not the best, and this news fed his infatuation and
gave it new growth, the rank unnatural growth of fantasy.
Before he had recovered enough from his illness to stand
steadily on his feet, Marie left for Frederiksborg. He must
follow her; he could not wait. He made a pretence of con-
sulting the wise woman in Lynge in order to regain his
strength and urged his sister Magnille to accompany him
and seek a cure for her weak eyes. Friends and neighbors
found this natural, and off they drove, Daniel and Magnille,
to Lynge. There he discovered Gyldenlöve's affair with
Karen Fiol, and there he confided all to Magnille, told
her of his strange love, declared that for him light and the
breath of life existed only where Marie Grubbe was, and
begged her to go with him to the village of Frederiksborg
that he might be near her who filled his mind so completely.

Magnille humored him. They took lodgings at Frederiksborg and had for days been shadowing Marie Grubbe
on her lonely morning walks. Thus the meeting had come
about.

CHAPTER XI

A FEW days later Ulrik Frederik was spending the morning at Lynge. He was crawling on all fours in the little garden outside of the house where Karen Fiol lived. One hand was holding a rose wreath, while with the other he was trying to coax or drag a little white lapdog from under the hazel bushes in the corner.

"Boncœur! Petit, petit Boncœur! Come, you little rogue, oh, come, you silly little fool! Oh, you brute, you — Boncœur, little dog — you confounded obstinate creature!"

Karen was standing at the window laughing. The dog would not come, and Ulrik Frederik wheedled and swore.

"Amy des morceaux délicats,"

sang Karen, swinging a goblet full of wine:

"Et de la débauche polie
Viens noyer dans nos Vins Muscats
Ta soif et ta mélancolie!"

She was in high spirits, rather heated, and the notes of her song rose louder than she knew. At last Ulrik Frederik caught the dog. He carried it to the window in triumph, pressed the rose chaplet down over its ears, and kneeling, presented it to Karen.

"Adorable Venus, queen of hearts, I beg you to accept from your humble slave this little innocent white lamb crowned with flowers—"

At that moment Marie Grubbe opened the wicket. When she saw Ulrik Frederik on his knees, handing a rose garland, or whatever it was, to that red laughing woman, she

turned pale, bent down, picked up a stone, and threw it
with all her might at Karen. It struck the edge of the
window and shivered the glass in fragments, which fell
rattling to the ground.

Karen darted back shrieking. Ulrik Frederik looked
anxiously in after her. In his surprise he had dropped the
dog, but he still held the wreath and stood dumbfounded,
angry and embarrassed, turning it round in his fingers.

"Wait, wait!" cried Marie. "I missed you this time, but
I'll get you yet! I'll get you!" She pulled from her hair
a long, heavy steel pin set with rubies, and holding it before
her like a dagger she ran toward the house with a queer
tripping, almost skipping gait. It seemed as though she were
blinded for she steered a strange meandering course up to
the door.

There Ulrik Frederik stopped her.

"Go away!" she cried almost whimpering, "you with
your chaplet! Such a creature"— she went on, trying to
slip past him, first on one side, then on the other, her eyes
fixed on the door—"such a creature you bind wreaths
for—rose wreaths, ay, here you play the lovesick shepherd! Have you not a flute too? Where's your flute?" she
repeated, tore the wreath from his hand, hurled it to the
ground, and stamped on it. "And a shepherd's crook—
Amaryllis—with a silk bow? Let me pass, I say!" She
lifted the pin threateningly.

He caught both her wrists and held her fast. "Would you
sting again?" he said sharply.

Marie looked up at him.

"Ulrik Frederik!" she said in a low voice, "I am your
wife before God and men. Why do you not love me any
more? Come with me! Leave the woman in there for what

she is, and come with me! Come, Ulrik Frederik, you little
know what a burning love I feel for you and how bitterly
I have longed and grieved! Come, pray come!"

Ulrik Frederik made no reply. He offered her his arm
and conducted her out of the garden to her coach, which
was waiting not far away. He handed her in, went to the
horses' heads and examined the harness, changed a buckle,
and called the coachman down under pretence of getting
him to fix the couplings. While they stood there he whispered, "The moment you get into your seat, you are to
drive on as hard as your horses can go and never stop
till you get home. Those are my orders, and I believe you
know me."

The man had climbed into his seat, Ulrik Frederik caught
the side of the coach as though to jump in, the whip cracked
and fell over the horses, he sprang back, and the coach
rattled on.

Marie's first impulse was to order the coachman to stop,
to take the reins herself, or to jump out, but then a strange
lassitude came over her, a deep unspeakable loathing, a
nauseating weariness, and she sat quite still, gazing ahead,
never heeding the reckless speed of the coach.

Ulrik Frederik was again with Karen Fiol.

When Ulrik Frederik returned to the castle that evening he
was in truth a bit uneasy — not exactly worried, but with
the sense of apprehension people feel when they know there
are vexations and annoyances ahead of them that cannot be dodged but must somehow be gone through with.
Marie had of course complained to the King. The King
would give him a lecture, and he would have to listen to it
all. Marie would wrap herself in the majestic silence of

offended virtue, which he would be at pains to ignore. The
whole atmosphere would be oppressive. The Queen would
look fatigued and afflicted—genteelly afflicted—and the
ladies of the court who knew nothing and suspected everything would sit silently, now and then lifting their heads
to sigh meekly and look at him with gentle upbraiding in
large, condoning eyes. Oh, he knew it all, even to the halo
of noble-hearted devotion with which the Queen's poor
groom of the chambers would try to deck his narrow head!
The fellow would place himself at Ulrik Frederik's side
with ludicrous bravado, overwhelming him with polite attentions and respectfully consoling stupidities while his
small, pale-blue eyes and every line of his thin figure
would cry out as plainly as words, "See, all are turning
from him, but *I,* never! Braving the King's anger and
the Queen's displeasure, I comfort the forsaken! I put
my true heart against—" Oh, how well he knew it all—
everything—the whole story!

Nothing of all this happened. The King received him
with a Latin proverb, a sure sign that he was in a good
humor. Marie rose and held out her hand to him as usual,
perhaps a little colder, a shade more reserved, but still in
a manner very different from what he had expected. Not
even when they were left alone together did she refer with
so much as a word to their encounter at Lynge, and Ulrik
Frederik wondered suspiciously. He did not know what to
make of this curious silence; he would almost rather she
had spoken.

Should he draw her out, thank her for not saying anything, give himself up to remorse and repentance, and play
the game that they were reconciled again?

Somehow he did not quite dare to try it, for he had

noticed that now and then she would gaze furtively at him with an inscrutable expression in her eyes as if she were looking through him and taking his measure with a calm wonder, a cool, almost contemptuous curiosity. Not a gleam of hatred or resentment, not a shadow of grief or reproach, not one tremulous glance of repressed sadness! Nothing of that kind, nothing at all!

Therefore he did not venture, and nothing was said. Once in a while as the days went by, his thoughts would dwell on the matter uneasily, and he would feel a feverish desire to have it cleared up. Still it was not done, and he could not rid himself of a sense that these unspoken accusations lay like serpents in a dark cave brooding over sinister treasures which grew as the reptiles grew, blood-red carbuncles rising on stalks of cadmium, and pale opal in bulb upon bulb slowly spreading, swelling, and breeding, while the serpents lay still but ceaselessly expanding, gliding forth in sinuous bend upon bend, lifting ring upon ring over the rank growth of the treasure.

She must hate him, must be harboring secret thoughts of revenge, for an insult such as he had dealt her could not forgotten. He connected this imagined lust for vengeance with the strange incident when she had lifted her hand against him and with Burrhi's warning. So he avoided her more than ever and wished more and more ardently that their ways might be parted.

But Marie was not thinking of revenge. She had forgotten both him and Karen Fiol. In that moment of unutterable disgust her love had been wiped out and left no traces, as a glittering bubble bursts and is no more. The glory of it is no more, and the iridescent colors it lent to every tiny picture mirrored in it are no more. They are

gone, and the eye which was held by their splendor and
beauty is free to look about and gaze far out over the world
which was once reflected in the glassy bubble.

The number of guests in the castle increased day by day.
The rehearsals of the ballet were under way, and the dancing masters and play-actors, Pilloy and Kobbereau, had
been summoned to give instruction as well as to act the
more difficult or less grateful rôles.

Marie Grubbe was to take part in the ballet and re-
hearsed eagerly. Since that day at Slangerup she had been
more animated and sociable and, as it were, more awake.
Her intercourse with those about her had always before
been rather perfunctory. When nothing special called her
attention or claimed her interest, she had a habit of slipping
back into her own little world, from which she looked
out at her surroundings with indifferent eyes; but now she
entered into all that was going on, and if the others had
not been so absorbed by the new and exciting events of
those days, they would have been astonished at her changed
manner. Her movements had a quiet assurance, her speech
an almost hostile subtlety, and her eyes observed everything. As it was, no one noticed her except Ulrik Frederik,
who would sometimes catch himself admiring her as if she
were a stranger.

Among the guests who came in August was Sti Högh,
the husband of Marie's sister. One afternoon, not long
after his arrival, she was standing with him on a hillock in
the woods from which they could look out over the village
and the flat, sun-scorched land beyond. Slow, heavy clouds
were forming in the sky, and from the earth rose a dry,
bitter smell like a sigh of drooping, withering plants for the

life-giving water. A faint wind, scarcely strong enough to
move the windmill at the crossroad below, was soughing
forlornly in the tree-tops like a timid wail of the forest burning under summer heat and sun-glow. As a beggar bares
his pitiful wound, so the parched, yellow meadows spread
their barren misery under the gaze of heaven.

The clouds gathered and lowered, and a few raindrops
fell, one by one, heavy as blows on the leaves and straws,
which would bend to one side, shake, and then be suddenly
still again. The swallows flew low along the ground, and
the blue smoke of the evening meal drooped like a veil over
the black thatched roofs in the village near by.

A coach rumbled heavily over the road, and from the
walks at the foot of the hill came the sound of low laughter
and merry talk, rustling of fans and silk gowns, barking
of tiny lapdogs, and snapping and crunching of dry twigs.
The court was taking its afternoon promenade.

Marie and Sti Högh had left the others to climb the
hill and were standing quite breathless after their hurried
ascent of the steep path.

Sti Högh was then a man in his early thirties, tall and
lean, with reddish hair and a long, narrow face. He was pale
and freckled, and his thin, yellow-white brows were arched
high over bright, light gray eyes which had a tired look
as if they shunned the light, a look caused partly by the
pink color that spread all over the lids and partly by his
habit of winking more slowly, or rather of keeping his eyes
closed longer, than other people did. The forehead was high,
the temples, well rounded and smooth. The nose was thin,
faintly arched, and rather long, the chin too long and too
pointed, but the mouth was exquisite, the lips fresh in color
and pure in line, the teeth small and white. Yet it was not

its beauty that drew attention to this mouth; it was rather
the strange, melancholy smile of the voluptuary, a smile
made up of passionate desire and weary disdain, at once
tender as sweet music and bloodthirsty as the low, satisfied
growl in the throat of the beast of prey when its teeth tear
the quivering flesh of its victim.

Such was Sti Högh—then.

"Madam," said he, "have you never wished that you
were sitting safe in the shelter of convent walls such as
they have them in Italy and other countries?"

"Mercy, no! How should I have such mad fancies!"

"Then, my dear kinswoman, you are perfectly happy?
Your cup of life is clear and fresh; it is sweet to your
tongue, warms your blood, and quickens your thoughts?
Is it, in truth, never bitter as lees, flat, and stale? Never
fouled by adders and serpents that crawl and mumble? If
so, your eyes have deceived me."

"Ah, you would fain bring me to confession!" laughed
Marie in his face.

Sti Högh smiled and led her to a little grass mound
where they sat down. He looked searchingly at her.

"Know you not," he began slowly and seeming to hesi-
tate whether to speak or be silent, "know you not, madam,
that there is in the world a secret society which I might call
'the melancholy company'? It is composed of people who
at birth have been given a different nature and constitution
from others, who yearn more and covet more, whose passions are stronger, and whose desires burn more wildly than
those of the vulgar mob. They are like Sunday children,
with eyes wider open and senses more subtle. They drink
with the very roots of their hearts that delight and joy of
life which others can only grasp between coarse hands."

He paused a moment, took his hat in his hand, and sat idly running his fingers through the thick plumes.

"But," he went on in a lower voice as speaking to himself, "pleasure in beauty, pleasure in pomp and all the things that can be named, pleasure in secret impulses and in thoughts that pass the understanding of man—all that which to the vulgar is but idle pastime or vile revelry—is to these chosen ones like healing and precious balsam. It is to them the one honey-filled blossom from which they suck their daily food, and therefore they seek flowers on the tree of life where others would never think to look, under dark leaves and on dry branches. But the mob— what does it know of pleasure in grief or despair?"

He smiled scornfully and was silent.

"But wherefore," asked Marie carelessly, looking past him, "wherefore name them 'the melancholy company' since they think but of pleasure and the joy of life but never of what is sad and dreary?"

Sti Högh shrugged his shoulders and seemed about to rise as though weary of the theme and anxious to break off the discussion.

"But wherefore?" repeated Marie.

"Wherefore!" he cried impatiently, and there was a note of disdain in his voice. "Because all the joys of this earth are hollow and pass away as shadows. Because every plea- sure, while it bursts into bloom like a flowering rosebush, in the selfsame hour withers and drops its leaves like a tree in autumn. Because every delight, though it glow in beauty and the fullness of fruition, though it clasp you in sound arms, is that moment poisoned by the cancer of death, and even while it touches your mouth, you feel it quivering in the throes of corruption. Is it joyful to feel thus? Must it not rather eat like reddest rust into every shining hour, ay, like frost nip unto death every fruitful sentiment of the soul and blight it down to its deepest roots?"

He sprang up from his seat and gesticulated down at her as he spoke. "And you ask why they are called 'the melancholy company' when every delight, in the instant you grasp it sheds its slough in a trice and becomes disgust, when all mirth is but the last woeful gasp of joy, when all beauty is beauty that passes, and all happiness is happiness that bursts like the bubble!"

He began to walk up and down in front of her.

"So it is this that leads your thoughts to the convent?" asked Marie, and looked down with a smile.

"It is so indeed, madam. Many a time have I fancied myself confined in a lonely cell or imprisoned in a high tower, sitting alone at my window, watching the light fade and the darkness well out, while the solitude, silent and calm and strong, has grown up around my soul and covered it like plants of mandrake pouring their drowsy juices in my blood. Ah, but I know full well that it is naught but an empty conceit; never could the solitude gain power over me! I should long like fire and leaping flame for life and what belongs to life—long till I lost my senses! But you understand nothing of all this I am prating. Let us go, *ma chère!* The rain is upon us; the wind is laid."

"Ah, no, the clouds are lifting. See the rim of light all around the heavens!"

"Ay, lifting and lowering."

"I say no," declared Marie, rising.

"I swear yes, with all deference."

Marie ran down the hill. "Man's mind is his kingdom. Come, now, down into yours!"

At the foot of the hill Marie turned into the path leading away from the castle, and Sti walked at her side.

"Look you, Sti Högh," said Marie, "since you seem
to think so well of me, I would have you know that I am
quite unlearned in the signs of the weather and likewise
in other people's discourse."

"Surely not."

"In what you are saying—yes."

"Nay."

"Now I swear yes."

"Oaths gouge no eye without fist follows after."

"Faith, you may believe me or not, but God knows I
ofttimes feel that great still sadness that comes we know
not whence. Pastor Jens was wont to say it was a longing for our home in the kingdom of heaven, which is the
true fatherland of every Christian soul, but I think it is
not that. We long and sorrow and know no living hope to
comfort us—ah, how bitterly have I wept! It comes over
one with such a strange heaviness and sickens one's heart,
and one feels so tired of one's own thoughts and wishes
one had never been born. But it is not the briefness of
these earthly joys that has weighed on my thoughts or
caused me grief. No, never! It was something quite different—but 't is quite impossible to give that grief a name.
Sometimes I have thought it was really a grief over some
hidden flaw in my own nature, some inward hurt that
made me unlike other people—lesser and poorer. Ah, no,
it passes everything how hard it is to find words—in just
the right sense. Look you, this life—this earth—seems
to me so splendid and wonderful I should be proud and
happy beyond words just to have some part in it. Whether
for joy or grief matters not, but that I might sorrow or

rejoice in honest truth, not in play like mummeries or shrovetide sports. I would feel life grasping me with such hard hands that I was lifted up or cast down until there was no room in my mind for aught else but that which lifted me up or cast me down. I would melt in my grief or burn together with my joy! Ah, you can never understand it! If I were like one of the generals of the Roman empire who were carried through the streets in triumphal chariots, I myself would be the victory and the triumph. I would be the pride and jubilant shouts of the people and the blasts of the trumpets and the honor and the glory — all, all in one shrill note. That is what I would be. Never would I be like one who merely sits there in his miserable ambition and cold vanity and thinks as the chariot rolls on how he shines in the eyes of the crowd and how helplessly the waves of envy lick his feet while he feels with pleasure the purple wrapping his shoulders softly and the laurel wreath cooling his brow. Do you understand me, Sti Högh? That is what I mean by life, that is what I have thirsted after, but I have felt in my own heart that such life could never be mine, and it was borne in on me that, in some strange manner I was myself at fault, that I had sinned against myself and led myself astray. I know not how it is, but it has seemed to me that this was whence my bitter sorrow welled, that I had touched a string which must not sound and its tone had sundered something within me that could never be healed. Therefore I could never force open the portals of life but had to stand without, unbidden and unsought, like a poor maimed bondwoman."

"You!" exclaimed Sti Högh in astonishment; then, his face changing quickly, he went on in another voice, "Ah, now I see it all!" He shook his head at her. "By my troth,

how easily a man may befuddle himself in these matters!
Our thoughts are so rarely turned to the road where every
stile and path is familiar, but more often they run amuck
wherever we catch sight of anything that bears a likeness
to a trail, and we're ready to swear it's the King's highway.
Am I not right, *ma chère?* Have we not both, each for
herself or himself, in seeking a source of our melancholy,
caught the first thought we met and made it into the one
and only reason? Would not anyone, judging from our
discourse, suppose that I went about sore afflicted and
weighed down by the corruption of the world and the
passing nature of all earthly things while you, my dear
kinswoman, looked on yourself as a silly old crone on
whom the door had been shut and the lights put out and all
hope extinguished! But no matter for that! When we get
to that chapter, we are easily made heady by our own words,
and ride hard on any thought that we can bit and bridle."

In the walk below the others were heard approaching,
and joining them, they returned to the castle.

At half-past the hour of eight in the evening of September
twenty-sixth, the booming of cannon and the shrill trumpet
notes of a festive march announced that both their Majesties, accompanied by his Highness Prince Johan, the Elector of Saxony, and his royal mother and followed by the
most distinguished men and women of the realm, were pro-
ceeding from the castle down through the park to witness
the ballet which was soon to begin.

A row of flambeaux cast a fiery sheen over the red wall,
made the yew and box glow like bronze, and lent all faces
the ruddy glow of vigorous health.

See, scarlet-clothed halberdiers are standing in double

rows, holding flower-wreathed tapers high against the dark
sky. Cunningly wrought lanterns and candles in sconces
and candelabra send their rays low along the ground and
high among the yellowing leaves, forcing the darkness
back and opening a shining path for the resplendent train.

The light glitters on gold and gilded tissue, beams
brightly on silver and steel, glides in shimmering stripes
down silks and sweeping satins. Softly as a reddish dew,
it is breathed over dusky velvet, and flashing white, it falls
like stars among rubies and diamonds. Reds make a brave
show with the yellows; clear sky blue closes over brown;
streaks of lustrous sea green cut their way through white
and violet blue; coral sinks between black and lavender;
golden brown and rose, steel gray and purple are whirled
about, light and dark, tint upon tint, in eddying pools of
color.

They are gone. Down the walk, tall plumes nod white,
white in the dim air. . . .

The ballet or masquerade to be presented is called *Die
Waldlust*. The scene is a forest. Crown Prince Christian,
impersonating a hunter, voices his delight in the free life of
the merry greenwood. Ladies walking about under leafy
crowns sing softly of the fragrant violets. Children play
at hide and seek and pick berries in pretty little baskets.
Jovial citizens praise the fresh air and the clear grape,
while two silly old crones are pursuing a handsome young
rustic with amorous gestures.

Then the goddess of the forest, the virginal Diana, glides
forward in the person of her Royal Highness the Princess
Anne Sofie. The Elector leaps from his seat with delight and
throws her kisses with both hands while the court applauds.

As soon as the goddess has disappeared, a peasant and

his goodwife come forward and sing a duet on the delights
of love. One gay scene follows another. Three young gentlemen are decking themselves with green boughs; five
officers are making merry; two rustics come rollicking
from market; a gardener's 'prentice sings, a poet sings, and
finally six persons play some sprightly music on rather
fantastic instruments.

This leads up to the last scene, which is played by eleven
shepherdesses: their Royal Highnesses the Princesses Anne
Sofie, Friderica Amalie, and Vilhelmina Ernestina, Madam
Gyldenlöve, and seven young maidens of the nobility.
With much skill they dance a pastoral dance in which
they pretend to tease Madam Gyldenlöve because she is
lost in thoughts of love and refuses to join their gay minuet.
They twit her with giving up her freedom and bending her
neck under the yoke of love, but she steps forward and in
a graceful *pas de deux* which she dances with the Princess
Anne Sofie reveals to her companion the abounding trans-
ports and ecstasies of love. Then all dance forward merrily,
winding in and out in intricate figures, while an invisible
chorus sings in their praise to the tuneful music of stringed
instruments:

"Ihr Nümphen hochberühmt, ihr sterblichen Göttinnen,
  Durch deren Treff'ligkeit sich lassen Heldensinnen
Ja auch die Götter selbst bezwingen für und für,
  Last nun durch diesen Tantz erblicken eure Zier
Der Glieder Hurtigkeit, die euch darum gegeben
  So schön und prächtig sind, und zu den End erheben
Was an euch göttlich ist, auff dass je mehr und mehr
  Man preisen mög an euch des Schöpfers Macht und Ehr."

This ended the ballet. The spectators dispersed through

the park, promenading through well-lit groves or resting
in pleasant grottos while pages dressed as Italian or Spanish fruit-venders offered wine, cake, and comfits from the
baskets they carried on their heads.

The players mingled with the crowd and were compli-
mented on their art and skill, but all were agreed that with
the exception of the Crown Princess and Princess Anne Sofie, none had acted better than Madam Gyldenlöve. Their
Majesties and the Electress praised her cordially, and the
King declared that not even Mademoiselle La Barre could
have interpreted the rôle with more grace and vivacity.

Far into the night the junketing went on in the lighted
park and the adjoining halls of the castle, where violins
and flutes called to the dance and groaning boards invited
to drinking and carousing. From the lake sounded the gay
laughter of revellers in gondolas strung with lamps. People
swarmed everywhere. The crowds were densest where the
light shone and the music played, more scattered where the
illumination was fainter, but even where darkness reigned
completely and the music was almost lost in the rustling of
leaves, there were merry groups and silent couples. One
lonely guest had strayed far off to the grotto in the eastern
end of the garden and had found a seat there, but he was
in a melancholy mood. The tiny lantern in the leafy roof
of the grotto shone on a sad mien and pensive brows —
yellow-white brows.

It was Sti Högh.

> " . . . E di persona
> Anzi grande, che no ; di vista allegra,
> Di bionda chioma, e colorita alquanto,"

he whispered to himself.

He had not come unscathed from his four or five weeks of
constant intercourse with Marie Grubbe. She had absolutely
bewitched him. He longed only for her, dreamed only of
her; she was his hope and his despair. He had loved before,
but never like this, never so timidly and weakly and hopelessly. It was not the fact that she was the wife of Ulrik
Frederik, nor that he was married to her sister, which robbed
him of his courage. No, it was in the nature of his love to
be faint-hearted—his calf-love, he called it bitterly. It had
so little desire, so much fear and worship, and yet so much
desire. A wistful, feverish languishing for her, a morbid
longing to live with her in her memories, dream her dreams,
suffer her sorrows, and share her sad thoughts, no more, no
less. How lovely she had been in the dance, but how distant and unattainable! The round gleaming shoulders, the
full bosom and slender limbs—they took his breath away.
He trembled before that splendor of body which made her
seem richer and more perfect and hardly dared to let himself be drawn under its spell. He feared his own passion and
the fire, hell-deep, heaven-high, that smouldered within
him. That arm around his neck, those lips pressed against
his—it was madness, imbecile dreams of a madman! This
mouth—

"Paragon di dolcezza!

·   ·   ·   ·   ·   ·   ·

. . . bocca beata,
. . . bocca gentil, che può ben dirsi
Conca d' Indo odorata
Di perle orientali e pellegrine:
E la porta, che chiude
Ed apre il bel tesoro,
Con dolcissimo mel porpora mista."

He started from the bench as with pain. No, no! He clung to his own humble longing and threw himself again in his thoughts at her feet, clutched at the hopelessness of his love, held up before his eyes the image of her indifference, and—Marie Grubbe stood there in the arched door of the grotto, fair against the outside darkness.

All that evening she had been in a strangely enraptured mood. She felt calm and sound and strong. The music and pomp, the homage and admiration of the men, were like a carpet of purple spread out for her feet to tread upon. She was intoxicated and transported with her own beauty. The blood seemed to shoot from her heart in rich, glowing jets and become gracious smiles on her lips, radiance in her eyes, and melody in her voice. Her mind held an exultant serenity, and her thoughts were clear as a cloudless sky. Her soul seemed to unfold its richest bloom in this blissful sense of power and harmony.

Never before had she been so fair as with that imperious smile of joy on her lips and the tranquillity of a queen in her eyes and bearing, and thus she stood in the arched door of the grotto, fair against the outside darkness. Looking down at Sti Högh, she met his gaze of hopeless adoration, and at that she bent down, laid her white hand as in pity on his hair, and kissed him. Not in love—no, no!—but as a king may bestow a precious ring on a faithful vassal as a mark of royal grace and favor, so she gave him her kiss in calm largesse.

As she did so, her assurance seemed to leave her for a moment, and she blushed while her eyes fell. If Sti Högh had tried to take her then or to receive her kiss as anything more than a royal gift, he would have lost her forever, but he knelt silently before her, pressed her hand gratefully

to his lips, then stepped aside reverently and saluted her
deeply with head bared and neck bent. She walked past
him proudly, away from the grotto and into the darkness.

CHAPTER XII

I N January of sixteen hundred and sixty-four, Ulrik
Frederik was appointed Viceroy of Norway, and in
the beginning of April the same year he departed for his
post. Marie Grubbe went with him.

The relation between them had not improved, except
in so far as the lack of mutual understanding and mutual
love had, as it were, been accepted by both as an unalter-
able fact and found expression in the extremely ceremonious manner they had adopted toward each other.

For a year or more after they had moved to Aggershus,
things went on much in the same way, and Marie for her
part desired no change. Not so Ulrik Frederik, for he had
again become enamored of his wife.

On a winter afternoon in the gloaming, Marie Grubbe
sat alone in the little parlor known from olden time as the
Nook. The day was cloudy and dark with a raw, bluster-
ing wind. Heavy flakes of melting snow were plastered into
the corners of the tiny window panes, covering almost half
the surface of the greenish glass. Gusts of wet, chilly wind
went whirling down between the high walls where they
seemed to lose their senses and throw themselves blindly
upon shutters and doors, rattling them fiercely, then flying
skyward again with a hoarse, dog-like whimper. Powerful
blasts came shrieking across the roofs opposite and hurled
themselves against windows and walls, pounding like waves,
then suddenly dying away. Now and again a squall would
come roaring down the chimney. The flames ducked their
frightened heads, and the white smoke, timidly curling
toward the chimney like the comb of a breaker, would
shrink back, ready to throw itself out into the room. Ah,

in the next instant it is whirled, thin and light and blue, up through the flue with the flames calling after it, leaping and darting, and sending sputtering sparks by the handful right in its heels. Then the fire began to burn in good earnest. With grunts of pleasure it spread over glowing coals and embers, boiled and seethed with delight in the innermost marrow of the white birch wood, buzzed and purred like a tawny cat, and licked caressingly the noses of blackening knots and smouldering chunks of wood.

Warm and pleasant and luminous the breath of the fire streamed through the little room. Like a fluttering fan of light it played over the parquet floor and chased the peaceful dusk which hid in tremulous shadows to the right and the left behind twisted chair legs or shrank into corners, lay thin and long in the shelter of mouldings or flattened itself under the large clothes press.

Suddenly the chimney seemed to suck up the light and heat with a roar. Darkness spread boldly across the floor on every board and square to the very fire, but the next moment the light leaped back again and sent the dusk flying to all sides with the light pursuing it up the walls and doors, above the brass latch. Safety nowhere! The dusk sat crouching against the wall, up under the ceiling, like a cat in a high branch, with the light scampering below, back and forth like a dog, leaping, running at the foot of the tree. Not even among the flagons and tumblers on the top of the press could the darkness be undisturbed, for red ruby glasses, blue goblets, and green Rhenish wineglasses lit iridescent fires to help the light search them out.

The wind blew and the darkness fell outside, but within the fire glowed, the light played, and Marie Grubbe was singing. Now and again she would murmur snatches of the words as they came to her mind, then again hum the melody alone. Her lute was in her hand, but she was not playing it, only touching the strings sometimes and calling out a few clear, long-sounding notes. It was one of those pleasant little pensive songs that make the cushions softer and the room warmer; one of those gently flowing airs that seem to sing themselves in their indolent wistfulness while they give the voice a delicious roundness and fullness of tone. Marie was sitting in the light from the fire, and its beams played around her while she sang in careless enjoyment, as if caressing herself with her own voice.

The little door opened, and Ulrik Frederik bent his tall form to enter. Marie stopped singing instantly.

"Ah, madam!" exclaimed Ulrik Frederik in a tone of gentle remonstrance, making a gesture of appeal as he came up to her. "Had I known that you would allow my presence to incommode you—"

"No, truly, I was but singing to keep my dreams awake."

"Pleasant dreams?" he asked, bending over the fire-dogs before the grate and warming his hands on the bright copper balls.

"Dreams of youth," replied Marie, passing her hand over the strings of the lute.

"Ay, that was ever the way of old age," and he smiled at her.

Marie was silent a moment, then suddenly spoke, "One may be full young and yet have old dreams."

"How sweet the odor of musk in here! But was my humble person along in these ancient dreams, madam?—if I may make so bold as to ask."

"Ah, no!"

"And yet there was a time—"

"Among all other times."

"Ay, among all other times there was once a wondrously fair time when I was exceeding dear to you. Do you bring to mind a certain hour in the twilight a sennight or so after our nuptials? 'T was storming and snowing—"

"Even as now."

"And you were sitting before the fire—"

"Even as now."

"Ay, and I was lying at your feet, and your dear hands were playing with my hair."

"Yes, then you loved me."

"Oh, even as now! And you—you bent down over me and wept till the tears streamed down your face, and you kissed me and looked at me with such tender earnestness it seemed you were saying a prayer for me in your heart, and then all of a sudden—do you remember?—you bit my neck."

"Ah, merciful God, what love I did bear to you, my lord! When I heard the clanging of your spurs on the steps, the blood pounded in my ears, and I trembled from head to foot and my hands were cold as ice. Then when you came in and pressed me in your arms—"

"*De grace*, madam!"

"Why, it's naught but dead memories of an *amour* that is long since extinguished."

"Alas, extinguished, madam? Nay, it smoulders hotter than ever."

"Ah, no, 'tis covered by the cold ashes of too many days."

"But it shall rise again from the ashes as the bird Phenix, more glorious and fiery than before—pray, shall it not?"

"No, love is like a tender plant; when the night frost

touches its heart, it dies from the blossom down to the root."

"No, love is like the herb named the rose of Jericho. In the dry months it withers and curls up, but when there is a soft and balmy night with a heavy fall of dew, all its leaves will unfold again, greener and fresher than ever before."

"It may be so. There are many kinds of love in the world."

"Truly there are, and ours was such a love."

"That yours was such you tell me now, but mine — never, never!

"Then you have never loved."

"Never loved? Now I shall tell you how I have loved. It was at Frederiksborg—"

"Oh, madam, you have no mercy!"

"No, no, that is not it at all. It was at Frederiksborg. Alas, you little know what I suffered there. I saw that your love was not as it had been. Oh as a mother watches over her sick child and marks every little change, so I kept watch over your love with fear and trembling, and when I saw in your cold looks how it had paled and felt in your kisses how feeble was its pulse it seemed to me I must die with anguish. I wept for this love through long nights; I prayed for it as if it had been the dearly loved child of my heart that was dying by inches. I cast about for aid and advice in my trouble and for physics to cure your sick love, and whatever secret potions I had heard of, such as love philtres, I mixed them betwixt hope and fear in your morning draught and your supper wine. I laid out your breastcloth under three waxing moons and read the marriage psalm over it, and on your bedstead I first painted with my own blood thirteen hearts in a cross, but all to no avail, my lord, for your love was sick unto death. Faith, that is the way you were loved."

"No. Marie, my love is not dead; it is risen again. Hear me, dear heart, hear me! for I have been stricken with blindness and with a mad distemper, but now, Marie, I kneel at your feet, and look, I woo you again with prayers and beseechings. Alack, my love has been like a wilful child, but now it is grown to man's estate. Pray give yourself trustingly to its arms, and I swear to you by the cross and the honor of a gentleman that it will never let you go again."

"Peace, peace, what help is in that!"

"Pray, pray believe me, Marie!"

"By the living God, I believe you. There is no shred nor thread of doubt in my soul. I believe you fully; I believe that your love is great and strong, but mine you have strangled with your own hands. It is a corpse, and however loudly your heart may call, you can never wake it again."

"Say not so, Marie, for those of your sex — I know there are among you those who when they love a man, even though he spurn them with his foot, come back ever and ever again, for their love is proof against all wounds."

"'Tis so indeed, my lord, and I — I am such a woman, I would have you know — but you are not the right kind of man."

May God in his mercy keep you, my dearly beloved sister, and be to you a good and generous giver of all those things which are requisite and necessary as well for the body as for the soul that I wish you from my heart.

To you, my dearly beloved sister, my one faithful friend from the time of my childhood, will I now relate what fine fruits I have of my elevation, which may it be cursed from the day it began; for it has, God knows, brought me naught but trouble and tribulation in brimming goblets.

Ay, it was an elevation for the worse, as you, my dearly beloved sister, shall now hear and as is probably known to you in part. For it cannot fail that you must have learned from your dear husband how, even at the time of our dwelling in Sjælland, there was a coolness between me and my noble lord and spouse. Now here at Aggershus matters have in no way mended, and he has used me so scurvily that it is past all belief but is what I might have looked for in so dainty a *junker*. Not that I care a rush about his filthy gallantries; it is all one to me, and he may run amuck with the hangman's wife if so be his pleasure. All I ask is that he do not come too near me with his tricks, but that is precisely what he is now doing, and in such manner that one might fain wonder whether he were stricken with madness or possessed of the devil. The beginning of it was on a day when he came to me with fair words and fine promises and would have all be as before between us, whereas I feel for him naught but loathing and contempt and told him in plain words that I held myself far too good for him. Then hell broke loose, for *wenn's de Düvel friert*, as the saying is, *macht er sein Hölle glühn*, and he made it hot for me by dragging into the castle swarms of loose women and filthy jades and entertaining them with food and drink in abundance, ay, with costly sweetmeats and expensive standdishes as at any royal banquet. And for this my flowered damask tablecloths, which I have gotten after our blessed mother, and my silk bolsters with the fringes were to have been laid out, but that did not come to pass inasmuch as I put them all under lock and key, and he had to go borrowing in the town for wherewithal to deck both board and bench.

My own dearly beloved sister, I will no longer fatigue you with tales of this vile company, but is it not shameful that such trulls, who if they were rightly served should have the lash laid on their back at the public whipping-post, now are queening it in the halls of his Majesty the King's Viceroy? I say 'tis so unheard of and so infamous that if it were to come to the ears of his Majesty, as with all my heart and soul I wish that it may come, he would talk to *mein guten Ulrik Friederich* in such terms as would give him but little joy to hear. The finest of all his tricks I have yet told you nothing of, and it is quite new, for it happened only the other day that I sent for a tradesman to bring me some Brabantian silk lace that I thought to put around the hem of a sack, but the man made answer that when I sent the money he would bring the goods, for the Viceroy had forbidden him to sell me anything on credit. The same word came from the milliner who had been sent for so it would appear that he has stopped my credit in the entire city, although I have brought to his estate thousands and thousands of rix-dollars. No more today. May we commit all unto the Lord, and may He give me ever good tidings of you.

Ever your faithful sister,

MARIE GRUBBE.

At Aggershus Castle, 12 December 1665.
The Honorable Mistress Anne Marie Grubbe, Styge Högh's, Magistrate of Laaland, my dearly beloved sister, graciously to hand.

God in his mercy keep you, my dearest sister, now and forever is my wish from a true heart, and I pray for you that you may be of good cheer and not let yourself be utterly cast down, for we have all our allotted portion of sorrow, and we swim and bathe in naught but misery.

Your letter, M. D. S., came to hand safe and unbroken in every way, and thence I have learned with a heavy heart what shame and dishonor your husband is heaping upon you, which it is a grievous wrong in his Majesty's Viceroy to behave as he behaves. Nevertheless, it behooves you not to be hasty, my duck, for you have cause for patience in that high position in which you have been placed, which it were not well to wreck but which it is fitting you should preserve with all diligence. Even though your husband consumes much wealth on his pleasures, yet is it of his own he wastes, while my rogue of a husband has made away with his and mine too. Truly it is a pity to see a man who should guard what God hath entrusted to us instead scattering and squandering it. If 't were but the will of God to part me from him by whatever means it might be that would be the greatest boon to me, miserable woman, for which I could never be sufficiently thankful; and we might as well be parted, since we have not lived together for upward of a year, for which may God be praised, and would that it might last! So you see, M. D. S., that neither is my bed decked with silk. But you must have faith that your husband will come to his senses in time and cease to waste his goods on wanton hussies and filthy rabble, and inasmuch as his office gives him a large income, you must not let your heart be troubled with his wicked wastefulness nor by his unkindness. God will help, I firmly trust. Farewell, my duck! I bid you a thousand good-nights.

Your faithful sister while I live,

ANNE MARIE GRUBBE.

At Vang, 6 February 1666.
Madam Gyldenlöve, my good friend and sister, written in all loving kindness.

May God in his mercy keep you, my dearly beloved sister, and be to you a good and generous giver of all those things which are requisite and necessary as well for the body as for the soul that I wish you from my heart.

My dearly beloved sister, the old saying that none is so mad but he has a glimmer of sense between St. John and Paulinus no longer holds good, for my mad lord and spouse is no more sensible than he was. In truth, he is tenfold, nay a thousandfold more frenzied than before, and that whereof I wrote you was but as child's play to what has now come to pass, which is beyond all belief. Dearest sister, I would have you know that he has been to Copenhagen, and thence —oh, fie, most horrid shame and outrage!— he has brought one of his old *canaille* women named Karen, whom he forthwith lodged in the castle, and she is set over everything and rules everything while I am let stand behind the door. But, my dear sister, you must now do me the favor to inquire of our dear father whether he will take my part, if so be it that I can make my escape from here, as he surely must, for none can behold my unhappy state without pitying me, and what I suffer is so past all endurance that I think I should but be doing right in freeing myself from it. It is no longer ago than the Day of the Assumption of Our Lady that I was walking in our orchard, and when I came in again, the door of my chamber was bolted from within. I asked the meaning of this and was told that Karen had taken for her own that chamber and the one next to it, and my bed was moved up into the western parlor, which is cold as a church when the wind is in that quarter, full of draughts, and the floor quite rough and has even great holes in it. But if I were to relate at length all the insults that are heaped upon me here, it would be as long as any Lenten sermon,

and if it is to go on much longer, my head is like to burst.
May the Lord keep us and send me good tidings of you.
Ever your faithful sister,

MARIE GRUBBE.

The Honorable Mistress Anne Marie Grubbe, Sti Högh's, Magistrate
of Laaland, my dearly beloved sister, graciously to hand.

Ulrik Frederik, if the truth were told, was as tired of the
state of affairs at the castle as Marie Grubbe was. He
had been used to refining more on his dissipations. They
were sorry boon companions, these poor, common officers
in Norway, and their soldiers' courtesans were not to be
endured for long. Karen Fiol was the only one who was
not made up of coarseness and vulgarity, and even her he
would rather bid good-by today than tomorrow.

In his chagrin at being repulsed by Marie Grubbe, he
had admitted these people into his company, and for a
while they amused him, but when the whole thing began
to pall and seem rather disgusting and when furthermore
he felt some faint stirrings of remorse, he had to justify
himself by pretending that such means had been necessary.
He actually made himself believe that he had been pursuing a plan in order to bring Marie Grubbe back repentant.
Unfortunately, her penitence did not seem to be forth-
coming, and so he had recourse to harsher measures in the
hope that, by making her life as miserable as possible, he
would beat down her resistance. That she had really ceased
to love him he never believed for a moment. He was con-
vinced that in her heart she longed to throw herself into his
arms, though she used his returning love as a good chance
to avenge herself for his faithlessness. Nor did he begrudge
her this revenge; he was pleased that she wanted it, if she

had only not dragged it out so long. He was getting bored in this barbarous land of Norway!

He had a sneaking feeling that it might have been wiser to have let Karen Fiol stay in Copenhagen, but he simply could not endure the others any longer; moreover, jealousy was a powerful ally, and Marie Grubbe had once been jealous of Karen; that he knew.

Time passed, and still Marie Grubbe did not come. He began to doubt that she ever would, and his love grew with his doubt. Something of the excitement of a game or a chase had entered into their relation. It was with an anxious mind and with a calculating fear that he heaped upon her one mortification after another, and he waited in suspense for even the faintest sign that his quarry was being driven into the right track, but nothing happened.

Ah, at last! At last something came to pass, and he was certain that it was the sign, the very sign he had been waiting for. One day when Karen had been more than ordinarily impudent, Marie Grubbe took a good strong bridle rein in her hand, walked through the house to the room where Karen just then was taking her after-dinner nap, fastened the door from within, and gave the dumbfounded strumpet a good beating with the heavy strap, then went quietly back to the western parlor past the speechless servants who had come running at the sound of Karen's screams.

Ulrik Frederik was downtown when it happened. Karen sent a messenger to him at once, but he did not hurry, and it was late afternoon before Karen, anxiously waiting, heard his horse in the courtyard. She ran down to meet him, but he put her aside quietly and firmly and went straight up to Marie Grubbe.

The door was ajar—then she must be out. He stuck his

head in, sure of finding the room empty, but she was there, sitting at the window asleep. He stepped in as softly and carefully as he could, for he was not quite sober.

The low September sun was pouring a stream of yellow and golden light through the room, lending color and richness to its poor tints. The plastered walls took on the whiteness of swans, the brown timbered ceiling glowed as copper, and the faded curtains around the bed were changed to wine-red folds and purple draperies. The room was flooded with light; even in the shadows it gleamed as through a shimmering mist of autumn yellow leaves. It spun a halo of gold around Marie Grubbe's head and kissed her white forehead, but her eyes and mouth were in deep shadow cast by the yellowing apple tree which lifted to the window branches red with fruit.

ıShe was asleep sitting in a chair, her hands folded in her lap. Ulrik Frederik stole up to her on tiptoe, and the glory faded as he came between her and the window.

He scanned her closely. She was paler than before. How kind and gentle she looked as she sat there, her head bent back, her lips slightly parted, her white throat uncovered and bare! He could see the pulse throbbing on both sides of her neck, right under the little brown birthmark. His eyes followed the line of the firm, rounded shoulder under the close-fitting silk, down the slender arm to the white, passive hand. And that hand was his! He saw the fingers closing over the brown strap, the white blue-veined arm growing tense and bright, then relaxing and softening after the blow it dealt Karen's poor back. He saw her jealous eyes gleaming with pleasure, her angry lips curling in a cruel smile at the thought that she was blotting out kiss after kiss with the leather rein. And she was his! He had been harsh and stern and ruthless; he had suffered these dear hands to be wrung with anguish and these dear lips to open in sighing.

His eyes took on a moist lustre at the thought, and he felt suffused with the easy, indolent pity of a drunken man. He stood there staring in sottish sentimentality until the rich flood of sunlight had shrunk to a thin bright streak high among the dark rafters of the ceiling.

Then Marie Grubbe awoke.

"You!" she almost screamed as she jumped up and darted back so quickly that the chair tumbled along the floor.

"Marie!" said Ulrik Frederik as tenderly as he could, and held out his hands pleadingly to her.

"What brings you here? Have you come to complain of the beating your harlot got?"

"No, no, Marie; let's be friends—good friends!"

"You are drunk," she said coldly, turning away from him.

"Ay, Marie, I'm drunk with love of you—I'm drunk and dizzy with your beauty, my heart's darling."

"Yes, truly, so dizzy that your eyesight has failed you, and you have taken others for me."

"Marie, Marie, leave your jealousy!"

She made a contemptuous gesture as if to brush him aside.

"Indeed, Marie, you were jealous. You betrayed yourself when you took that bridle rein, you know. But now let the whole filthy rabble be forgotten as dead and given over to the devil. Come, come, cease playing unkind to me as I have played the faithless rogue to you with all these make-believe pleasures and gallantries. We do nothing but prepare each other a pit of hell whereas we might have an Eden of delight. Come, whatever you desire, it shall be yours. Would you dance in silks as thick as chamlet, would you have pearls in strings as long as your hair, you shall have them, and rings, and tissue of gold in whole webs, and plumes, and precious stones, whatever you will— nothing is too good to be worn by you."

He tried to put his arm around her waist, but she caught his wrist and held him away from her.

"Ulrik Frederik," she said, "let me tell you something. If you could wrap your love in ermine and marten, if you could clothe it in sable and crown it with gold, ay, give it shoes of purest diamond, I would cast it away from me like filth and dung, for I hold it less than the ground I tread with my feet. There's no drop of my blood that's fond of you, no fibre of my flesh that doesn't cry out upon you. Do you hear? There's no corner of my soul where you're not called names. Understand me aright! If I could free your body from the pangs of mortal disease and your soul from the fires of hell by being as yours, I would not do it."

"Yes, you would, woman, so don't deny it!"

"No, and no, and more than no!"

"Then begone! Out of my sight in the accursed name of hell!"

He was white as the wall and shook in every limb. His voice sounded hoarse and strange, and he beat the air like a madman.

"Take your foot from my path! Take your—take your —take your foot from my path, or I'll split your skull! My blood's lusting to kill, and I'm seeing red. Begone—out of the land and dominion of Norway, and hell-fire go with you! Begone—"

For a moment Marie stood looking at him in horror, then ran as fast as she could out of the room and away from the castle.

When the door slammed after her, Ulrik Frederik seized the chair in which she had been sitting when he came in and hurled it out of the window, then caught the curtains from the bed and tore the worn stuff into shreds and tatters, storming round the room all the while. He threw himself on the floor and crawled around, snarling like a wild beast, and pounding with his fists till the knuckles were bloody. Exhausted at last, he crept over to the bed and flung himself face downward in the pillows, called Marie tender names, and wept and sobbed and cursed her, then again began to talk in low, wheedling tones as if he were fondling her.

That same night Marie Grubbe for fair words and good pay got a skipper to sail with her to Denmark.

The following day Ulrik Frederik turned Karen Fiol out of the castle, and a few days later he himself left for Copenhagen.

CHAPTER XIII

ONE fine day Erik Grubbe was surprised to see Madam Gyldenlöve driving in to Tjele. He knew at once that something was wrong, since she came thus without servants or anything, and when he learned the facts, it was no warm welcome he gave her. In truth, he was so angry that he went away, slamming the door after him, and did not appear again that day. When he had slept on the matter, however, he grew more civil and even treated his daughter with an almost respectful affection while his manner took on some of the formal graces of the old courtier. It had occurred to him that, after all, there was no great harm done, for even though there had been some little disagreement between the young people, Marie was still Madam Gyldenlöve, and no doubt matters could easily be brought back into the old rut again.

To be sure, Marie was clamoring for a divorce and would not hear of a reconciliation, but it would have been unreasonable to expect anything else from her in the first heat of her anger with all her memories like sore bruises and gaping wounds, so he did not lay much stress upon that. Time would cure it, he felt sure.

There was another circumstance from which he hoped much. Marie had come from Aggershus almost naked, without clothes or jewels, and she would soon miss the luxury which she had learned to look upon as a matter of course. Even the plain food and poor service, the whole simple mode of living at Tjele would have its effect on her by making her long for what she had left. On the other hand, Ulrik Frederik, however angry he might be, could not well think of a divorce. His financial affairs were hardly in such a state that he could give up Marie's fortune, for twelve thousand rix-dollars was a large sum in ready money, and gold, landed estates, and manorial rights were hard to part with when once acquired.

For upward of six months all went well at Tjele. Marie felt a sense of comfort in the quiet country place where day after day passed all empty of events. The monotony was something new to her, and she drank in the deep peace with dreamy, passive enjoyment. When she thought of the past, it seemed to her like a weary struggle, a restless pressing onward without a goal in the glare of smarting, stinging light, deafened by intolerable noise and hubbub. A delicious feeling of shelter and calm stole over her, a sense of undisturbed rest in a grateful shadow, in a sweet and friendly silence, and she liked to deepen the peace of her refuge by picturing to herself the world outside where people were still striving and struggling while she had, as it were, slipped behind life and found a safe little haven where none could discover her or bring unrest into her sweet twilight solitude.

As time went on, however, the silence became oppressive, the peace dull, and the shadow dark. She began to listen for sounds of living life from without. So it was not unwelcome to her when Erik Grubbe proposed a change. He wished her to reside at Kalö manor, the property of her husband, and he pointed out to her that as Ulrik Frederik had her entire fortune in his possession and yet did not send anything for her maintenance, it was but fair she should be supported from his estate. There she would be in clover; she might have a houseful of servants and live in the elegant and costly fashion to which she was accustomed far better than at Tjele, which was quite too poor for her. Moreover,

the King, as a part of his wedding gift, had settled upon
her in case of Ulrik Frederik's death an income equal to
that at which Kalö was rated and in doing so he had
clearly had Kalö in mind, since it was conveyed to Ulrik
Frederik six months after their marriage. If they should
not patch up their difference, Ulrik Frederik would very
likely have to give up to her the estate intended for her
dowager seat, and she might as well become familiar
with it. It would be well too that Ulrik Frederik should
get used to knowing her in possession of it; he would
then the more readily resign it to her.

What Erik Grubbe really had in mind was to rid himself
of the expense of keeping Marie at Tjele and to make the
breach between Ulrik Frederik and his wife less evident in
the eyes of the world. It was at least a step toward reconciliation, and there was no knowing what it might lead to.

So Marie went to Kalö, but she did not live in the style
she had pictured to herself, for Ulrik Frederik had given
his bailiff, Johan Utrecht, orders to receive and entertain
Madam Gyldenlöve but not to give her a stiver in ready
money. Besides Kalö was, if possible, even more tiresome
than Tjele, and Marie would probably not have remained
there long if she had not had a visitor who was soon to
become more than a visitor to her.

His name was Sti Högh.

Since the night of the ballet in Frederiksborg Park,
Marie had often thought of her brother-in-law and always
with a warm sense of gratitude. Many a time at Aggershus,
when she had been wounded in some particularly galling
manner, the thought of Sti's reverent, silently adoring
homage had comforted her, and he treated her in precisely
the same way now that she was forgotten and forsaken as

in the days of her glory. There was the same flattering
hopelessness in his mien and the same humble adoration
in his eyes.

He would never remain at Kalö for more than two or
three days at a time; then he would leave for a week's visit
in the neighborhood, and Marie learned to long for his coming and to sigh when he went away, for he was practically
the only company she had. They became very intimate,
and there was but little they did not confide to each other.

"Madam," said Sti one day, "is it your purpose to return to his Excellency if he make you full and proper
apologies?"

"Even though he were to come here crawling on his
knees," she replied, "I would thrust him away. I have
naught but contempt and loathing for him in my heart, for
there's not a faithful sentiment in his mind, not one honest drop of warm blood in his body. He is a slimy, cursed
harlot and no man. He has the empty, faithless eyes of
a harlot and the soulless, clammy desire of a harlot. There
has never a warm-blooded passion carried him out of himself, never a heartfelt word cried from his lips. I hate him,
Sti, for I feel myself besmirched by his stealthy hands and
bawdy words."

"Then, madam, you will sue for a separation?"

Marie replied that she would, and if her father had only
stood by her, the case would have been far advanced, but
he was in no hurry, for he still thought the quarrel could be
patched up, though it never would be.

They talked of what maintenance she might look for
after the divorce, and Marie said that Erik Grubbe meant
to demand Kalö on her behalf. Sti thought this was ill-con-
sidered. He forecast a very different lot for her than sitting

as a dowager in an obscure corner of Jutland and at last, perhaps, marrying a country squire, which was the utmost she could aspire to if she stayed. Her rôle at court was played out, for Ulrik Frederik was in such high favor that he would have no trouble in keeping her away from it and it from her. No, Sti's advice was that she should demand her fortune in ready money and, as soon as it was paid her, leave the country, never to set foot in it again. With her beauty and grace she could win a fairer fate in France than here in this miserable land with its boorish nobility and poor little imitation of a court.

He told her so, and the frugal life at Kalö made a good background for the alluring pictures he sketched of the splendid and brilliant court of Louis the Fourteenth. Marie was fascinated and came to regard France as the theatre of all her dreams.

Sti Högh was as much under the spell of his love for Marie as ever, and he often spoke to her of his passion, never asking or demanding anything, never even expressing hope or regret, but taking for granted that she did not return his love and never would. At first Marie heard him with a certain uneasy surprise, but after a while she became absorbed in listening to these hopeless musings on a love of which she was the source, and it was not without a certain intoxicating sense of power that she heard herself called the lord of life and death to so strange a person as Sti Högh. Before long, however, Sti's lack of spirit began to irritate her. He seemed to give up the fight merely because the object of it was unattainable and to accept tamely the fact that too high was too high. She did not exactly doubt that there was real passion underneath his strange words or grief behind his melancholy looks, but she wondered whether he did not speak more strongly than he felt. A hopeless passion that did not defiantly close its eyes to its own hopelessness and storm ahead—she could not understand it and did not believe in it. She formed a mental picture of Sti Högh as a morbid nature, everlastingly fingering himself and hugging the illusion of being richer and bigger and finer than he really was. Since no reality bore out this conception of himself, he seemed to feed his imagination with great feelings and strong passions that were, in truth, born only in the fantastic pregnancy of his over-busy brain. His last words to her—for at her father's request she was returning to Tjele, where he could not follow her—served to confirm her in the opinion that this mental portrait resembled him in every feature.

He had bid her good-by and was standing with his hand on the latch, when he turned back to her, saying, "A black leaf of my book of life is being turned now that your Kalö days are over, madam. I shall think of this time with longing and anguish, as one who has lost all earthly happiness and all that was his hope and desire, and yet, madam, if such a thing should come to pass as that there were reason to think you loved me and if I were to believe it, then God only knows what it might make of me. Perhaps it might rouse in me those powers which have hitherto failed to unfold their mighty wings. Then perhaps the part of my nature that is thirsting after great deeds and burning with hope might be in the ascendant and make my name famous and great. Yet it might as well be that such unutterable happiness would slacken every high-strung fibre, silence every crying demand, and dull every hope. Thus the land of my happiness might be to my gifts and powers a lazy Capua. . . ."

No wonder Marie thought of him as she did, and she realized that it was best so. Yet she sighed.

She returned to Tjele by Erik Grubbe's desire, for he was afraid that Sti might persuade her to some step that did not fit into his plans, and besides he was bound to try whether he could not talk her into some compromise by which the marriage might remain in force. This proved fruitless, but still Erik Grubbe continued to write Ulrik Frederik letters begging him to take back Marie. Ulrik Frederik never replied. He preferred to let the matter hang fire as long as possible, for the sacrifice of property that would have to follow a divorce was extremely inconvenient for him. As for his father-in-law's assurances of Marie's conciliatory state of mind, he did not put any faith in them. Squire Erik Grubbe's untruthfulness was too well known.

Meanwhile Erik Grubbe's letters grew more and more threatening, and there were hints of a personal appeal to the King. Ulrik Frederik realized that matters could not go on this way much longer, and while in Copenhagen, he wrote his bailiff at Kalö, Johan Utrecht, ordering him to find out secretly whether Madam Gyldenlöve would meet him there unknown to Erik Grubbe. This letter was written in March of sixty-nine. Ulrik Frederik hoped by this meeting to learn how Marie really felt, and in case he found her compliant, he meant to take her back with him to Aggershus. If not, he would make promises of steps leading to an immediate divorce and so secure for himself as favorable terms as possible. But Marie Grubbe refused to meet him, and Ulrik Frederik was obliged to go back to Norway with nothing accomplished.

Still Erik Grubbe went on with his futile letter writing, but in February of sixteen hundred and seventy, they had tidings of the death of Frederik the Third, and then Erik Grubbe felt the time had come to act. King Frederik had always held his son Ulrik Frederik in such high regard and had such a blind fondness for him that in a case like this he would no doubt have laid all the blame on the other party. King Christian might be expected to take a different attitude, for though he and Ulrik Frederik were bosom friends and boon companions, a tiny shadow of jealousy might lurk in the mind of the King, who had often in his father's time been pushed aside for his more gifted and brilliant half-brother. Besides, young rulers liked to show their impartiality and would often in their zeal for justice be unfair to the very persons whom they might be supposed to favor. So it was decided that in the spring they should both go to Copenhagen. In the meantime Marie was to try to get from Johan Utrecht two hundred rix-dollars to buy mourning so that she could appear properly before the new king, but as the bailiff did not dare to pay out anything without order from Ulrik Frederik, Marie had to go without the mourning, for her father would not pay for it and thought the lack of it would make her pitiful condition the more apparent.

They arrived in Copenhagen toward the end of May, and when a meeting between father and son-in-law had proved fruitless, Erik Grubbe wrote to the King that he had no words to describe in due submission the shame, disgrace, and dishonor with which his Excellency Gyldenlöve had some years ago driven his wife, Marie Grubbe, out of Aggershus and had given her over to the mercies of wind and weather and freebooters who at that time infested the sea, there being a burning feud between Holland and England. God in his mercy had preserved her from the

above-mentioned mortal dangers, and she had returned to
his home in possession of life and health. Nevertheless,
it was an unheard-of outrage that had been inflicted upon
her, and he had time and again with letters, supplications,
and tears of weeping besought his noble and right honorable son, my lord his Excellency, that he would consider
of this matter and either bring proofs against Marie why
the marriage should be annulled or else take her back, but
all in vain. Marie had brought him a fortune of many thousand rix-dollars, and she had not even been able to get two
hundred rix-dollars with which to buy mourning dress. In
brief, her misery was too manifold to be described, wherefore they now addressed themselves to his Majesty the King,
appealing to the natural kindness and condescension of
their most gracious sovereign with the prayer that he would
for God's sake have mercy upon him, Erik Grubbe, for his
great age, which was seven and sixty years, and upon her
for her piteous condition and be graciously pleased to command his Excellency Gyldenlöve that he should either bring
proof against Marie of that for which Christ said married
persons should be parted, which, however, he would never
be able to do, or else take her back, whereby the glory
of God would be furthered, the state of marriage held in
honor as God had Himself ordained, great cause of offence
removed, and a soul be saved from perdition.

Marie at first refused to put her name to this document,
since she was determined not to live with Ulrik Frederik
whatever happened, but her father assured her that the
appeal to her husband to take her back was merely a matter
of form. The fact was that Ulrik Frederik now wanted a
divorce at any price and the wording of the petition would
put the onus of demanding it upon him, thus securing for

her better terms. Marie finally yielded and even added a postscript, written according to her father's dictation as follows:

I would fain have spoken with your Royal Majesty, but, miserable woman that I am, I have no dress proper to appear among people. Have pity on my wretchedness, most gracious Monarch and King, and help me! God will reward you.

MARIE GRUBBE.

As she did not put much faith in Erik Grubbe's assurances, she managed to get a private letter into the hands of the King through one of her old friends at court. In this she told him plainly how she loathed Ulrik Frederik, how eagerly she longed to be legally parted from him, and how she shrank from having even the slightest communication with him in regard to the settlement of money matters.

Yet Erik Grubbe had for once spoken the truth. Ulrik Frederik really wanted a divorce. His position at court as the King's half-brother was very different from that of the King's favorite son. He could no longer trust to fatherly partiality but simply had to compete with the men about him for honor and emoluments. To have such a case as this pending did not help to strengthen his position. It would be much better to make an end of it as quickly as possible and seek compensation in a new and wiser marriage for whatever the divorce might cost him in fortune or reputation. So he brought all his influence to bear to reach this end.

The King laid the case before the Consistory, and this body delivered a report, following which the marriage was dissolved by judgment of the Supreme Court, October fourteenth, sixteen hundred and seventy. Both parties were to have the right to marry again, and Marie Grubbe's twelve thousand rix-dollars were to be refunded to her with all her other dowry of jewels and estates. As soon as the money had been paid over to her, she began preparations to leave the country without listening to her father's remonstrances. As for Ulrik Frederik, he wrote his half-sister, wife of Johan Georg, Elector of Saxony, telling her of his divorce and asking if she would show him so much sisterly kindness that he might flatter himself with the hope of receiving a bride from her royal hands.

CHAPTER XIV

M ARIE GRUBBE had never had money of her own, and the possession of a large sum gave her a sense of powers and possibilities without limit. Indeed, it seemed to her that a veritable magic wand had been placed in her hands, and she longed like a child to wave it round and round and bring all the treasures of the earth to her feet.

Her most immediate wish was to be far away from the towers of Copenhagen and the meadows of Tjele, from Erik Grubbe and Aunt Rigitze. She waved the wand once, and lo! she was carried by wheel and keel over water and way from the land of Sjælland to Lübeck town. Her whole retinue consisted of the maid Lucie, whom she had persuaded her aunt to let her have, and a trader's coachman from Aarhus, for the real outfitting for her trip was to be done at Lübeck.

It was Sti Högh who had put into her head the idea of travelling, and in doing so, he had hinted that he might himself leave the country to seek his fortune abroad and had offered his services as courier. Summoned by a letter from Copenhagen, he arrived in Lübeck a fortnight after Marie and at once began to make himself useful by attending to the preparations necessary for so long a journey.

In her secret heart Marie had hoped to be a benefactor to poor Sti Högh. She meant to use some of her wealth to lighten his expenses on the trip and in France until it should appear whether some other fountain would well in his behalf. But when poor Sti Högh came, he surprised her by being splendidly attired, excellently mounted, attended by two magnificent grooms, and altogether looking as if his purse by no means needed to be swelled by her gold.

More astonishing yet was the change in his state of mind.
He seemed lively, even merry. In the past he had always
looked as if he were marching with stately step in his own
funeral procession, but now he trod the floor with the
air of a man who owned half the world and had the other
half coming to him. In the old days there had always
been something of the plucked fowl about him, but now
he seemed like an eagle, with spreading plumage and sharp
eyes hinting of still sharper claws.

Marie at first thought the change was due to his relief in
casting behind him past worries and his hope of winning a
future worth while, but when he had been with her several
days and had not opened his lips to one of the love-sick,
dispirited words she knew so well, she began to believe he
had conquered his passion and now, in the sense of proudly
setting his heel on the head of the dragon love, felt free and
strong and master of his own fate. She grew quite curious
to know whether she had guessed aright and thought with
a slight feeling of pique that the more she saw of Sti Högh,
the less she knew him.

This impression was confirmed by a talk she had with
Lucie. The two were walking in the large hall which formed
a part of every Lübeck house, serving as entry and living-
room, as playground for the children and the scene of the
chief household labors, besides being used sometimes for
dining room and storehouse. This particular hall was intended chiefly for warm weather and was furnished only
with a long white-scoured deal table, some heavy wooden
chairs, and an old cupboard. At the farther end some boards
had been put up for shelves, and there cabbages lay in long
rows over red mounds of carrots and bristling bunches
of horse-radish. The outer door was wide open and showed

the wet, glistening street, where the rain splashed in shining rivulets.

Marie Grubbe and Lucie were both dressed to go out, the former in a fur-bordered cloak of broadcloth, the latter in a cape of gray russet. They were pacing the red brick floor with quick, firm little steps as though trying to keep their feet warm while waiting for the rain to stop.

"Pray, d' you think it 's a safe travelling companion you 've got?" asked Lucie.

"Sti Högh? Safe enough, I suppose. Why not?"

"Faith, I hope he won't lose himself on the way, that 's all."

"Lose himself?"

"Ay, among the German maidens—or the Dutch, for the matter of that. You know 'tis said of him his heart is made of such fiery stuff it bursts into flame at the least flutter of a petticoat."

"Who 's taken you to fools' market with such fables?"

"Merciful! Did you never hear that? Your own brother-in-law? Who 'd have thought that could be news to you! Why, I 'd as lief have thought to tell you the week had seven days."

"Come, come, what ails you today? You run on as if you 'd had Spanish wine for breakfast."

"One of us has, that 's plain. Pray have you never heard tell of Ermegaard Lynow?"

"Never."

"Then ask Sti Högh if he should chance to know her. And name to him Jydte Krag and Christence Rud and Edele Hansdaughter and Lene Poppings if you like. He might happen to know some fables, as you call it, about them all."

Marie stopped and looked long and fixedly through the
open door at the rain. "Perhaps you know," she said as
she resumed her walk, "perhaps you know some of these
fables so that you can tell them."

"Belike I do."

"Concerning Ermegaard Lynow?"

"Concerning her in particular."

"Well, let's have it."

"Why, it had to do with one of the Höghs — Sti, I think
his name was — tall, red-haired, pale — "

"Thanks, but all that I know already."

"And do you know about the poison too?"

"Nay, nothing."

"Nor the letter?"

"What letter?"

"Faugh, 't is such an ugly story!"

"Out with it!"

"Why, this Högh was a very good friend — this happened before he was married — and he was the very best of
friends with Ermegaard Lynow. She had the longest hair
of any lady — she could well-nigh walk on it, and she was
red and white and pretty as a doll, but he was harsh and
barbarous to her, they said, as if she'd been an unruly
staghound and not the gentle creature she was, and the
more inhumanly he used her, the more she loved him. He
might have beaten her black and blue — and belike he did
— she would have kissed him for it. To think that one
person can be so bewitched by another, it's horrible! But
then he got tired of her and never even looked at her, for
he was in love with someone else, and Mistress Ermegaard
wept and came nigh breaking her heart and dying of grief,
but still she lived, though forsooth it was n't much of a life.

At last she could n't bear it any longer, and when she saw Sti Högh riding past, so they said, she ran out after him and followed alongside of his horse for a mile, and he never so much as drew rein nor listened to her crying and pleading but rode on all the faster and left her. That was too much for her, and so she took deadly poison and wrote Sti Högh that she did it for him, and she would never stand in his way; all that she asked was that he would come and see her before she died."

"And then?"

"Why, God knows if it 's true what people say, for if it is, he 's the wickedest body and soul hell is waiting for. They say he wrote back that his love would have been the best physic for her, but as he had none to give her, he 'd heard that milk and white onions were likewise good and he 'd advise her to take some. That 's what he said. Now, what do you think of that? Could anything be more inhuman?"

"And Mistress Ermegaard?"

"Mistress Ermegaard?"

"Ay, what of her?"

"Well, no thanks to him, but she had n't taken enough poison to kill her, though she was so sick and wretched they thought she 'd never be well again."

"Poor little lamb!" said Marie laughing.

Almost every day in the time that followed brought some change in Marie's conception of Sti Högh and her relation to him. Sti was no dreamer; that was plain from the forethought and resourcefulness he displayed in coping with the innumerable difficulties of the journey. It was evident too, that in manners and mind he was far above even the most distinguished of the noblemen they met on their way.

What he said was always new and interesting and different; he seemed to have a shortcut, known only to himself, to an understanding of men and affairs, and Marie
was impressed by the audacious scorn with which he
owned his belief in the power of the beast in man and the
scarcity of gold amid the dross of human nature. With
cold, passionless eloquence he tried to show her how little
consistency there was in man, how incomprehensible and
uncomprehended, how weak-kneed and fumbling and altogether the sport of circumstance that which was noble
and that which was base fought for ascendancy in his soul.
The fervor with which he expounded this seemed to her
great and fascinating, and she began to believe that rarer
gifts and greater powers had been given him than usually
fell to the lot of mortals. She bowed down in admiration,
almost in worship, before the tremendous force she imagined him possessed of. Yet withal there lurked in her soul
a still small doubt which was never shaped into a definite
thought but hovered as an instinctive feeling, whispering
that perhaps his power was a power that threatened and
raged, that coveted and desired, but never swooped down,
never took hold.

In Lohendorf, about three miles from Vechta, there was an
old inn near the highway, and there Marie and her travelling companions sought shelter an hour or two after sun-
down.

In the evening when the coachmen and grooms had gone
to bed in the outhouses, Marie and Sti Högh were sitting at
the little red-painted table before the great stove in a corner of the tap-room chatting with two rather oafish Old-
enborg noblemen. Lucie was knitting and looking on from

her place at the end of a bench where she sat leaning against the edge of the long table running underneath the windows. A tallow dip in a yellow earthenware candlestick on the gentlefolk's table cast a sleepy light over their faces and woke greasy reflections in a row of pewter plates ranged above the stove. Marie had a small cup of warm wine before her, Sti Högh a larger one, while the two Oldenborgers were sharing a huge pot of ale, which they emptied again and again and which was as often filled by the slovenly drawer who lounged on the goose-bench at the farther end of the room.

Marie and Sti Högh would both have preferred to go to bed, for the two rustic noblemen were not very stimulating company, and no doubt they would have gone had not the bedrooms been icy cold and the disadvantages of heating them even worse than the cold, as they found when the innkeeper brought in the braziers, for the peat in that part of the country was so saturated with sulphur that no one who was not accustomed to it could breathe where it was burning.

The Oldenborgers were not merry, for they saw that they were in very fine company and tried hard to make their conversation as elegant as possible; but as the ale gained power over them, the rein they had kept on themselves grew slacker and slacker and was at last quite loose. Their language took on a deeper local color, their playfulness grew massive, and their questions impudent.

As the jokes became coarser and more insistent, Marie stirred uneasily, and Sti's eyes asked across the table whether they should not retire. Just then the fairer of the two strangers made a gross insinuation. Sti gave him a frown and a threatening look, but this only egged him on, and he re-

peated his foul jest in even plainer terms whereupon Sti
promised that at one more word of the same kind he would
get the pewter cup in his head.

At that moment Lucie brought her knitting up to the
table to look for a dropped stitch, and the other Olden-
borger availed himself of the chance to catch her round the
waist, force her down on his knee, and imprint a sounding
kiss on her lips.

This bold action fired the fair man, and he put his arm
around Marie Grubbe's neck.

In the same second Sti's goblet hit him in the forehead with such force and such sureness of aim that he sank
down on the floor with a deep grunt.

The next moment Sti and the dark man were grappling
in the middle of the floor while Marie and her maid fled
to a corner.

The drawer jumped up from the goose-bench, bellowed
something out at one door, ran to the other and bolted it
with a two-foot iron bar just as someone else could be
heard putting the latch on the postern. It was a custom in
the inn to lock all doors as soon as a fight began so no one
could come from outside and join in the fracas, but this was
the only step for the preservation of peace that the inn-
people took. As soon as the doors were closed, they would
sneak off to bed; for he who has seen nothing can testify
to nothing.

Since neither party to the fight was armed, the affair had
to be settled with bare fists, and Sti and the dark man stood
locked together wrestling and cursing. They dragged each
other back and forth, turned in slow, tortuous circles, stood
each other up against walls and doors, caught each other's
arms, wrenched themselves loose, bent and writhed, each

with his chin in the other's shoulder. At last they tumbled
down on the floor, Sti on top. He had knocked his adver-
sary's head heavily two or three times against the cold
clay floor when suddenly he felt his own neck in the grip
of two powerful hands. It was the fair man, who had picked
himself up.

Sti choked, his throat rattled, he turned giddy, and his
limbs relaxed. The dark man wound his legs around him
and pulled him down by the shoulders; the other still
clutched his throat and dug his knees into his sides.

Marie shrieked and would have rushed to his aid, but
Lucie had thrown her arms around her mistress and held
her in such a convulsive grip that she could not stir.

Sti was on the point of fainting when suddenly, with one
last effort of his strength, he threw himself forward, knock-
ing the head of the dark man against the floor. The fingers
of the fair man slipped from his throat, opening the way
for a bit of air. Sti bounded up with all his force, hurled
himself at the fair man, threw him down, bent over the
fallen man in a fury, but in the same instant got a kick in
the pit of the stomach that almost felled him. He caught
the ankle of the foot that kicked him; with the other hand
he grasped the boot-top, lifted the leg, and broke it over his
outstretched thigh until the bones cracked in the boot and
the fair man sank down in a swoon. The dark man, who
lay staring at the scene still dizzy from the blows in his
head, gave vent to a yell of agony as if he had himself been
the maltreated one and crawled under the shelter of the
bench beneath the windows. With that the fight was ended.

The latent savagery which this encounter had called out
in Sti had a strange and potent effect on Marie. That
night when she laid her head on the pillow, she told her-

self that she loved him, and when Sti, perceiving a change in her eyes and manner that boded good for him, begged for her love, a few days later, he got the answer he longed for.

CHAPTER XV

THEY were in Paris. A half year had passed, and the bond of love so suddenly tied had loosened, and at last been broken. Marie and Sti Högh were slowly slipping apart. Both knew it, though they had not put the fact into words. The confession hid so much pain and bitterness, so much abasement and self-scorn, that they shrank from uttering it.

In this they were one, but in their manner of bearing their distress they were widely different. Sti Högh grieved ceaselessly in impotent misery, dulled by his very pain against the sharpest stings of that pain, despairing like a captured animal that paces back and forth, back and forth, in its narrow cage. Marie was more like a wild creature escaped from captivity, fleeing madly without rest or pause, driven on and ever on by frantic fear of the chain that drags clanking in its track.

She wanted to forget, but forgetfulness is like the heather: it grows of its own free will, and not all the care and labor in the world can add an inch to its height. She poured out gold from overflowing hands and purchased luxury. She caught at every cup of pleasure that wealth could buy or wit and beauty and rank could procure, but all in vain. There was no end to her wretchedness, and nothing, nothing could take it from her. If the mere parting from Sti Högh could have eased her pain or even shifted the burden, she would have left him long ago, but no, it was all the same, no spark of hope anywhere. As well be together as apart since there was no relief either way.

Yet the parting came, and it was Sti Högh who proposed it. They had not seen each other for several days when Sti came into the drawing room of the magnificent apartment they had rented from Isabel Gilles, the landlady of *La Croix de Fer*. Marie was sitting there in tears. Sti shook his head drearily and took a chair at the other end of the room. It was hard to see her weep and to know that every word of comfort from his lips, every sympathetic sigh or compassionate look merely added bitterness to her grief and made her tears flow faster.

He went up to her.

"Marie," he said in a low, husky voice, "let us have one more talk and then part."

"What is the good of that?"

"Nay, Marie, there are yet happy days awaiting you; even now they are coming thick and fast."

"Ay, days of mourning and nights of weeping in an endless, unbreakable chain."

"Marie, Marie, have a care what you say, for I understand the meaning of your words as you never think to have me, and they wound me cruelly."

"I reck but little of wounds that are stung with words for daggers. It was never in my mind to spare you them."

"Then drive the weapon home, and do not pity me — not for one instant. Tell me that my love has besmirched you and humbled you in the dust! Tell me that you would give years of your life to tear from your heart every memory of me! And make a dog of me and call me cur. Call me by every shameful name you know, and I will answer to every one and say you are right; for I know you are right, you are, though it's torture to say so! Hear me, Marie, hear me and believe if you can: though I know you loathe yourself because you have been mine and sicken in your soul when you think of it and frown with disgust and remorse, yet do I love you still — I do indeed. I love you with all my might and soul, Marie."

"Fie, shame on you, Sti Högh! Shame on you! You know not what you are saying. And yet — God forgive me — but 'tis true, fearful as it seems! Oh, Sti, Sti, why are you such a varlet soul? Why are you such a miserable, cringing worm that doesn't bite when it's trodden underfoot? If you knew how great and proud and strong I believed you — you who are so weak! It was your sounding phrases that lied to me of a power you never owned; they spoke loud of everything your soul never was and never could be. Sti, Sti, was it right that I should find weakness instead of strength, abject doubt instead of brave faith, and pride — Sti, where was your pride?"

"Justice and right are but little mercy, but I deserve naught else, for I have been no better than a counterfeiter with you, Marie. I never believed in your love; no, even in the hour when you first vowed it to me, there was no faith in my soul. Oh! how I wanted to believe but could not! I could not down the fear that lifted its dark head from the ground, staring at me with cold eyes, blowing away my rich, proud dreams with the breath from its bitterly smiling mouth. I could not believe in your love, and yet I grasped the treasure of it with both hands and with all my soul. I rejoiced in it with a timid, anxious happiness as a thief might feel joy in his golden booty, though he knew the rightful owner would step in the next moment and tear the precious thing from his hands. For I know the man will come who will be worthy of you, or whom you will think worthy, and he will not doubt, not tremble and entreat. He will mould you like pure gold in his hands and set his foot on your will, and you will obey him, humbly and

street leading up to the castle in the house known as von
Karndorf's, a feast was held that same evening. The guests
were sitting around the table, merry and full of food and
drink. All but one were men who had left youth behind,
and this one was but eighteen years. He wore no periwig,
but his own hair was luxuriant enough, long, golden, and
curly. His face was fair as a girl's, white and red, and his
eyes were large, blue, and serene. They called him the
golden Remigius, golden not only because of his hair but
because of his great wealth. For all his youth he was the
richest nobleman in the Bavarian forest—for he hailed
from the Bavarian forest.

They were speaking of female loveliness, these gay gentlemen around the groaning board, and they all agreed that
when they were young, the world was swarming with
beauties beside whom those who laid claim to the name
in these days were as nothing at all.

"But who knew the pearl among them all?" asked a
chubby, red-faced man with tiny, sparkling eyes. "Who
ever saw Dorothea von Falkenstein of the Falkensteiners
of Harzen? She was red as a rose and white as a lamb. She
could clasp her waist round with her two hands and have
an inch to spare, and she could walk on larks' eggs without
crushing them so light of foot was she. But she was none
of your scrawny chicks for all that; she was as plump as a
swan swimming in a lake and firm as a roe deer running
in the forest."

They drank to her.

"God bless you all, gray though you be!" cried a tall,
crabbed old fellow at the end of the table. "The world is
getting uglier every day. We have but to look at ourselves"
—his glance went round the table—"and think what

dashing blades we once were. Well, no matter for that!
But where in the name of everything drinkable—can anyone say? huh? can you?—who can?—can anyone tell
me what 's become of the plump landladies with laughing
mouths and bright eyes and dainty feet and the landladies'
daughters with yellow, yellow hair and eyes so blue—
what 's become of them? huh? Or is 't a lie that one could
go to any tavern or wayside inn or ordinary and find them
there? Oh, misery of miseries and wretchedness! Look at
the hunchbacked jades the tavern people keep in these days
—with pig's eyes and broad in the beam! Look at the
toothless, bald-pated hags that get the king's license to
scare the life out of hungry and thirsty folks with their sore
eyes and grubby hands! Faugh, I 'm as scared of an inn
as of the devil himself, for I know full well the tapster is
married to the living image of the plague from Lübeck,
and when a man 's as old as I am, there 's something about
memento mori that he 'd rather forget than remember."

Near the centre of the long table sat a man of strong
build with a face rather full and yellow as wax, bushy eyebrows, and clear, searching eyes. He looked not exactly
ill, but as if he had suffered great bodily pain, and when he
smiled, there was an expression about his mouth as though
he were swallowing something bitter. He spoke in a soft,
low, rather husky voice. "The brown Euphemia of the
Burtenbacher stock was statelier than any queen I ever saw.
She could wear the stiffest cloth of gold as if it were the easi-
est house-dress. Golden chains and precious stones hung
round her neck and waist and rested on her bosom and hair
as lightly as berries the children deck themselves with when
they play in the forest. There was none like her. The other
young maidens would look like reliquaries weighed down

by necklaces of gold and clasps of gold and jewelled roses, but she was fair and fresh and festive and light as a banner that flies in the wind. There was none like her, nor is there now."

"Ay, and a better one," cried young Remigius jumping up. He bent forward across the table, supporting himself with one hand while the other swung a bright goblet, from which the golden grape brimmed over wetting his fingers and wrist and falling in clear drops from his full white lace ruffles. His cheeks were flushed with wine, his eyes shone, and he spoke in an unsteady voice.

"Beauty! Are you blind, one and all, or have you never even seen the Lady from Denmark— not so much as seen Mistress Marie! Her hair is like the sunlight on a field when the grain is ripe. Her eyes are bluer than a steel blade, and her lips are like the bleeding grape. She walks like a star in the heavens, and she is straight as a sceptre and stately as a throne, and all, all charms and beauties of person are hers like rose upon rose in flowering splendor. But there is that about her loveliness which makes you feel when you see her as on a holy morn when they blow the trumpets from the tower of the cathedral. A stillness comes over you, for she is like the sacred Mother of Sorrows on the beauteous painting; there is the same noble grief in her clear eyes and the same hopeless, patient smile around her lips."

He was quite moved. Tears came to his eyes, and he tried to speak but could not and remained standing, struggling with his voice to utter the words. A man sitting near him laid a friendly hand on his shoulder and made him sit down. They drank together goblet after goblet until all was well. The mirth of the old fellows rose high as before, and nothing was heard but laughter and song and revelry.

Marie Grubbe was at Nürnberg. After the parting from Sti
Högh she had roamed about from place to place for almost
a year and had finally settled there. She was very much
changed since the night she danced in the ballet at Frederiksborg park. Not only had she entered upon her thirtieth
year, but the affair with Sti Högh had made a strangely deep
impression upon her. She had left Ulrik Frederik urged on
partly by accidental events but chiefly because she had kept
certain dreams of her early girlhood of the man a woman
should pay homage to, one who should be to her like a god
upon earth from whose hands she could accept, lovingly
and humbly, good and evil according to his pleasure. And
now, in a moment of blindness, she had taken Sti for that
god, him who was not even a man. These were her thoughts.
Every weakness and every unmanly doubt in Sti she felt
as a stain upon herself that could never be wiped out. She
loathed herself for that short-lived love and called it base
and shameful names. The lips that had kissed him, would
that they might wither! The eyes that had smiled on him,
would that they might be dimmed! The heart that had loved
him, would that it might break! Every virtue of her soul—
she had smirched it by this love; every feeling—she had
desecrated it. She lost all faith in herself, all confidence in
her own worth, and as for the future, it kindled no beacon
of hope.

Her life was finished, her course ended. A quiet nook
where she could lay down her head, never to lift it again
was the goal of all her desires.

Such was her state of mind when she came to Nürnberg.
By chance she met the golden Remigius, and his fervent
though diffident adoration—the idolatrous worship of fresh
youth—his exultant faith in her and his happiness in this

faith —were to her as the cool dew to a flower that has been
trodden under foot. Though it cannot rise again, neither
does it wither; it still spreads delicate, brightly tinted petals
to the sun and is still fair and fragrant in lingering freshness. So with her. There was balm in seeing herself pure
and holy and unsullied in the thoughts of another person.
It well-nigh made her whole again to know that she could
rouse that clear-eyed trust, that fair hope and noble longing which enriched the soul of him in whom they awoke.
There was comfort and healing in hinting of her sorrows
in shadowy images and veiled words to one who, himself
untried by grief, would enter into her suffering with a
serene joy, grateful to share the trouble he guessed but did
not understand and yet sympathized with. Ay, it was a
comfort to pour out her grief where it met reverence and
not pity, where it became a splendid queenly robe around her
shoulders and a tear-sparkling diadem around her brow.

Thus Marie little by little grew reconciled to herself, but
then it happened one day, when Remigius was out riding
that his horse shied, threw him from the saddle, and dragged
him to death by the stirrups.

When the news was brought to Marie, she sank into
a dull, heavy, tearless misery. She would sit for hours staring straight before her with a weary, empty look, silent as
if she had been bereft of the power of speech and refusing
to exert herself in any way. She could not even bear to be
spoken to; if anyone tried it, she would make a feeble gesture of protest and shake her head as if the sound pained her.

Time passed, and her money dwindled until there was
barely enough left to take them home. Lucie never tired of
urging this fact upon her, but it was long before she could
make Marie listen.

At last they started. On the way Marie fell ill, and the journey dragged out much longer than they had expected. Lucie was forced to sell one rich gown and precious trinket after the other to pay their way. When they reached Aarhus Marie had hardly anything left but the clothes she wore. There they parted; Lucie returned to Mistress Rigitze, and Marie went back to Tjele.

This was in the spring of seventy-three.

CHAPTER XVI

A FTER she came back to Tjele, Mistress Marie Grubbe remained in her father's household until sixteen hundred and seventy-nine, when she was wedded to Palle Dyre, counsellor of justice to his Majesty the King, and with him she lived in a marriage that offered no shadow of an event until sixteen hundred and eighty-nine. This period of her life lasted from the time she was thirty till she was forty-six—full sixteen years.

Full sixteen years of petty worries, commonplace duties, and dull monotony with no sense of intimacy or affection to give warmth, no homelike comfort to throw a ray of light. Endless brawling about nothing, noisy hectoring for the slightest neglect, peevish fault-finding, and coarse jibes were all that met her ears. Every sunlit day of life was coined into dollars and shillings and pennies; every sigh uttered was a sigh for loss; every wish a wish for gain; every hope, a hope of more. All around her was shabby parsimony; in every nook and corner, busyness that chased away all pleasure; from every hour stared the wakeful eye of greed. Such was the existence Marie Grubbe led.

In the early days she would sometimes forget the hubbub and bustle all around her and sink into waking dreams of beauty, changing as clouds, teeming as light. There was one that came oftener than others. It was a dream of a sleeping castle hidden behind roses. Oh, the quiet garden of that castle with stillness in the air and in the leaves, with silence brooding over all like a night without darkness! There the odors slept in the flower-cups and the dewdrops on the bending blades of grass. There the violet drowsed with mouth half open under the curling leaves of the fern while a thou-

sand bursting buds had been lulled to sleep in the fullness
of spring at the very moment when they quickened on the
branches of the moss green trees. She came up to the palace.
From the thorny vines of the rose bushes, a flood of green
billowed noiselessly down over walls and roofs, and the
flowers fell like silent froth, sometimes in masses of bloom,
sometimes flecking the green like pale pink foam. From
the mouth of the marble lion a fountain jet shot up like a
tree of crystal with boughs of cobweb, and shining horses
mirrored breathless mouths and closed eyes in the dor-
mant waters of the porphyry basin while the page rubbed
his eyes in sleep.

She feasted her eyes on the tranquil beauty of the old
garden where fallen petals lay like a rose-flushed snowdrift
high against walls and doors, hiding the marble steps. Oh,
to rest! To let the days glide over her in blissful peace hour
after hour and to feel all memories, longings, and dreams
flowing away out of her mind in softly lapping waves —
that was the most beautiful of all the dreams she knew.

This was true at first, but her imagination tired of flying
unceasingly toward the same goal like an imprisoned bee
buzzing against the windowpane, and all other faculties of
her soul wearied too. As a fair and noble edifice in the hands
of barbarians is laid waste and spoiled, the bold spires made
into squat cupolas, the delicate, lace-like ornaments broken
bit by bit, and the wealth of pictures hidden under layer
upon layer of deadening whitewash, so was Marie Grubbe
laid waste and spoiled in those sixteen years.

Erik Grubbe, her father, was old and decrepit, and age
seemed to intensify all his worst traits just as it sharpened
his features and made them more repulsive. He was grouchy
and perverse, childishly obstinate, quick to anger, extremely

suspicious, sly, dishonest, and stingy. In his later days he always had the name of God on his lips, especially when the harvest was poor or the cattle were sick, and he would address the Lord with a host of cringing, fawning names of his own invention. It was impossible that Marie should either love or respect him, and besides she had a particular grudge against him because he had persuaded her to marry Palle Dyre by dint of promises that were never fulfilled and by threats of disinheriting her, turning her out of Tjele, and withdrawing all support from her. In fact her chief motive for the change had been her hope of making herself independent of the paternal authority, though this hope was frustrated, for Palle Dyre and Erik Grubbe had agreed to work the farms of Tjele and Nörbæk — which latter was given Marie as a dower on certain conditions — together, and as Tjele was the larger of the two and Erik Grubbe no longer had the strength to look after it, Marie and her husband spent more time under her father's roof than under their own.

Palle Dyre was the son of Colonel Clavs Dyre of Sandvig and Krogsdal, later of Vinge, and his wife Edele Pallesdaughter Rodtsteen. He was a thickset, shortnecked little man, brisk in all his motions and with a rather forceful face, which, however, was somewhat marred by a hemorrhage in the lungs that had affected his right cheek.

Marie despised him. He was as stingy and greedy as Erik Grubbe himself. Yet he was really a man of some ability, sensible, energetic, and courageous, but he simply lacked any sense of honor whatever. He would cheat and lie whenever he had a chance and was never in the least abashed when found out. He would allow himself to be abused like a dog and never answer back if silence could bring him a penny's profit. Whenever a relative or friend commissioned him to buy or sell anything or entrusted any other business to him, he would turn the matter to his own advantage without the slightest scruple. Though his marriage had been in the main a bargain, he was not without a sense of pride in winning the divorced wife of the Viceroy; but this did not prevent him from treating her and speaking to her in a manner that might have seemed incompatible with such a feeling. Not that he was grossly rude or violent—by no means. He simply belonged to the class of people who are so secure in their own sense of normal and irreproachable mediocrity that they cannot refrain from asserting their superiority over the less fortunate and naïvely setting themselves up as models. As for Marie, she was, of course, far from unassailable; her divorce from Ulrik Frederik and her squandering of her mother's fortune were but too patent irregularities.

This was the man who became the third person in their life at Tjele. Not one trait in him gave grounds for hope that he would add to it any bit of brightness or comfort. Nor did he. Endless quarrelling and bickering, mutual sullenness and fault-finding were all that the passing days brought in their train.

Marie was blunted by it. Whatever had been delicate and flowerlike in her nature, all the fair and fragrant growth which heretofore had entwined her life as with luxurious though fantastic and even bizarre arabesques, withered and died the death. Coarseness in thought as in speech, a low and slavish doubt of everything great and noble, and a shameless self-scorn were the effect of these sixteen years at Tjele. And yet another thing: she developed a thick-blooded sensuousness, a hankering for the good things of life, a lusty appetite for food and drink, for soft chairs and soft beds, a voluptuous pleasure in spicy, narcotic scents, and a craving for luxury which was neither ruled by good taste nor refined by love of the beautiful. True, she had scant means of gratifying these desires, but that did not lessen their force.

She had grown fuller of form and paler, and there was a slow languor in all her movements. Her eyes were generally quite empty of expression, but sometimes they would grow strangely bright, and she had fallen into the habit of setting her lips in a meaningless smile.

There came a time when they wrote sixteen hundred and eighty-nine. It was night, and the horse-stable at Tjele was on fire. The flickering flames burst through the heavy clouds of brown smoke; they lit up the grassy courtyard, shone on the low outhouses and the white walls of the manor house, and even touched with light the black crowns of the trees in the garden where they rose high above the roof. Servants and neighbors ran from the well to the fire with pails and buckets full of water glittering red in the light of the flames. Palle Dyre was here, there, and everywhere, tearing wildly about, his hair flying, a red wooden rake in his hand. Erik Grubbe lay praying over an old chaff bin which had been carried out. He watched the progress of the fire from beam to beam, his agony growing more intense every moment, and he groaned audibly whenever the flames leaped out triumphantly and swung their spirals high above the house in a shower of sparks.

Marie too was there, but her eyes sought something besides the fire. They were fixed on the new coachman, who was taking the frightened horses out from the smoke-filled stable. The doorway had been widened to more than double

its usual size by lifting off the frame and tearing down a bit
of the frail wall on either side, and through this opening
he was leading the animals, one by either hand. They were
crazed with the smoke, and when the stinging, flickering
light of the flames met their eyes, they reared wildly and
threw themselves to one side until it seemed the man must
be torn to pieces or be trampled down between the powerful
brutes. Yet he neither fell nor lost his hold; he forced their
noses down on the ground and ran with them, half driving,
half dragging them across the courtyard to the gate of the
garden where he let them go.

There were many horses at Tjele, and Marie had plenty
of time to admire that beautiful, gigantic form in changing
postures as he struggled with the spirited animals, one moment hanging from a straight arm, almost lifted from the
ground by a rearing stallion, the next instant thrown violently down and gripping the earth with his feet, then again
urging them on by leaps and bounds always with the same
peculiarly quiet, firm, elastic movements seen only in very
strong men. His short cotton breeches and blue-gray shirt
looked yellow where the light fell on them but black in the
shadows and outlined sharply the vigorous frame, making a
fine, simple background for the ruddy face with its soft, fair
down on lip and chin and the great shock of blonde hair.

This giant of two-and-twenty was known as Sören Overseer. His real name was Sören Sörensen Möller, but the
title had come down to him from his father, who had been
overseer on a manor in Hvornum.

The horses were all brought out at last. The stable burned
to the ground, and when the fire still smouldering on the site
had been put out, the servants went to get a little morning
nap after a wakeful night.

Marie Grubbe too went to bed, but she could not sleep. She lay thinking, sometimes blushing at her own fancies, then tossing about as if she feared them. It was late when she rose. She smiled contemptuously at herself as she dressed. Her every-day attire was usually careless, even slovenly, though on special occasions she would adorn herself in a manner more showy than tasteful, but this morning she put on an old though clean gown of blue homespun, tied a little scarlet silk kerchief round her neck, and took out a neat, simple little cap; then she suddenly changed her mind again and chose instead one with a turned-up rim of yellow and brown flowered stuff and a flounce of imitation silver brocade in the back which went but poorly with the rest. Palle Dyre supposed she wanted to go to town and gossip about the fire, and he thought to himself there were no horses to drive her there. She stayed home, however, but somehow she could not work. She would take up one thing after another only to drop it as quickly. At last she went out into the garden, saying that she meant to set to rights what the horses had trampled in the night, but she did not accomplish much; for she sat most of the time in an arbor with her hands in her lap, gazing thoughtfully into the distance.

The unrest that had come over her did not leave her but grew worse day by day. She was suddenly seized with a desire for lonely walks in the direction of Fastrup Grove or in the more distant parts of the outer garden. Her father and husband both scolded her, but when she turned a deaf ear and did not even answer them, they finally made up their minds that it was best to let her go her own way for a short time, all the more as it was not the busy season.

About a week after the fire she was taking her usual walk

out Fastrup way, and was skirting the edge of a long copse
of stunted oaks and dogrose that reached almost to her
shoulder when suddenly she caught sight of Sören Overseer stretched at full length in the edge of the copse, his
eyes closed as if he were asleep. A scythe was lying at his
side, and the grass had been cut for some distance around.

Marie stood for a long time gazing at his large, regular
features, his broad, vigorously breathing chest, and his dark,
full-veined hands, which were clasped above his head. But
Sören was drowsing rather than sleeping, and suddenly he
opened his eyes, wide awake, and looked up at her. He was
startled at being found by one of the family sleeping when
he should have been cutting hay, but the expression in
Marie's eyes amazed him so much that he did not come to
his senses until she blushed, said something about the heat,
and turned to go. He jumped up, seized his scythe and whet-
stone, and began to rub the steel until it sang through the
warm, tremulous air. Then he went at the grass, slashing
as if his life were at stake.

After a while he saw Marie crossing the stile into the
grove, and at that he paused. He stood a moment staring
after her, his arms resting on his scythe, then suddenly
flung it away with all his strength, sat down with legs
sprawling, mouth open, palms flat out on the grass, and thus
he sat in silent amazement at himself and his own strange
thoughts.

He looked like a man who had just dropped down from
a tree.

His head seemed to be teeming with dreams. What if anyone had cast a spell over him? He had never known anything like the way things swarmed and swarmed inside of
his head as if he could think of seven things at once, and

he couldn't get the hang of them—they came and went as
if he 'd nothing to say about it. It surely was queer the way
she 'd looked at him, and she had n't said anything about his
sleeping this way in the middle of the day. She had looked
at him so kindly, straight out of her clear eyes, and—just
like Jens Pedersen's Trine she had looked at him. Her ladyship! Her ladyship! There was a story about a lady at Nörbæk manor who had run away with her gamekeeper. Had he
got such a look when he was asleep? Her ladyship! Maybe
he might get to be good friends with her ladyship, just as
the gamekeeper did. He could n't understand it—was he
sick? There was a burning spot on each of his cheeks, and
his heart beat, and he felt so queer it was hard to breathe.
He began to tug at a stunted oak, but he could not get a grip
on it where he was sitting; he jumped up, tore it loose, and
threw it away, caught his scythe, and cut till the grass flew
in the swath.

In the days that followed, Marie often came near Sören,
who happened to have work around the house, and he always stared at her with an unhappy, puzzled, questioning
expression as if imploring her to give him the answer to the
riddle she had thrown in his way, but Marie only glanced
furtively in his direction and turned her head away.

Sören was ashamed of himself and lived in constant fear
that his fellow-servants would notice there was something
the matter with him. He had never in all his life before been
beset by any feeling or longing that was in the least fantastic, and it made him timid and uneasy. Maybe he was getting addled or losing his wits. There was no knowing how
such things came over people, and he vowed to himself that
he would think no more about it, but the next moment his
thoughts were again taking the road he would have barred

them from. The very fact that he could not get away from these notions was what troubled him most, for he remembered that he had heard tales of Cyprianus, whom you could burn and drown, yet he always came back. In his heart of hearts he really hoped that the fancies would not leave him, for life would seem very dreary and empty without them, but this he did not admit to himself. In fact his cheeks flushed with shame whenever he soberly considered what he really had in mind.

About a week after the day when she had found Sören asleep, Marie Grubbe was sitting under the great beech on the heathery hill in Fastrup Grove. She sat leaning her back against the trunk and held an open book in her hand, but she was not reading. With dreamy eyes she followed intently a large, dark bird of prey, which hung in slowly gliding, watchful flight over the unending, billowing surface of the thick, leafy treetops.

The air was drenched with light and sun, vibrant with the drowsy, monotonous hum of myriad invisible insects. The sweet—too sweet—odor of yellow-flowered broom and the spicy fragrance of sun-warmed birch-leaves mingled with the earthy smell of the forest and the almond scent of white meadowsweet in the hollows.

Marie sighed.

"Petits oiseaux des bois,"

she whispered plaintively,

"que vous estes heureux,
De plaindre librement vos tourmens amoreux.
Les valons, les rochers, les forests et les plaines
Sçauent également vos plaisirs et vos peines."

She sat a moment trying to remember the rest, then took
the book and read in a low, despondent tone:

> "Vostre innocente amour ne fuit point la clarté,
> Tout le monde est pour vous un lieu de liberté,
> Mais ce cruel honneur, ce fléau de nostre vie,
> Sous de si dures loix la retient asservie. . . ."

She closed the book with a bang and almost shouted:

> "Il est vray je ressens une secrète flame
> Qui malgré ma raison s'allume dans mon âme
> Depuis le jour fatal que je vis sous l'ormeau
> Alcidor, qui dançoit au son du chalumeau."

Her voice sank, and the last lines were breathed forth softly,
almost automatically, as if her fancy were merely using the
rhythm as an accompaniment to other images than those
of the poem. She leaned her head back and closed her eyes.
It was so strange and disturbing now that she was middle-
aged to feel herself again in the grip of the same breathless
longing, the same ardent dreams and restless hopes that had
thrilled her youth. But would they last? Would they not be
like the short-lived bloom that is sometimes quickened by
a sunny week in autumn, the after-bloom that sucks the
very last strength of the flower only to give it over, feeble
and exhausted, to the mercy of winter? For they were dead,
these longings, and had slept many years in silent graves.
Why did they come again? What did they want of her?
Was not their end fulfilled so they could rest in peace and
not rise again in deceitful shapes of life to play the game
of youth once more?

So ran her thoughts, but they were not real. They were

quite impersonal, as if she were making them up about someone else, for she had no doubt of the strength and lasting power of her passion. It had filled her so irresistibly and completely that there was no room left in her for reflective amazement. Yet for a moment she followed the train of theoretical reasoning, and she thought of the golden Remigius and his firm faith in her, but the memory drew from her only a bitter smile and a forced sigh, and the next moment her thoughts were caught up again by other things.

She wondered whether Sören would have the courage to make love to her. She hardly believed he would. He was only a peasant, and she pictured to herself his slavish fear of the gentlefolks, his dog-like submission, his cringing servility. She thought of his coarse habits and his ignorance, his peasant speech and poor clothes, his toil-hardened body and his vulgar greediness. Was she to bend beneath all this, to accept good and evil from this black hand? In this self-abasement there was a strange, voluptuous pleasure which was in part gross sensuality but in part akin to whatever is counted noblest and best in woman's nature. For such was the manner in which the clay had been mixed out of which she was fashioned. . . .

A few days later, Marie Grubbe was in the brewing house at Tjele mixing mead; for many of the beehives had been injured on the night of the fire. She was standing in the corner by the hearth, looking at the open door, where hundreds of bees, drawn by the sweet smell of honey, were swarming, glittering like gold in the strip of sunlight that pierced the gloom.

Just then Sören came driving in through the gate with an empty coach in which he had taken Palle Dyre to Viborg. He caught a glimpse of Marie and made haste to unharness and stable the horses and put the coach in its place. Then he strutted about a little while, his hands buried deep in the pockets of his long livery coat, his eyes fixed on his great boots. Suddenly he turned abruptly toward the brewhouse, swinging one arm resolutely, frowning, and biting his lips like a man who is forcing himself to an unpleasant but unavoidable decision. He had in fact been swearing to himself all the way from Viborg to Foulum that this must end, and he had kept up his courage with a little flask, which his master had forgotten to take out of the coach.

He took off his hat when he came into the house but said nothing, simply stood passing his fingers awkwardly along the edge of the brewing vat.

Marie asked whether Sören had any message to her from her husband.

No.

Would Sören taste her brew, or would he like a piece of sugar honey?

Yes, thank you—or that is, no, thanks—that wasn't what he'd come for.

Marie blushed and felt quite uneasy.

Might he ask a question?

Ay, indeed he might.

Well, then, all he wanted to say was this, with her kind permission, that he wasn't in his right mind, for waking or sleeping he thought of nothing but her ladyship, and he couldn't help it.

Ah, but that was just what Sören ought to do.

No, he wasn't so sure of that, for 'twas not in the way of tending to his work that he thought of her ladyship. 'Twas quite different; he thought of her in the way of what folks called love.

He looked at her with a timid, questioning expression and seemed quite crestfallen as he shook his head when Marie replied that it was quite right; that was what the pastor said they should all do.

No, 'twasn't in that way either; 'twas kind of what you might call sweethearting. But of course there wasn't any cause for it—he went on in an angry tone as if to pick a quarrel—he s'posed such a fine lady would be afraid to come near a poor common peasant like him, though to be sure peasants were kind of half way like people too and didn't have either water or sour gruel for blood anymore than gentlefolks. He knew the gentry thought they were of a kind by themselves, but really they were made about the same way as others, and sure he knew they ate and drank and slept and all that sort of thing just like the lowest, commonest peasant lout. And so he didn't think it would hurt her ladyship if he kissed her mouth anymore than if a gentleman had kissed her. Well, there was no use her looking at him like that even if he was kind of free in his talk, for he didn't care what he said anymore, and she was welcome to make trouble for him if she liked, for when he left her, he was going straight to drown himself in the miller's pond or else put a rope around his neck.

He mustn't do that, for she never meant to say a word against him to any living creature.

So she didn't? Well, anybody could believe that who was simple enough, but no matter for that. She'd made trouble enough for him, and 'twas nobody's fault but hers that he was going to kill himself, for he loved her beyond anything.

He had seated himself on a bench and sat gazing at her with a mournful look in his good, faithful eyes while his lips trembled as if he were struggling with tears.

She could not help going over to him and laying a comforting hand on his shoulder.

She'd best not do that. He knew very well that when she put her hand on him and said a few words quietly to herself she could read the courage out of him, and he would n't let her. Anyhow, she might as well sit down by him, even if he was nothing but a low peasant, seeing that he'd be dead before nightfall.

Marie sat down.

Sören looked at her sideways and moved a little farther away on the bench. Now he s'posed he'd better say good-by and thank her ladyship for all her kindness in the time they'd known each other, and maybe she'd say good-by from him to his cousin Anne—the kitchen-maid at the manor.

Marie held his hand fast.

Well, now he was going.

No, he must stay; there was no one in all the world she loved like him.

Oh, that was just something she said because she was afraid he'd come back and haunt her, but she might make herself easy on that score, for he did n't bear any grudge against her and would never come near her after he was dead; that he'd both promise and perform if she would only let him go.

No, she would never let him go.

Then if there was nothing else for it—Sören tore his hand away and ran out of the brew house and across the yard.

Marie was right on his heels when he darted into the menservants' quarters, slammed the door after him, and set his back against it.

"Open the door, Sören, open the door or I'll call the servants!"

Sören made no answer but calmly took a bit of pitchy twine from his pocket and proceeded to tie the latch with it while he held the door with his knee and shoulder. Her threat of calling the other servants did not alarm him, for he knew they were all haymaking in the outlying fields.

Marie hammered at the door with all her might.

"Merciful God!" she cried. "Why don't you come out! I love you as much as it's possible for one human being to love another! I love you, love you, love you — oh, he doesn't believe me! What shall I do — miserable wretch that I am!"

Sören did not hear her, for he had passed through the large common room into the little chamber in the rear, where he and the gamekeeper usually slept. This was where he meant to carry out his purpose, but then it occurred to him that it would be a pity for the gamekeeper; it would be better if he killed himself in the other room where a number of them slept together. He went out into the large room again.

"Sören, Sören, let me in, let me in! Oh, please open the door! No, no, oh, he's hanging himself, and here I stand. Oh, for God Almighty's sake, Sören, open the door! I have loved you from the first moment I saw you! Can't you hear me? There's no one I'm so fond of as you, Sören, no one — no one in the world, Sören!"

"Is't true?" asked Sören's voice, hoarse and unrecognizable, close to the door.

"Oh, God be praised for evermore! Yes, yes, yes, it *is* true, it *is* true; I swear the strongest oath there is in the world that I love you with my whole soul. Oh, God be praised for evermore —"

Sören had untied the twine, and the door flew open. Marie rushed into the room and threw herself on his breast, sobbing and laughing. Sören looked embarrassed and hardly knew how to take it.

"Oh, Heaven be praised that I have you once more!" cried Marie. "But where were you going to do it? Tell me!" She looked curiously around the room at the unmade beds where faded bolsters, matted straw, and dirty leather sheets lay in disorderly heaps.

But Sören did not answer; he gazed at Marie angrily. "Why didn't you say so before?" he said and struck her arm.

"Forgive me, Sören, forgive me!" wept Marie pressing close to him while her eyes sought his pleadingly.

Sören bent down wonderingly and kissed her. He was utterly amazed.

"And it's neither play-acting nor visions?" he asked, half to himself.

Marie smiled and shook her head.

"The devil! Who'd 'a' thought—"

At first the relation between Marie and Sören was carefully concealed, but when Palle Dyre had to make frequent trips to Randers in his capacity of royal commissioner, his lengthy absences made them careless, and before long it was no secret to the servants at Tjele. When the pair realized that they were discovered, they took no pains to keep the affair hidden but behaved as if Palle Dyre were at the other end of the world instead of at Randers. Erik Grubbe they recked nothing of. When he threatened Sören with his crutch, Sören would threaten him with his fist, and when he scolded Marie and tried to bring her to her senses, she would tease him by reeling off long speeches without rais-

ing her voice, as was necessary now if he were to hear
her, for he had become quite deaf, and besides he was wont
to protect his bald head with a skull-cap with long earlaps,
which did not improve his hearing.

It was no fault of Sören's that Palle Dyre too did not
learn the true state of affairs, for in the violence of his youthful passion, he did not stick at visiting Marie even when
the master was at home. At dusk, or whenever he saw his
chance, he would seek her in the manor house itself, and
on more than one occasion it was only the fortunate loca-
tion of the stairway that saved him from discovery.

His sentiment for Marie was not always the same, for
once in a while he would be seized with the idea that she was
proud and must despise him. Then he would become capricious, tyrannical, and unreasonable and treated her much
more harshly and brutally than he really meant simply in
order to have her sweetness and submissiveness chase away
his doubts. Usually, however, he was gentle and easily led,
so long as Marie was careful not to complain too much
of her husband and her father or picture herself as too
much abused, for then he would wax furious and swear that
he would blow out Palle Dyre's brains and put his hands
around Erik Grubbe's thin neck, and he would be so intent
on carrying out his threat that she had to use prayers and
tears to calm him.

The most serious element of disturbance in their relation was the persistent baiting of the other servants. They
were of course highly incensed at the lovemaking between
mistress and coachman, which put their fellow-servant in
a favored position and—especially in the absence of the
master—gave him an influence to which he had no more
rightful claim than they. So they harassed and tortured poor

Sören until he was quite beside himself and thought sometimes that he would run away and sometimes that he would
kill himself.

The maids were of course his worst tormentors.

One evening they were busy making candles in the hall
at Tjele. Marie was standing beside the straw-filled vat in
which the copper mould was placed. She was busy dipping
the wicks while the kitchen maid, Anne Trinderup, Sören's
cousin, was catching the drippings in an earthenware dish.
The cook was carrying the trays back and forth, hanging
them up under the frame, and removing the candles when
they were thick enough. Sören sat at the hall table looking
on. He wore a gold-laced cap of red cloth trimmed with
black feathers. Before him stood a silver tankard full of
mead, and he was eating a large piece of roast meat which
he cut in strips with his clasp-knife on a small pewter plate.
He ate very deliberately, sometimes taking a draught from
his cup and now and then answering Marie's smile and
nod with a slow, appreciative movement of his head.

She asked him if he was comfortable.

H'm, it might have been better.

Then Anne must go and fetch him a cushion from the
maids' room.

She obeyed, but not without a great many signs to the
other maid behind Marie's back.

Did Sören want a piece of cake?

Yes, that might n't be out of the way.

Marie took a tallow dip and went to get the cake but
did not return immediately. As soon as she was out of the
room, the two girls began to laugh uproariously as if by
agreement. Sören gave them an angry, sidelong glance.

"Dear Sören," said Anne imitating Marie's voice and manner, "won't you have a serviette, Sören, to wipe your dainty fingers, Sören, and a bolstered foot-stool for your feet, Sören? And are you sure it's light enough for you to eat with that one thick candle, Sören, or shall I get another for you? And there's a flowered gown hanging up in master's chamber, shan't I bring it in? 'T would look so fine with your red cap, Sören!"

Sören did not deign to answer.

"Ah, won't your lordship speak to us?" Anne went on. "Common folk like us would fain hear how the gentry talk, and I know his lordship's able, for you've heard, Trine, that his sweetheart's given him a compliment-book, and sure it can't fail that such a fine gentleman can read and spell both backwards and forwards."

Sören struck the table with his fist and looked wrathfully at her.

"Oh, Sören," began the other girl, "I'll give you a bad penny for a kiss. I know you get roast meat and mead from the old—"

At that moment Marie came in with the cake and set it down before Sören, but he threw it along the table.

"Turn those women out!" he shouted.

But the tallow would get cold.

He didn't care if it did.

The maids were sent away.

Sören flung the red cap from him, cursed and swore and was angry. He didn't want her to go there and stuff him with food as if he was an unfattened pig, and he wouldn't be made a fool of before people with her making play-actor caps for him, and there'd have to be an end to this. He'd have her know that he was the man, and didn't care to have her coddle him, and he'd never meant it that way. He wanted to rule, and she'd have to mind him; he wanted to give, and she should take. Of course he knew he didn't have anything to give, but that was no reason why she should make nothing of him by giving to him. If she wouldn't go with him through fire and flood, they'd have to part. He couldn't stand this. She'd have to give herself into his power and run away with him; she shouldn't sit there and be your ladyship and make him always look up to her. He needed to have her be a dog with him—be poor, so he could be good to her and have her thank him, and she must be afraid of him and not have anyone to put her trust in but him.

A coach was heard driving in at the gate. They knew it must be Palle Dyre, and Sören stole away to the men-servants' quarters.

Three of the men were sitting there on their beds, besides the gamekeeper, Sören Jensen, who stood up.

"Why, there's the baron!" said one of the men as the coachman came in.

"Hush, don't let him hear you," exclaimed the other with mock anxiety.

"Ugh," said the first speaker, "I wouldn't be in his shoes fer 's many rosenobles as you could stuff in a mill-sack."

Sören looked around uneasily and sat down on a chest that was standing against the wall.

"It must be an awful death," put in the man who had not yet spoken and shuddered.

Sören Gamekeeper nodded gravely to him and sighed.

"What 're you talkin' about?" asked Sören with pretended indifference.

No one answered.

"Is't here?" said the first man passing his fingers across his neck.

"Hush!" replied the gamekeeper, frowning at the questioner.

"Ef it's me you're talkin' about," said Sören, "don't set there an' cackle but say what you got to say."

"Ay," said the gamekeeper, laying great stress on the word and looking at Sören with a serious air of making up his mind. "Ay, Sören, it *is* you we're talkin' about. Good Lord!" he folded his hands and seemed lost in dark musings. "Sören," he began, "it's a hangin' matter what ye're doin', and I give you warnin'"—he spoke as if reading from a book—"mend your ways, Sören! There stands the gallows and the block"—he pointed to the manor house—"and there a Christian life an' a decent burial"—he waved his hand in the direction of the stable. "For you must answer with your neck, that's the sacred word of the law, ay, so it is, so it is, think o' that!"

"Huh!" said Sören defiantly. "Who'll have the law on me?"

"Ay," repeated the gamekeeper in a tone as if something had been brought forward that made the situation very much worse. "Who'll have the law on you? Sören, Sören, who'll have the law on you? But devil split me, you're a fool," he went on in a voice from which the solemnity had flown, "an' it's fool's play to be runnin' after an old woman when there's such a risk to it. If she'd been young! An' such an ill-tempered satan too—let Blue-face keep *her* in peace; there's other women in the world besides her, Heaven be praised."

Sören had neither courage nor inclination to explain to them that he could no longer live without Marie Grubbe.

In fact, he was almost ashamed of his foolish passion, and he knew that if he confessed the truth, it would only mean that the whole pack of men and maids would hound him so he lied and denied his love.

"'T is a wise way you 're pointin', but look 'ee here, folks, I 've got a rix-dollar when you have n't any, an' I 've got a bit of clothes an' another bit an' a whole wagon-load, my dear friends, and once I get my purse full, I 'll run away just as quiet, an' then one o' you can try your luck."

"All well an' good," answered Sören Gamekeeper, "but it 's stealin' money with your neck in a noose, I say. It 's all very fine to have clothes and silver given you for a gift an' most agreeable to lie in bed here an' say you 're sick an' get wine an' roasted meat an' all kinds o' belly-cheer sent down, but it won't go long here with so many people round. It 'll get out some day, an' then you 're sure o' the worst that can befall anyone."

"Oh, they won't let things come to such a pass," said Sören, a little crestfallen.

"Well, they 'd both like to get rid o' her, and her sisters and her brothers-in-law are not the kind o' folks who 'd stand between if there 's a chance o' getting her disinherited."

"O jeminy, she 'd help me."

"You think so? She may ha' all she can do helpin' herself; she's been in trouble too often fer anyone to help her wi' so much as a bucket o' oats."

"Hey-day," said Sören making for the inner chamber, "a threatened man may live long."

From that day on Sören was pursued by hints of the gallows and the block and the red-hot pincers wherever he went. The consequence was that he tried to drive away fear and keep up his courage with brandy, and as Marie often gave him money, he was never forced to stay sober. After a while he grew indifferent to the threats, but he was much more cautious than before, kept more to the other servants, and sought Marie more rarely.

A little before Christmas Palle Dyre came home and remained there, which put a stop to the meetings between Sören and Marie. In order to make the other servants believe that all was over and so keep them from telling tales to the master, Sören began to play sweethearts with Anne Trinderup, and he deceived them all, even Marie, although he had told her of his plan.

On the third day of Christmas, when most of the people were at church, Sören was standing by the wing of the manor house playing with one of the dogs when suddenly he heard Marie's voice calling him, it seemed to him under the ground.

He turned and saw Marie standing in the low trap-door leading to the salt cellar. She was pale and had been weeping, and her eyes looked wild and haunted under eyebrows that were drawn with pain.

"Sören," she said, "what have I done, since you no longer love me?"

"But I do love you! Can't you see I must have a care, fer they're all thinkin' o' nothin' but how they can make trouble fer me an' get me killed. Don't speak to me; let me go, ef ye don't want to see me dead!"

"Tell me no lies, Sören; I can see what is in your heart, and I wish you no evil, not for a single hour, for I am not your equal in youth, and you have always had a kindness for Anne, but it's a sin to let me see it, Sören; you shouldn't do that. Don't think I am begging you to take me, for

I know full well the danger 't would put you in and the
labor and wear and tear that would be needed if we were
to become a couple by ourselves, and 't is a thing hardly to
be wished either for you or me, though I can't help it."

"But I don't want Anne now or ever, the country jade
she is! I 'm fond o' you an' no one else in the world, let 'em
call you old and wicked an' what the devil they please."

"I can't believe you, Sören, much as I wish to."

"You don't believe me?"

"No, Sören, no. My only wish is that this might be my
grave, the spot where I stand. Would that I could close the
door over me and sit down to sleep forever in the darkness."

"I 'll make you believe me!"

"Never, never! there is nothing in all the world you can
do to make me believe you, for there is no reason in it."

"You make me daft wi' your talk, and you 'll live to be
sorry, for I 'm goin' to make you believe me, even ef they
burn me alive or do me to death fer it."

Marie shook her head and looked at him sadly.

"Then it must be, come what may," said Sören and
ran away.

He stopped at the kitchen door, asked for Anne Trinderup, and was told that she was in the garden. Then he went
over to the menservants' quarters, took a loaded old gun
of the gamekeeper's, and made for the garden.

Anne was cutting kale when Sören caught sight of her.
She had filled her apron with the green stuff and was holding the fingers of one hand up to her mouth to warm them
with her breath. Slowly Sören stole up to her, his eyes fixed
on the edge of her dress, for he did not want to see her face.

Suddenly Anne turned and saw Sören. His dark looks,
the gun, and his stealthy approach alarmed her, and she

called to him: "Oh, don't, Sören, please don't!" He lifted the gun, and Anne rushed off through the snow with a wild, shrill scream.

The shot fell; Anne went on running, then put her hand to her cheek and sank down with a cry of horror.

Sören threw down the gun and ran to the side of the house. He found the trap-door closed. Then on to the front door, in and through all the rooms till he found Marie.

" 'Tis all over!" he whispered, pale as a corpse.

"Are they after you, Sören?"

"No, I've shot her."

"Anne? Oh, what will become of us! Run, Sören, run —take a horse and get away, quick, quick! Take the gray one!"

Sören fled. A moment later he was galloping out of the gate. He was scarcely halfway to Foulum when people came back from church. Palle Dyre at once asked where Sören was going.

"There is someone lying out in the garden, moaning," said Marie. She trembled in every limb and could hardly stand on her feet.

Palle and one of the men carried Anne in. Her screams could be heard far and wide, but the hurt was not really serious. The gun had only been loaded with grapeshot, of which a few had gone through her cheek and a few more had settled in her shoulder, but as she bled freely and cried piteously, a coach was sent to Viborg for the barber-surgeon.

When she had gathered her wits together a little, Palle Dyre questioned her about how it had happened and was told not only that but the whole story of the affair between Sören and Marie.

As soon as he came out of the sick-room, all the servants

crowded around him and tried to tell him the same tale,
for they were afraid that if they did not, they might be pun-
ished. Palle refused to listen to them, saying it was all gossip and stupid slander. The fact was the whole thing was
extremely inconvenient to him: divorce, journeys to court,
lawsuit, and various expenditures—he preferred to avoid
them. No doubt the story could be hushed up and smoothed
over and all be as before. Marie's unfaithfulness did not
in itself affect him much; in fact, he thought it might be
turned to advantage by giving him more power over her
and possibly also over Erik Grubbe, who would surely be
anxious to keep the marriage unbroken, even though it had
been violated.

When he had talked with Erik Grubbe, however, he
hardly knew what to think, for he could not make out the
old man. He seemed furious and had instantly sent off
four mounted men with orders to take Sören dead or alive,
which was certainly not a good way of keeping matters
dark, for many other things might come up in a trial for
attempted murder.

In the evening of the following day, three of the men
returned. They had caught Sören at Dallerup, where the
gray horse had fallen under him, and had brought him to
Skanderborg, where he was now held for trial. The fourth
man had lost his way and did not return until a day later.

In the middle of January Palle Dyre and Marie moved
to Nörbæk manor. He thought the servants would more
easily forget when their mistress was out of their sight, but
in the latter part of February they were again reminded
of the affair when a clerk came from Skanderborg to ask
whether Sören had been seen in the neighborhood, for he
had broken out of the arrest. The clerk came too early, for

not until a fortnight later did Sören venture to visit Nörbæk one night and to rap on Marie's chamber window. His
first question when Marie opened it was whether Anne
was dead, and it seemed to relieve his mind of a heavy
burden when he heard that she had quite recovered. He
lived in a deserted house on Gassum heath and often came
again to get money and food. The servants, as well as
Palle Dyre, knew that he was in the habit of visiting the
house, but Palle took no notice, and the servants did not
trouble themselves in the matter, when they saw the
master was indifferent.

At haymaking time, the master and mistress moved back
to Tjele, where Sören did not dare to show himself. His
absence, added to her father's taunts and petty persecu-.
tion, irritated and angered Marie until she gave her feelings
vent by scolding Erik Grubbe, in private two or three
times, as if he had been her foot-boy. The result was that,
in the middle of August Erik Grubbe sent a letter of com-
plaint to the King. After recounting at great length all her
misdeeds, which were a sin against God, a scandal before
men, and an offence to all womanhood, he ended the epistle
saying:

Whereas she hath thus grievously disobeyed and miscon-
ducted herself, I am under the necessity of disinheriting
her, and I do humbly beseech Your Royal Majesty that You
will graciously be pleased to ratify and confirm this my
action and that Your Royal Majesty will furthermore be
pleased to issue Your most gracious command to Governor
Mogens Scheel that he may make inquiry concerning her
aforesaid behavior toward me and toward her husband
and that because of her wickedness she be confined at

Borringholm, the expense to be borne by me, in order that
the wrath and visitation of God may be upon her as a dis-
obedient creature, a warning unto others, and her own
soul possibly unto salvation. Had I not been hard pressed,
I should not have made so bold as to come before You with
this supplication, but I live in the most humble hope of
Your Royal Majesty's most gracious answer, acknowledg-
ment, and aid, which God shall surely reward. I live and
die

> Your Royal Majesty's
> Most humble and most devoted
> true hereditary subject

ERIK GRUBBE.

Tjele, August 14, 1690.

The King desired a statement in the matter from the Honorable Palle Dyre, and this was to the effect that Marie
did not conduct herself toward him as befitted an honest
wife, wherefore he petitioned the King to have the marriage
annulled without process of law. This was not granted,
and the couple were divorced by a decree of the court on
March twenty-third, sixteen hundred and ninety-one. Erik
Grubbe's supplication that he might lock her up and dis-
inherit her was also refused, and he had to content himself with keeping her a captive at Tjele, strictly guarded
by peasants while the trial lasted, and indeed it must be
admitted that he was the last person who had any right to
cast at her the stone of righteous retribution.

As soon as judgment had been pronounced, Marie left
Tjele with a poor bundle of clothes in her hand. She met
Sören on the heath to the south, and he became her third
husband.

CHAPTER XVII

ABOUT a month later, on an April evening, there was a crowd gathered outside of Ribe cathedral. The Church Council was in session, and it was customary, while that lasted, to light the tapers in church three times a week at eight o'clock in the evening. The gentry and persons of quality in town, as well as the respectable citizens, would assemble and walk up and down in the nave while a skilful musician would play for them on the organ. The poorer people had to be content to listen from the outside.

Among the latter were Marie Grubbe and Sören.

Their clothing was coarse and ragged, and they looked as if they had not had enough to eat every day; and no wonder, for it was not a profitable trade they plied. In an inn between Aarhus and Randers, Sören had met a poor, sick German who for twenty marks had sold him a small, badly battered hurdy-gurdy, a motley fool's suit, and an old checked rug. With these he and Marie gained their livelihood, going from market to market; she would turn the hurdy-gurdy, and he would stand on the checked rug, dressed in the motley clothes lifting and doing tricks with some huge iron weights and long iron bars which they borrowed of the tradesmen.

It was the market that had brought them to Ribe.

They were standing near the door where a faint, faded strip of light shone on their pale faces and the dark mass of heads behind them. People were coming singly or in pairs or small groups, talking and laughing in well-bred manner to the very threshold of the church, but there they suddenly became silent, gazed gravely straight before them, and changed their gait.

Sören was seized with a desire to see more of the show,

and whispered to Marie that they ought to go in; there was no harm in trying; nothing worse could happen to them than to be turned out. Marie shuddered inwardly at the thought that *she* should be turned out from a place where common artisans could freely go, and she held back Sören, who was trying to draw her on; but suddenly she changed her mind, pressed eagerly forward pulling Sören after her, and walked in without the slightest trace of shrinking timidity or stealthy caution; indeed, she seemed determined to be noticed and turned out. At first no one stopped them, but just as she was about to step into the well-lit, crowded nave, a church warden who was stationed there, caught sight of them. After casting one horrified glance up through the church, he advanced quickly upon them with lifted and outstretched hands as if pushing them before him to the very threshold and over it. He stood there for a moment, looking reproachfully at the crowd as if he blamed it for what had occurred, then returned with measured tread, and took up his post, shuddering.

The crowd met the ejected ones with a burst of jeering laughter and a shower of mocking questions, which made Sören growl and look around savagely, but Marie was content; she had bent to receive the blow which the respectable part of society always has ready for such as he, and the blow had fallen.

On the night before St. Oluf's market, four men were sitting in one of the poorest inns at Aarhus playing cards.

One of the players was Sören. His partner, a handsome man with coal-black hair and a dark skin, was known as Jens Bottom and was a juggler. The other two members of the party were joint owners of a mangy bear. Both were unusually hideous: one had a horrible harelip while the other was one-eyed, heavy jowled, and pock-marked, and was known as Rasmus Squint, plainly because the skin around the injured eye was drawn together in such a manner as to give him the appearance of being always ready to peer through a keyhole or some such small aperture.

The players were sitting at one end of the long table which ran under the window and held a candle and an earless cruse. Opposite them was a folding table fastened up against the wall with an iron hook. A bar ran across the other end of the room, and a thin, long-wicked candle, stuck into an old inverted funnel threw a sleepy light over the shelf above, where some large square flasks of brandy and bitters, some quart and pint measures, and half a dozen glasses had plenty of room beside a basket full of mustard seed and a large lantern with panes of broken glass. In one corner outside of the bar sat Marie Grubbe, knitting and drowsing, and in the other sat a man with body bent forward and elbows resting on his knees. He seemed intent on pulling his black felt hat as far down over his head as possible, and when that was accomplished, he would clutch the wide brim, slowly work the hat up from his head again, his eyes pinched together and the corners of his mouth twitching, probably with the pain of pulling his hair, then presently begin all over again.

"Then this is the last game to play," said Jens Bottom, whose lead it was.

Rasmus Squint pounded the table with his knuckles as a sign to his partner Salmand to cover.

Salmand played two of trumps.

"A two!" cried Rasmus; "have you nothing but twos and threes in your hand?"

"Lord," growled Salmand, "there's always been poor folks and a few beggars."

Sören trumped with a six.

"Oh, oh," Rasmus moaned, "are you goin' to let him have it for a six? What the devil are you so stingy with your old cards for, Salmand?"

He played, and Sören won the trick.

"Kerstie Meek," said Sören, playing four of hearts.

"And her half-crazy sister," continued Rasmus, putting on four of diamonds.

"Maybe an ace is good enough," said Sören, covering with ace of trumps.

"Play, man, play if you never played before!" cried Rasmus.

"That's too costly," whimpered Salmand, taking his turn.

"Then I'll put on my seven and another seven," said Jens.

Sören turned the trick.

"And then nine of trumps," Jens went on, leading.

"Then I'll have to bring on my yellow nag," cried Salmand, playing two of hearts.

"You'll never stable it," laughed Sören, covering with four of spades.

"Forfeit!" roared Rasmus Squint, throwing down his cards. "Forfeit with two of hearts, that's a good day's work! Nay, nay, 'tis a good thing we're not goin' to play anymore. Now let them kiss the cards that have won."

They began to count the tricks, and while they were busy with this, a stout, opulently dressed man came in. He went at once to the folding table, let it down, and took a seat nearest the wall. As he passed the players, he touched his hat with his silver-knobbed cane, and said, "Good even to the house!"

"Thanks," they replied, and all four spat.

The newcomer took out a paper full of tobacco and a long clay pipe, filled it, and pounded the table with his cane.

A barefoot girl brought him a brazier full of hot coals and a large earthenware cruse with a pewter cover. He took out from his vest-pocket a pair of small copper pincers, which he used to pick up bits of coal and put them in his pipe, drew the cruse to him, leaned back, and made himself as comfortable as the small space would allow.

"How much do you have to pay for a paper o' tobacco like the one you've got there, master?" asked Salmand, as he began to fill his little pipe from a sealskin pouch held together with a red string.

"Sixpence," said the man, adding as if to apologize for such extravagance, "it's very good for the lungs, as you might say."

"How's business?" Salmand went on, striking fire to light his pipe.

"Well enough, and thank you kindly for asking, well enough, but I'm getting old, as you might say."

"Well," said Rasmus Squint, "but then you've no need to run after customers since they're all brought to you."

"Ay," laughed the man, "in respect of that it's a good business and, moreover, you don't have to talk yourself hoarse persuading folks to buy your wares; they have to take 'em as they come; they can't pick and choose."

"And they don't want anything thrown in," Rasmus went on, "and don't ask for more than what's rightly comin' to 'em."

"Master, do they scream much?" asked Sören in a half whisper.

"Well, they don't often laugh."

"Faugh, what an ugly business!"

"Then there's no use my counting on one of you for help, I suppose."

"Are you countin' on us to help you?" asked Rasmus and rose angrily.

"I'm not counting on anything, but I'm looking for a young man to help me and to take the business after me; that's what I'm looking for, as you might say."

"And what wages might a man get for that?" asked Jens Bottom earnestly.

"Fifteen dollars per annum in ready money, one-third of the clothing, and one mark out of every dollar earned according to the fixed rate."

"And what might that be?"

"The rate is this, that I get five dollars for whipping at the post, seven dollars for whipping from town, four dollars for turning out of the county, and the same for branding with hot iron."

"And for the bigger work?"

"Alack, that does not come so often, but it's eight dollars for cutting off a man's head, that is with an axe— with a sword it's ten, but that may not occur once in seven years. Hanging is fourteen rix-dollars, ten for the job itself and four for taking the body down from the gallows. Breaking on the wheel is seven dollars, that is for a whole body, but I must find the stake and put it up too. And now is there anything more? Ay, crushing arms and legs according to the new German fashion and breaking on the wheel, that's fourteen—that's fourteen, and for quartering and

breaking on the wheel I get twelve, and then there's pinch-
ing with red-hot pincers—that's two dollars for every
pinch—and that's all; there's nothing more except such
extras as may come up."

"It can't be very hard to learn, is it?"

"The business? Well, anyone can do it, but how—
that's another matter. There's a certain knack about it
that one gets with practice just like any other handicraft.
There's whipping at the post; that's not so easy if 'tis
to be done right—three flicks with each whip, quick and
light like waving a bit of cloth and yet biting the flesh
with due chastisement, as the rigor of the law and the betterment of the sinner require."

"I think I might do it," said Jens, sighing as he spoke.

"Here's the earnest-penny," tempted the man at the
folding-table, putting a few bright silver coins out before
him.

"Think well!" begged Sören.

"Think and starve, wait and freeze—that's two pair of
birds that are well mated," answered Jens, rising. "Farewell as an honest and true guild-man," he went on, giving
Sören his hand.

"Farewell, guild-mate, and godspeed," replied Sören.

He went round the table with the same farewell and
got the same answer. Then he shook hands with Marie and
with the man in the corner, who had to let go his hat for the
moment.

Jens proceeded to the man at the folding table, who settled his face in solemn folds and said, "I, Master Herman
Köppen, executioner in the town of Aarhus, take you in
the presence of these honest men a journeyman to be and
a journeyman's work to perform to the glory of God, your

own preferment, and the benefit of myself and the honorable office of executioner," and as he made this unnecessarily pompous speech, which seemed to give him immense satisfaction, he pressed the bright earnest-penny into Jens's hand. Then he rose, took off his hat, bowed, and asked whether he might not have the honor of offering the honest men who had acted as witnesses a drink of half and half.

The three men at the long table looked inquiringly at one another, then nodded as with one accord.

The barefoot girl brought a clumsy earthenware cruse and three green glasses on which splotches of red and yellow stars were still visible. She set the cruse down before Jens and the glasses before Sören and the bear-baiters and fetched a large wooden mug from which she filled first the glasses of the three honest men, then the earthenware cruse, and finally Master Herman's private goblet.

Rasmus drew his glass toward him and spat, the two others followed suit, and they sat a while looking at one another as if none of them liked to begin drinking. Meanwhile, Marie Grubbe came up to Sören and whispered something in his ear to which he replied by shaking his head. She tried to whisper again, but Sören would not listen. For a moment she stood uncertain, then caught up the glass and emptied the contents on the floor, saying that he mustn't drink the hangman's liquor. Sören sprang up, seized her arm in a hard grip, and pushed her out of the door, gruffly ordering her to go upstairs. Then he called for a half pint of brandy and resumed his place.

"I'd like to ha' seen my Abelone—God rest her soul—try a thing like that on me," said Rasmus, drinking.

"Ay," said Salmand, "she can thank the Lord she isn't

my woman; I'd ha' given her somethin' else to think o'
besides throwin' the gifts o' God in the dirt."

"But look 'ee, Salmand," said Rasmus with a sly glance
in Master Herman's direction, " your wife she is n't a fine
lady of the gentry; she's only a poor common thing like
the rest of us, and so she gets her trouncin' when she needs
it, as the custom is among common people; but if instead
she'd been one of the quality, you 'd never ha' dared to flick
her noble back; you'd ha' let her spit you in the face if
she pleased."

"No, by the Lord Harry, I wouldn't," swore Salmand;
"I'd ha' dressed her down till she couldn't talk or see, and
I 'd ha' picked the maggots out o' her. You just ask mine if
she knows the thin strap bruin's tied up in — you 'll see it 'll
make her back ache just to think of it. But if she 'd tried
to come as I 'm sitting here and pour my liquor on the floor,
I 'd ha' trounced her if she was the emperor's own daughter,
as long 's I could move a hand or there was breath in my
body. What is she thinking about, — the fine doll— does
she think she 's better than anybody else's wife since she 's
got the impudence to come here and put shame on her husband in the company of honest men? Does she s'pose it 'ud
hurt her if you came near her after drinkin' the liquor of
this honorable man? Mind what I say, Sören, and" — he
made a motion as if he were beating someone — "or else
you 'll never in the wide world get any good out of her."

"If he only dared," teased Rasmus, looking at Sören.

"Careful, Squint, or I 'll tickle your hide."

With that he left them. When he came into the room
where Marie was, he closed the door after him with a kick
and began to untie the rope that held their little bundle of
clothing.

Marie was sitting on the edge of the rough board frame that served as a bed. "Are you angry, Sören?" she said.

"I'll show you," said Sören.

"Have a care, Sören! No one yet has offered me blows since I came of age, and I will not bear it."

He replied that she could do as she pleased; he meant to beat her.

"Sören, for God's sake, for God's sake don't lay violent hands on me; you will repent it!"

But Sören caught her by the hair and beat her with the rope. She did not cry out but merely moaned under the blows.

"There!" said Sören, and threw himself on the bed.

Marie lay still on the floor. She was utterly amazed at herself. She expected to feel a furious hatred against Sören rising in her soul, an implacable, relentless hatred, but no such thing happened. Instead she felt a deep, gentle sorrow, a quiet regret at a hope that had burst—how could he?

CHAPTER XVIII

I N May of sixteen hundred and ninety-five Erik Grubbe died at the age of eighty-seven. The inheritance was promptly divided among his three daughters, but Marie did not get much as the old man before his death had issued various letters of credit in favor of the other two, thus withdrawing from the estate the greater part of his property to the disadvantage of Marie.

Even so, her portion was sufficient to make her and her husband respectable folk instead of beggars, and with a little common sense they might have secured a fair income to the end of their days. Unluckily Sören made up his mind to become a horse-dealer, and it was not long before he had squandered most of the money. Still there was enough left so they could buy the Burdock House at the Falster ferry.

In the early days they had a hard time, and Marie often had to lend a hand at the oars, but later on her chief task was to mind the alehouse which was a part of the ferry privileges. On the whole, they were very happy, for Marie still loved her husband above everything else in the world, and though he would sometimes get drunk and beat her, she did not take it much to heart. She realized that she had enrolled in a class where such things were an everyday matter, and though she would sometimes feel irritated, she would soon get over it by telling herself that this man who could be so rough and hard was the same Sören who had once shot a human being for her sake.

The people they ferried over were generally peasants and cattlemen, but occasionally there would come someone who was a little higher up in the world. One day Sti Högh passed that way. Marie and her husband rowed him across, and he sat in the stern of the boat where he could talk with Marie, who had the oar nearest him. He recognized her at once but showed no signs of surprise; perhaps he had known that he would find her there. Marie had to look twice before she knew him, for he was very much changed. His face was red and bloated, his eyes were watery; his lower jaw dropped as if the corners of his mouth were paralyzed, his legs were thin and his stomach hung down —in short, he bore every mark of a life spent in stupefying debauchery of every kind, and this had, as a matter of fact, been his chief pursuit ever since he left Marie. As far as the external events went, he had for a time been *gentilhomme* and *maître d'hôtel* in the house of a royal cardinal in Rome, had gone over to the Catholic Church, had joined his brother, Just Högh, then ambassador to Nimeguen, had been converted back to the Lutheran religion again and returned to Denmark, where he was living on the bounty of his brother.

"Is this," he asked nodding in the direction of Sören — "is this the one I foretold was to come after me?"

"Ay, he is the one," said Marie hesitating a little, for she would have preferred not to reply.

"And he is greater than I — was?" he went on, straightening himself in his seat.

"Nay, you can't be likened to him, your lordship," she answered, affecting the speech of a peasant woman.

"Oh, ay, so it goes—you and I have indeed cheapened ourselves — we've sold ourselves to life for less pay than we had thought to, you in one manner, I in another."

"But your lordship is surely well enough off?" asked Marie in the same simple tone.

"Well enough," he laughed, "well enough is more than half ill; I am indeed well enough off. And you, Marie?"

"Thank you kindly for asking; we've got our health, and when we keep tugging at the oars every day, we've got bread and brandy too."

They had reached land, and Sti stepped out and said good-by.

"Lord," said Marie looking after him pityingly, "he's certainly been shorn of crest and wings too."

Peacefully and quietly the days passed at the Burdock House with daily work and daily gain. Little by little the pair improved their condition, hired boatmen to do the ferrying, carried on a little trade, and built a wing on their old house. They lived to the end of the old century and ten years into the new. Marie turned sixty, and she turned sixty-five, and still she was as brisk and merry at her work as if she had been on the sunny side of sixty. But then it happened, on her sixty-eighth birthday in the spring of seventeen hundred and eleven, that Sören accidentally shot and killed a skipper from Dragör under very suspicious circumstances and in consequence was arrested.

This was a hard blow to Marie. She had to endure a long suspense for judgment was not pronounced until midsummer of the following year, and this, together with her anxiety lest the old affair of his attempt on the life of Anne Trinderup should be taken up again, aged her very much.

One day in the beginning of this period of waiting, Marie went down to meet the ferry just as it was landing. There were two passengers on board, and one of these, a journeyman, absorbed her attention by refusing to show his passport, declaring that he had shown it to the boatmen when he went on board, which they, however, denied. When she threatened to charge him full fare unless he would produce his passport as proof of his right as a journeyman to travel for half price, he had to give in. This matter being settled, Marie turned to the other passenger, a little slender man who stood pale and shivering after the seasickness he had just endured, wrapped in his mantle of coarse, greenish-black stuff and leaning against the side of a boat that had been dragged up on the beach. He asked in a peevish voice whether he could get lodgings in the Burdock House, and Marie replied that he might look at their spare room.

She showed him a little chamber which besides bed and chair, contained a barrel of brandy with funnel and wastecup, some large kegs of molasses and vinegar, and a table with legs painted in pearl-color and a top of square tiles on which scenes from the Old and New Testament were drawn in purplish black. The stranger at once noticed that three of the tiles represented Jonah being thrown on land from the mouth of the whale, and when he put his hand on them, he shuddered, declaring he was sure to catch a cold if he should be so careless as to sit and read with his elbows on the table.

When Marie questioned him, he explained that he had left Copenhagen on account of the plague and meant to stay until it was over. He ate only three times a day, and he could not stand salt meat or fresh bread. As for the rest, he was a master of arts at present fellow at Borch's Collegium, and his name was Holberg, Ludvig Holberg.

Master Holberg was a very quiet man of remarkably youthful appearance. At first glance he appeared to be about eighteen or nineteen years old, but upon closer examination his mouth, his hands, and the inflection of his voice showed that he must be a good deal older. He kept

to himself, spoke but little, and that little — so it seemed —
with reluctance. Not that he avoided other people, but he
simply wanted them to leave him in peace and not draw
him into conversation. When the ferry came and went with
passengers or when the fishermen brought in their catch,
he liked to watch the busy life from a distance and to listen
to the discussions. He seemed to enjoy the sight of people
at work, whether it was ploughing or stacking or launching
the boats, and whenever anyone put forth an effort that
showed more than common strength, he would smile with
pleasure and lift his shoulders in quiet delight. When he
had been at the Burdock House for a month, he began to approach Marie Grubbe, or rather he allowed her to approach
him, and they would often sit talking in the warm summer evenings, for an hour or two at a time in the common
room, where they could look out through the open door
over the bright surface of the water to the blue, hazy out-
lines of Möen.

One evening after their friendship had been well estab-
lished, Marie told him her story, and ended with a sigh
because they had taken Sören away from her.

"I must own," said Holberg, "that I am utterly unable
to comprehend how you could prefer an ordinary groom and
country oaf to such a polished gentleman as his Excellency the Viceroy, who is praised by everybody as a past
master in all the graces of fashion, nay as the model of
everything that is elegant and pleasing."

"Even though he had been as full of it as the book they
call the *Alamodische Sittenbuch*, it would not have mattered
a rush, since I had once for all conceived such an aversion
and loathing for him that I could scarce bear to have him
come into my presence; and you know how impossible it is

to overcome such an aversion—so that if one had the virtue and principles of an angel, yet this natural aversion would be stronger. On the other hand, my poor present husband woke in me such an instant and unlooked-for inclination that I could ascribe it to nothing but a natural attraction which it would be in vain to resist."

"Ha! That were surely well reasoned! Then we have but to pack all morality into a strong chest and send it to Hekkenfell and live on according to the desires of our hearts, for then there is no lewdness to be named but we can dress it up as a natural and irresistible attraction, and in the same manner there is not one of all the virtues but we can easily escape from the exercise of it; for one may have an aversion for sobriety, one for honesty, one for modesty, and such a natural aversion, he would say, is quite irresistible so one who feels it is quite innocent. But you have altogether too clear an understanding, goodwife, not to know that all this is naught but wicked conceits and bedlam talk."

Marie made no answer.

"But do you not believe in God, goodwife," Master Holberg went on, "and in the life everlasting?"

"Ay, God be praised, I do. I believe in our Lord."

"But eternal punishment and eternal reward, good-wife?"

"I believe every human being lives his own life and dies his own death; that is what I believe."

"But that is no faith; do you believe we shall rise again from the dead?"

"How shall I rise? As the young, innocent child I was when I first came out among people, or as the honored and envied favorite of the King and the ornament of the court, or as poor old hopeless Ferryman's Marie? And shall I answer for what the others, the child and the woman in the fullness of life, have sinned, or shall one of them answer for me? Can you tell me that, Master Holberg?"

"Yet you have had but one soul, goodwife!"

"Have I indeed?" asked Marie and sat musing for a while. "Let me speak to you plainly, and answer me truly as you think. Do you believe that one who his whole life has sinned grievously against God in heaven and who in his last moment, when he is struggling with death, confesses his sin from a true heart, repents, and gives himself over to the mercy of God without fear and without doubt, do you think such a one is more pleasing to God than another who has likewise sinned and offended against Him but then for many years of her life has striven to do her duty, has borne every burden without a murmur, but never in prayer or open repentance has wept over her former life, do you think that she who has lived as she thought was rightly lived but without hope of any reward hereafter and without prayer, do you think God will thrust her from Him and cast her out, even though she has never uttered a word of prayer to Him?"

"That is more than any man may dare to say," replied Master Holberg and left her.

Shortly afterwards he went away.

In August of the following year judgment was pronounced against Sören Ferryman, and he was sentenced to three years of hard labor in irons at Bremerholm.

It was a long time to suffer, longer to wait, yet at last it was over. Sören came home, but the confinement and harsh treatment had undermined his health, and before Marie had nursed him for a year, they bore him to the grave.

For yet another long, long year Marie had to endure this life. Then she suddenly fell ill and died. Her mind was wandering during her illness, and the pastor could neither pray with her nor give her the sacrament.

On a sunny day in summer they buried her at Sören's side, and over the bright waters and the golden grain-fields sounded the hymn, as the poor little group of mourners, dulled by the heat, sang without sorrow and without thought:

"Lord God, in mercy hear our cry before Thee;
Thy bloody scourge lift from us, we implore Thee;
Turn Thou from us Thy wrath all men pursuing
For their wrongdoing.

"If Thou regard alone our vile offending,
If upon us true justice were descending,
Then must the earth and all upon it crumble,
Yea, proud and humble."

THE END

NOTES

NOTES

THE historical setting of *Marie Grubbe* centres around the siege of Copenhagen, when the gallant resistance of the citizens saved the national existence of Denmark. It was the turning point in a contest extending over several generations. Christian the Fourth (1588–1648), though a gifted and energetic monarch devoted throughout his long reign to the welfare of his people and idolized by them, was unable to stem the tide of Sweden's advance, and by the peace of Brömsebro, 1645, the supremacy in the North passed definitely from Denmark to Sweden. His son and successor, Frederik the Third (1648–1670), hoped to regain what was lost, and seized the opportunity in 1657, when Sweden was engaged elsewhere, to make the declaration of war which is discussed in the opening chapter of *Marie Grubbe*. The attempt was disastrous, and in 1658 he had to conclude the short-lived peace of Roskilde, by which Denmark was still further shorn of her possessions. Yet the Swedish king, Carl Gustaf, was not satisfied with the punishment he had inflicted, and in the same year broke the peace without warning. Kronborg fell easily into his hands, but in Copenhagen he met unexpected resistance. Frederik the Third refused to listen to prudent counsellors who advised him to flee. The suburbs were burned and the ramparts hastily strengthened. For a year and a half the citizens endured the siege and, with the aid of a mere handful of soldiers, beat back the repeated attacks of the seasoned Swedish warriors. Finally, after a furious fight in the night of February 11, 1660, the enemy had to retire with great loss.

One effect of the war was to strengthen the King and the citizens and to weaken correspondingly the overweening power of the nobility. The States-General was called in September 1660, at the request of the citizens of Copenhagen, but unfortunately they did not know how to seize the golden moment and enact their temporary privileges into a law of the realm. Frederik the Third, on the other hand, had his programme ready. Egged on by his ambitious wife, the German princess Sofie Amalie, he succeeded in making himself an absolute autocrat and the crown hereditary in his line. He used his unlimited power wisely, checked the nobility, and unified and strengthened the kingdom. His policy was continued by his son, Christian the Fifth (1670–1699).

All the important characters in *Marie Grubbe* are historical, and Jacobsen has followed the facts when known. Regarding the heroine herself we have few data beyond what may be gleaned from the documents in connection with her three marriages and two divorces; indeed, it seems strange that a career so extraordinary should have elicited so little comment from contemporaries. We do not even know how she met her first husband, Ulrik Frederik Gyldenlöve, but the fact that she, a little country maiden from Jutland, could charm this experienced gallant is sufficient testimony to her beauty. The bridegroom's royal father, Frederik the Third, was so pleased with the marriage that he wrote a congratulatory poem in German which was printed on white satin. We are told that she was clever in repartee and that even in her old age she spoke French fluently. She died in 1718 "at a great age, but in a very poor and miserable condition." Her history has been written by Severin Kjær in his *Erik Grubbe til Tjele og hans tre Dötre* (1904), to which the translator is indebted for the notes relating to the Grubbes and their connections. The notes about the various old songs that occur in the text are condensed from those of the author.

$\cdot\ \cdot$

Page 8.
Tjele Manor is still standing, situated a few miles to the northeast of Viborg. The south wing, a massive structure with walls ten feet thick, dates from the thirteenth century. The main building was erected in 1585 by Jörgen Skram and his wife Hilleborg Daa, whose arms may be seen above the portal. The manor passed afterwards into the hands of the Below family, from whom Erik Grubbe bought it in 1635. It is a splendid edifice characterized by a stepped gable and some interesting interior decorations. The estate at present is entailed in the Lütti-

chau family, and the owners have taken care to keep up and extend
the fine old garden. A lane of shade trees leads up to the entrance.
Erik Grubbe came of an old noble family and received a good edu-
cation, which included foreign travel. He inherited large holdings of
land, which his forbears had taken from the peasants by fair means
or foul, and he devoted his life to increasing his estates. As *lensmand*
in Aarhus, he gained an unsavory reputation for profligacy as well
as for harshness and avarice. In 1651 he retired from the service of
the Crown and went to spend the remainder of his long life at Tjele.
His wife, Marie Juul, had died four years earlier, leaving him the two
daughters, Anne Marie and Marie. At Tjele Erik Grubbe took as
concubine a peasant woman, Anne Jensdaughter, who bore him a
daughter, Anne. He lies buried at Tjele.

Page 18.
Gyldenlöve was the name bestowed by four successive Danish kings on
their illegitimate children.
Rigitze Grubbe was a distant cousin of Erik Grubbe. She married
Hans Ulrik Gyldenlöve, a natural son of Christian the Fourth, and
after his death lived many years as a widow in Copenhagen. It is
thought that Marie Grubbe may have visited her there. In 1678 she
was banished for life to the island of Bornholm for an attempt at
poisoning a noblewoman, Birgitte Skeel.

Page 24.
Ulrik Frederik. See note under page 41.

Page 40.
Ulrik Christian Gyldenlöve was a member of the war party, made up
chiefly of the younger nobility. See note under page 55.

Page 41.
Ulrik Frederik Gyldenlöve was the son of Frederik the Third and Margrethe Pappen. His marriage to Sofie Urne during the siege of Copenhagen and his marriage to Marie Grubbe shortly afterwards without
dissolving the first contract are historical. It has been surmised that
the King, his father, may not have been aware that the first marriage
actually took place. Gyldenlöve did not acknowledge Sofie Urne's two
sons until more than twenty years later, and of Sofie herself we hear
no more except that she died in retirement, in 1714. Ulrik Frederik divorced Marie Grubbe in 1670 for her alleged relations with Sti Högh,
and afterwards married the Countess Antonette Augusta of Alden-

burg. He was a brave officer and a capable official. As Viceroy of Norway he ruled well, defended the peasants against extortion, and tried in every way to strengthen the autonomy of the country. He is still mentioned with affection as the best friend the common people in Norway had during the union with Denmark. He retired upon the death of his half-brother, Christian the Fifth, and went to spend the rest of his days in Hamburg, where he died in 1704, sixty-three years old. His body was brought to Copenhagen in a war-ship and buried in Vor Frue Church. The portrait of him at Frederiksborg shows great physical and mental vigor marred by a certain grossness and sensuality.

Page 49.
In a boat sat Phyllis fair. A pastoral song translated from the German and very popular at the time.

Page 55.
Ulrik Christian Gyldenlöve was the son of Christian the Fourth and Vibeke Kruse and hence the half-brother of Frederik the Third and the uncle of Ulrik Frederik Gyldenlöve, whose senior he was by eight years. When only seventeen years old, he went abroad and served in Spain under Condé. He was called home to take part in the war against the Swedes and acquitted himself brilliantly. His entire fortune was spent in the cause. During the siege of Copenhagen he seemed to embody in himself all that youthful enthusiasm and patriotism which made victory possible, and he naturally became a popular idol. He died during the early months of the siege, only twenty-eight years old. The death-bed repentance, which Jacobsen has used with such dramatic effect, is historical. His portrait, painted by Abraham Wuchters, hangs in Rosenborg Castle. It shows a pleasing, rather pensive countenance, not at all what one would expect in the rough, profligate soldier, and no doubt it suggested to Jacobsen the sympathetic description of Ulrik Christian as he appeared to Marie Grubbe in Mistress Rigitze's parlor.

Page 75.
Corfitz Ulfeldt was married to Christian the Fourth's favorite daughter, the beautiful and gifted Eleonore Christine, and was the leader of the "son-in-law" party in the upper nobility. Frederik the Third disliked him, and there is no doubt that he tried to deliver his countrymen into the hands of the Swedes. He was sentenced for treason in 1663 and was beheaded in effigy; his house in Copenhagen was levelled with

the ground and a shame-pillar erected on the site. Whether his wife shared his guilt or was merely the victim of the Queen's jealousy may never be known. Certain it is that she was kept in harsh captivity for twenty-two years and only released after the death of Sofie Amalie, then dowager queen.

Page 91.
Hans Nansen was chief mayor of Copenhagen and a leader of the citizen party. The other persons mentioned are likewise historical : *Axel Urup,* Councillor of the Realm; *Joachim Gersdorf,* High Steward of the Realm; *Hans Schack,* Governor and defender of the city; *Frederik Thuresen,* commander of the citizens' militia; *Peder Retz,* Chancellor and chief pillar of royalty.

Page 113.
Burrhi. The Italian physician and alchemist Francesco Borri or Burrhi afterwards came to Denmark and gained much influence over Frederik the Third.

Page 145.
Sti Högh, known also as Stycho or Stygge Höegh, was the son of the famous Just Högh, Chancellor of the Realm. He was an accomplished linguist and an eloquent speaker, but in ill repute for his somewhat hysterical nature and his atheistical opinions. He married Erik Grubbe's eldest daughter, Anne Marie, but neglected both his family and his office as magistrate of Laaland. He was always in debt and borrowing money. A contemporary, Matthias Skaanlund, whose chronicle has been published under the title *Gyldenlöves Lakaj,* writes of him: "Guldenlew and Sti Högh they were very fine friends, but it was said that Sti Högh had a little more inclination toward Guldenlew's consort [Marie Grubbe] than was proper, and when his High Excellency found this out, he at once divorced her, and Sti Högh had to leave his wife and immediately depart out of the King's land and dominions." Anne Marie divorced Sti Högh in 1674. We hear of him later in the staff of his brother, Just Högh, ambassador to Nimeguen, then a very important post. Sti was incorrigible, however, and his scandalous conduct made him always a thorn in the side of his respectable brother.

Page 154.
Mademoiselle La Barre was a French singer who appeared at the Danish court in the fifties.

E di persona. The verses Sti quotes to himself are from Guarini's famous pastoral play in which Myrtill wants to give his life for the beloved Amaryllis although he believes himself spurned by her.

Page 158.
Aggershus. The modern spelling is Akershus.

Page 167.
Between St. John and Paulinus. From June 24 to June 23 of the following year.
The Day of the Assumption of Our Lady. August 15.

Page 181.
Erik Grubbe's letters to the King are historical. The other letters in the book are Jacobsen's own creation.

Page 186.
The plucked fowl. The word *Hög* in Danish signifies a falcon.

Page 215.
Petits oiseaux des bois. Marie is reading to herself a passage from Racan's pastoral play, *Les Bergeries,* in which the heroine Arténice is destined for the hand of the wealthy Lucidas, but is in love with the poor young shepherd Alcidor.

Page 234.
Divorced by a decree of the court. The trial was held in Viborg by a Commission consisting of the bishop, the dean, and the civil governor of the diocese. Many witnesses were called, and others flocked in voluntarily. The records of the Commission are preserved in *Dansk Musæum,* and from them Jacobsen has gleaned such details as Sören's attempt upon the life of Anne Trinderup and the incident of the candle-making. Among the presents Marie gave Sören were not only the red cap, but one of green satin with gold lace and many other articles of personal adornment, as well as household goods, besides an ivory comb a tooth-brush and ivory tooth-picks in a little case, the "compliment book" about which the maids tease Sören, and a book of devotion called "A Godly Voice for each of the Twelve Months," which Jacobsen uses in the earlier part of the book as one of the volumes conned by Marie in her girlhood.

Page 248.

Ludvig Holberg really visited Marie Grubbe. He writes in his Eighty-ninth Epistle : "An example from the history of our own time is a lady of the high nobility who had an invincible loathing for her first husband, although he was first among all subjects and moreover the most gallant gentleman of the realm, and this went on until it resulted in a divorce, and after a second marriage, which was likewise unhappy, she entered the married estate for the third time with a common tar, with whom, though he abused her daily, she herself said that she lived in much greater content than in her first marriage. I have this from her own mouth, for I visited her house at the Falster ferry at a time when her husband was arrested for a crime."